Deadly ground

Bolan swam to the shore and pulled himself out of the water. He stayed in the shadows of buildings and pulled the windbreaker tighter, trying to find warmth though everything was wet.

Armando's motive for kidnapping Nicky DeVincenzo was apparent now, but Bolan had no clue about the Romanians'. There was a storm brewing over Venice, and the warrior knew it reached into Eastern Europe. He didn't know how, but he was certain Julia DeVincenzo was near the eye of it. And whether she was innocent or guilty it was going to roll over her.

DON PENDLETON's
MACK BOLAN®

DEAD CENTER

A GOLD EAGLE BOOK FROM
WORLDWIDE®

TORONTO • NEW YORK • LONDON
AMSTERDAM • PARIS • SYDNEY • HAMBURG
STOCKHOLM • ATHENS • TOKYO • MILAN
MADRID • WARSAW • BUDAPEST • AUCKLAND

First edition June 1996

ISBN 0-373-61448-9

Special thanks and acknowledgment to
Mel Odom for his contribution to this work.

DEAD CENTER

Whose games were empires, whose stakes were
   thrones,
Whose table earth—whose dice were human
   bones.

> —Lord Byron
> *The Age of Bronze,* 1823

Those who play high-stakes games with other people's
lives do not care for the casualties of their ruthless
ambitions. But someone has to lay his life on the line
for the innocents. It's the only thing that keeps this world
civilized.

> —Mack Bolan

PROLOGUE

Venice
10:43 p.m.

Somewhere in the house, porcelain shattered against the wooden floor.

Julia DeVincenzo came awake in her bedroom at once. She knew from the sound that the breakage was porcelain and not glass. Her grandfather had loved the delicate miniatures Venice was so famous for, and had bought several of them from Palazzo Rezzonico just down the canal.

Thoughts of her grandfather's funeral earlier that day, as well as all the long visits from relatives, vanished as she forced herself from bed, leaving only the cold thought that she and Nicky were no longer as protected as they had been.

Julia DeVincenzo knew the bedroom from memory and instinct. She reached for the intercom unit beside the huge four-poster and thumbed the button. The orange power button showed that it was in working order.

"Carmelo."

There was no reply.

She didn't wait long before switching to another channel. Her heart beat rapidly. Though she wore only a silk T-shirt and panties to sleep in, the temperature inside the room was comfortable. Still, a chill thrilled through her, scratching at the insides of her skin with tiny lizards' claws. "Armando."

"Yes, Mrs. DeVincenzo," came the formal response, reflecting her grandfather's insistence on the proper decorum. He'd been a very powerful man, a man most others could never say no to.

"I heard something break inside the house, and I can't get Carmelo to answer."

"I will check on it, Mrs. DeVincenzo. Please stay in your room."

"Like hell," she replied without the benefit of the intercom. Her son was just down the hall from where the noise had originated. She slipped a hand inside the nightstand drawer and pulled out a small Beretta .380. As she flicked off the safety, she was already moving.

The hallway was dark and narrow. She kept two hands on the pistol. Usually a night-light was left on for Nicky, in case he had bad dreams. Julia's heart felt like a frozen lump, and she had to restrain herself to keep from breaking into a run.

Armando came into view at the other end of the hallway, silhouetted by the moonlight playing against the blinds covering the window behind him. At first he covered her with his pistol, then recognized her and shook his head. Two other housemen were behind him.

"You shouldn't be here," Armando whispered.

Julia nodded toward the empty chair in front of Nicky's room. "Carmelo should."

A tight expression filled the man's face. He was five-eight and built like a fire hydrant, with broad features and receding black hair lacquered to perfection. Julia was the same height, but slender, pretty, and her dark red hair was cut short, almost mannish.

With a sweep of his arm, Armando tucked Julia behind him, then advanced on the bedroom door. The knob turned easily, and the door opened inward on oiled hinges.

The strong, briny stench of the Rio di San Barnaba canal filled the room and told Julia at once that something was wrong. She followed Armando into the room.

The maids kept Nicky's room in order despite his best efforts. Nicky was five, and his great-grandfather had spoiled him all his life. Treasures lined the walls, from Power Rangers dolls to Dr. Seuss books, including porcelain figures of fantasy creatures.

One of those figures lay in colorful pieces on the polished wooden floor. Julia recognized it as one of Nicky's favorites, a detailed representation of Sauron, from the *Lord of the Rings*. His great-grandfather had often read him bits and pieces from the book while he sat on Papa Pietro's knee.

Breath caught in her throat, Julia turned toward her son's bed. It sat low on the floor, shaped like a Lamborghini and painted a fiery red. Carmelo lay draped over one end of it, most of his head shot away. Blood stained the sheets. Bullet holes pocked the wall, echoing the violence.

"Nicky." Julia moved forward, afraid to look.

"Not here." Armando raked the sheets and comforter from the bed.

The cool breeze that wafted over her drew Julia's attention to the open window. She crossed the room and shoved between the two housemen who stood there with guns in their fists.

Outside, splintered moonlight spilled over the dark water of the canal three stories below. The three- and four-story buildings on either side of the canal showed only a few yellow lights here and there. Less than a dozen people strolled the walkways.

Two men sprinted for an unmarked black boat riding low in the water. One of them carried a small figure over his shoulder.

"Nicky," Julia breathed. She leaned farther out the window and saw the rope ladder that trailed to the ground. As she reached for it, the man beside her suddenly jerked back with a painful grunt. Something warm splattered over Julia's arm. When she looked, she saw the bright crimson of blood just before the sound of the rifle shot reached her ears.

More shots hammered through the window and took out the second houseman. She knew she could have easily been dead even as Armando swept her to the floor with a massive arm. The sniper deliberately hadn't killed her.

Before the sound of the shots had drifted away, she heard the boat's engine sputter into vigorous life. She struggled out from Armando's grip. "Stop," she ordered. "They don't want me dead."

"Maybe," Armando agreed. "And maybe you were just lucky, Mrs. DeVincenzo."

Cold as steel and hard as iron, every inch the woman she'd become by being Pietro Magaddino's granddaughter and wife and widow of Stefan DeVincenzo, Julia walked to the window and glared out. The boat sped east, toward Palazzo Rezzonico and the Canal Grande. Its running lights were indistinguishable from those of other boats on the waterway.

"They took my son," Julia said.

"I know, Mrs. DeVincenzo."

"I want him back, safe and sound. I'm willing to do anything for that—lie, cheat, pay ransom ... or kill. You understand?"

"Yes."

"And put out the word," she added, "that the Magaddino ways haven't changed." The vendetta of the Magaddino Family was something most people knew and feared. Julia meant to show her son's kidnappers that her grandfather's death didn't lessen that.

With the same self-control that had kept her intact through her grandfather's and husband's violent trade, she left the room. She felt certain the kidnappers would be in touch, but there were some calls she needed to make first. She wasn't as weak as the men who'd targeted her had thought. Nor was she without resources.

11:08 p.m.

"A KIDNAPPING, EH?" Stepping from the police boat onto the stone piling, Detective Giacomo Canova glanced up at the three-story house. Whitish gray in the moonlight, with a wrought iron trellis linking the rooftop and the patio thrusting out from the second floor, it didn't look out of the ordinary. "What makes this so special that I have to be roused from my bed in the middle of the night?"

The uniformed policeman in charge of the scene gave Canova a scowl. No longer a young man, he had cynicism stamped all over him. "This kid is Pietro Magaddino's great-grandson."

"Ah." Canova nodded in understanding. He was in his late fifties with gray hair and a short, neat, black mustache. "The widow DeVincenzo's son."

"Yes."

"How old is the boy?" Canova started for the dwelling, ducking through the yellow tape and around sawhorses that had been placed there to keep out the curious.

"Five."

"Anyone hurt?"

"Two men inside the house were killed. One is pretty badly wounded."

"The kidnappers?"

The policeman shook his head. "Sadly, no."

"Does anyone have an idea who's behind the kidnapping?" Canova asked.

"The security guards here say no."

"And what does the widow DeVincenzo say?"

"She says no."

"But she might say that anyway."

"Yes."

Canova gazed at the ornate door leading into the house. For years the home had been off-limits to police, a sanctuary of power that coursed through the underworld and spanned continents. Yet tonight he was freely being given entrance. But he would be lied to. He was certain of that.

"The funeral was this morning, wasn't it?" Canova asked.

"Magaddino's? Yeah."

Suddenly the door opened, and a medical team emerged with a sheet-covered body on a creaking gurney. Canova glanced away from the bloodstains to the rope ladder waving gently in the breeze. "The vultures didn't wait long to start picking over the bones, did they?"

"Personally," the policeman said, "I wouldn't care if the whole lot of them killed each other. Save us a lot of trouble. But using a kid like that, I draw the line there. I have children of my own. If somebody took one of my kids, I'd kill the bastard."

"Probably the widow DeVincenzo's sentiments exactly." Canova touched his hat brim and stepped into the house. For years, so the rumors went, Pietro Magaddino had worked diligently to make sure none of his business had ever slopped over onto his only granddaughter. But now he was no longer around to protect her. His death had caused a rift, a shift in power. It remained to be seen who would live as the balance was restored. And who would die.

Vatican City
11:56 p.m.

GERALD "JERICHO" LIGHT ran as if all the hosts of hell were on his heels. But it wasn't flight. He was pushing himself hard. In the quiet dark that had fallen over Vatican City, his footsteps slapped rhythmically against the pavement.

Perspiration covered his body. He wore a black sweat suit despite the evening's warmth. Shorts weren't allowed in Vatican City. He moved with the instinctive coordination of a deer, one giant step beyond that of a trained athlete. With his six-foot-seven-inch height and a football linebacker's build, most people wouldn't have thought him capable.

He made the corner onto Via di Porta Angelica, almost at the end of his run around Vatican City. Ahead of him he could see the outermost wall of the quadruple colonnade surrounding St. Peter's Square. Upon the balustrade were the saints' statues. He tried to remember them in order to keep his mind off his burning lungs.

Then the cellular flip-phone in his fist buzzed for attention. He came to a stop and breathed deeply twice, then flipped the phone open and said, "Light."

A handful of people were still about, and they gazed at him in open curiosity. Light turned from them and continued walking toward St. Anne's Gate.

"Are you through with your run then, my son?" The voice was low and authoritative.

"Almost." Light consumed air in great drafts. His fair hair was silver in the moonlight and lent his face a chiseled look that drained away the carefree youth his twenty-seven years might have otherwise held. His eyes were so dark and intense that they might have been black.

"Do you need some time to recover?"

"No. I can listen." Light concentrated on breathing out. Breathing in was natural and took no real effort.

"Good. I'm afraid things in Venice haven't progressed as well as His Holiness would like. Nor to my satisfaction, for that matter. There have been recent complications."

"I see." Light knew that the events hadn't been a large surprise. Everyone involved had been expecting something to go wrong. That was why he'd been sent to Vatican City from his most recent post in Boston. He'd only been to the Vatican once before, and that was for a short visit.

"It's imperative that you leave as quickly as possible."

"Of course." Automatically he turned his steps toward his apartment, moving rapidly.

"We have arranged for a helicopter to take you to Venice," the voice went on.

"What should I do when I arrive?"

"Wait, watch. You'll be contacted. We've just found out that Mrs. DeVincenzo's son was kidnapped. Opening negotiations at this time would be most awkward."

Light silently agreed.

"Perhaps we would even be suspected in the matter. Other steps would have to be taken if that happened. Whatever the cost, the papacy's interests must be protected."

"Yes."

"Call me when you are ready."

"Of course." The connection broke, and Light flipped the phone closed. He reached his apartment in minutes and started packing a worn leather rucksack. After a quick shower and shave, he shrugged into a black suit. He left the apartment without looking back.

Moving almost at a jog, his long stride eating up the distance, Light moved directly into St. Peter's, going through the central door where cherubs larger than man-size clung to the massive column to his right.

He kept walking, becoming part of the silence that surrounded him, turning in at the Chapel of the Holy Sacrament and passing through the gates designed by Borromini. His eyes wandered to the Trinity by de Cortona against the opposite wall, then to the chairs in front of them.

A man sat there by himself, dressed in the robes of a priest.

"Father," Light said in a low voice. He took a seat behind the priest.

"My son," the man replied in his authoritative voice. He didn't turn around. He was in his sixties, thin and balding, with a blade of a nose beneath his deep-set eyes. "You are ready for your journey."

"Yes. But before I go, I would like to make a confession." Light shrugged out of the rucksack and dropped to his knees, his big hands gripping the back of the priest's chair.

"Have you sinned, my son?"

"No."

"Then why confess?"

"I would ask forgiveness for the things I may have to do," Light answered.

There was a moment of silence. The priest shifted uncomfortably. "You are a warrior of the church, Jericho, and you are on a holy mission to return that which was lost to us for almost sixty years. You can do no wrong in the sight of God."

"Still." There were things that could happen that he might have no control over at all. These were dangerous men, used to violence.

"As you wish," the priest said. "Lead us, then, in the Twenty-third Psalm, Father. I think it's fitting."

Eyes shut, his concentration complete, Father Gerald "Jericho" Light bowed his head and began.

CHAPTER ONE

Venice
7:18 p.m.

The predator's stance and body language gave him away. Mack Bolan had been clued in by his combat senses and figured the guy for a pickpocket or mugger. Either was possible among the two hundred plus tourists and passengers packed aboard the *vaporetti*. Neither posed a direct threat to him.

But as the water bus chugged toward the pilings off Molo Riva in front of Palazzo Ducale, the predator glanced toward the night-shrouded shoreline and blinked a green-colored penlight in his cupped palm. A green blink answered him from the eleven-o'clock position. Three beats, then it faded, lost in the yellow glow of streetlights and the oil lamps hanging from the phalanx of gondolas tied up along the stands.

A small boy tugged on the predator's pants leg and pointed to the penlight as the man pocketed it. With an irritable scowl, the man slapped the boy's hand away. He was thin and wiry, somewhere near six feet in height. To the trained eye, his suit wasn't tailored well enough to hide the shoulder holster under his left arm.

Pushing his way through the throng of people moving up to the front of the *vaporetti,* he caught the attention of three more men and shook his head at each one in turn. All of them began circling through the crowd, looking intently at faces.

Bolan drew back against the water bus's wall. He was dressed in black jeans, rubber boots and a red-and-black flannel shirt with a brown bomber jacket to break the April chill. It was a little early for tourist season to begin in earnest, and there were still plenty of cold fronts and fogs.

His trip from Denmark had been unplanned, starting the race against an unknown clock. There hadn't been time to arrange for armament. The Swiss army knife in his pocket was the most customs would have allowed.

The papers he was traveling under listed him as Mike McKay, a free-lance photographer and journalist. The identity had occasionally served him in the past and couldn't be traced back to the Executioner. The message that had been waiting for him at the drop required subtlety and a low profile.

The *vaporetti* was less than a hundred yards from the slender dock thrusting out into the canal. On the shoreline Palazzo Ducale and the buildings around it offered refuge and shadows where he could lose himself once he got off the boat.

He didn't know for sure if the men were searching for him, but he didn't want to be found anyway. He slid the straps of the backpack he carried in one fist into a new position and tried the heft of it. The backpack wouldn't be damaging, but it might buy some time.

Less than six feet away, the predator came to a stop in front of a short man with dark hair and a mustache. Even without his white Stetson, the man was obviously American. A brown-haired woman and two teenage kids stood beside him. All of them looked tired.

"You are American, yes?" the predator asked as he stood in a ready stance in front of the man.

"All my life," the man said in a Texas drawl. Unconsciously he took a step forward in front of his wife. The threat the man presented was immediately apparent.

"I need to see your papers."

"Why?"

"Don't ask questions. I don't have the time." The predator's hand was inside his jacket.

The Texan stood his ground defiantly. "Yeah, well, make the time, buddy. I didn't come all this way to get shoved around by a jerk with a tinhorn-dictator complex. And if you don't get out of my face right now, I'm gonna call for the captain of this here boat and get this shit straight in about a heartbeat."

The predator jerked his head to one of his companions. The remaining two were circling around the other side of the *vaporetti*. Stepping forward, the man reached for the Texan's wife and roughly took her arm.

She yelped in surprise and pain.

"Why, you—" The Texan balled up a fist and stepped forward.

"I wouldn't," the predator said, pulling the pistol from his shoulder rig. It was a Heckler & Koch P-7 K-3 chambered in .380. With a brutal, short snout, the pistol was ugly and vicious up close, but wasn't accurate at a distance.

"David, don't," his wife implored.

The Texan froze.

Silently Bolan made his way through the crowd. Most of the passengers had their attention fixed on the shoreline, and only a handful seemed to notice the confrontation. None of those appeared willing to help.

Low profile or not, the warrior knew he couldn't stand idly by. He came up on the first predator from behind.

"I have his wallet, Marco," the second man said in Italian.

"Open it."

"It says his name is David Phillips."

"But he looks like the man we are searching for," Marco insisted.

"Yes." The second man shone a small penlight in the Texan's eyes. He compared the man's features to the picture in his palm. The image was of a short, stocky man with a mustache and unruly hair. He wore a trench coat and was standing in front of a white gazebo.

Bolan recognized the face in the photograph at once. Leo Turrin was an old friend in his wars. He was also the one who'd left the message at the drop.

The warrior flipped open the Swiss army knife's long blade with a thumbnail and kept it hidden at his side. He closed in on Marco.

"This man is close," the second man said, stepping back, "but I don't think he is the one we're searching for." He smiled at the Texan's wife. "Pity we can't take them in for further questioning."

Though he probably didn't speak the language, the Texan understood the implications of the smile easily enough. With a quick turn, he launched a right hook at the second man's head and connected solidly.

As his partner slammed up against the *vaporetti*'s cabin, the predator pushed his pistol out before him and took aim. The Texan's wife shrilled out an alarm, and she gathered her children in a big hug, pulling them out of the line of fire.

The Texan spun but he was caught flat-footed. A sick expression twisted his features.

"Die, you pathetic fool," the predator snarled in English.

Without hesitation Bolan jerked the Swiss army knife up into the predator's armpit. The sharp blade penetrated the flesh easily and skated along bone.

A sudden scream of pain ripped from Marco's throat. Paralyzed by the assault, he dropped the small automatic, and it clattered against the deck.

Not allowing time for recovery, Bolan yanked the knife blade out and managed an armlock that provided enough leverage to heave the man over the *vaporetti*'s side. Most of the water bus passengers were now aware of the violence breaking out in their midst, and pushed away from it.

The man the Texan had punched had recovered. Instinctively his hand reached for the back of his pants.

Bolan dived for the loose pistol as it slid across the deck. He closed his fist around the P-7 K-3's butt as the other man produced a full-size Beretta. Still prone on the deck, Bolan fired from the point. A trio of .380 rounds smacked into the gunner's face and sent him sprawling back against the cabin.

The screaming then broke out in earnest from all corners.

At the other end of the *vaporetti,* the two remaining men were moving roughly through the frightened crowd, shoving anyone who got in their way.

Glancing over his shoulder, Bolan saw the shoreline only twenty-five yards away. The water bus had already reversed engines in preparation for docking. The vibration and pull in the opposite direction made the deck rock more vigorously.

He knew he would only draw fire toward the innocents, and he didn't have a clear shot at either of his attackers. Abandoning the backpack, he pushed himself to his feet and dived over the *vaporetti*'s side. Nothing in the backpack would tie up with either the McKay cover or the Executioner. He kept the pistol clenched in his fist and oriented himself with the shoreline. He had a brief impression of a flurry of activity along the docks. Some of it was simply confused milling about by those waiting on the passengers. But some of it looked deliberate and definitely hostile.

Grimly aware that he wasn't clear of the hot zone, Bolan hit the canal as shots cracked out above his head. The black, cold water flooded over him as he went down.

AT THE SOUND OF GUNSHOTS coming from the approaching *vaporetti,* Leo Turrin uncurled himself from where he'd been slouched against one of the castle's arches. Moving forward with the rest of the crowd, he peered across the gloom at the two gunners standing at the side of the water bus and firing down into the canal. The disembarking passengers split around them like the Red Sea.

Dressed in a long raincoat and snap-brim hat against the possible threat of inclement weather, Turrin blended in with the crowd. He kept his movements slow enough not to draw too much unwanted attention but fast and sharp enough to get him near the front of the dock.

The *vaporetti* made an ungainly stop against the dock, bobbing like a child's bathtub toy. The shouts and screams ripped out over the landing.

Turrin cursed. He'd noticed the men lurking along the canal awaiting the arrival of the *vaporetti,* but hadn't connected it with his presence or Bolan's. With Pietro Magaddino's death, covert hostilities seemed to be the name of the game around Venice and other parts of Italy.

He reached into the raincoat pocket and fisted the S&W .38 Airweight Bodyguard pistol he carried there. Two speedloaders were clipped to his belt under a loose knit shirt, and a handful of shells were in the other coat pocket.

Scanning the stream of passengers coming from the *vaporetti,* he searched for Bolan but didn't spot him. Then the canal surface broke less than ten feet away, and a man stroked for the shore.

"There he is!" a man screamed in Italian from behind Turrin. "Kill him!"

Swiveling, taking advantage of one of the slender gondola stands, Turrin located the speaker. The guy was swarthy and lean, looking feral in the dark suit he wore. A burn scar made a satanic eyebrow over his right eye. He led three more men as they shoved their way through the crowd waiting to greet the arrivals.

Bullets thwacked into the water near Bolan's position, and he dived again.

Turrin lifted the Bodyguard and assumed a Weaver's stance behind the gondola stand. Squeezing the revolver through on double action, he brought the trigger to the breaking point, centered the sights on the man in front of the scar-faced gunner and dropped the hammer.

The .38 hollowpoint round punched through the man's cheekbone, and he tumbled to the ground, throwing one of his companions off stride. Reacting to the immediacy of the new threat, the scar-faced man dropped to a prone position with his Glock pistol thrust before him.

Four 9 mm parabellum rounds zinged past Turrin's position. Two of them yanked at his coat, and the other two ricocheted from the gondola stand, making the pole quiver.

Turrin stood his ground grimly, assuming the Weaver's stance again despite a primitive instinct to flee. He squeezed the trigger twice more, working to make his shots count. The first round sparked on the pavement to the right of his target, while the second caught another gunner in the thigh.

The wounded man rolled down the incline toward the canal. Bystanders who had dropped to the ground near him when the firing started now slithered away on their stomachs.

Turrin regretted that the situation had gone ballistic with so many people around, but there hadn't been a choice. At least one innocent life was already hanging in the balance. He fired his remaining two rounds at the scar-faced man but missed by inches.

Still turned sideways to the hostile guns, he broke the Bodyguard open and shook the hot brass from the cylinder. A practiced twist with one of the speedloaders put five fresh shells into the revolver. He brought it up, spotting the two men charging his position at once.

He fired a double-tap into the center mass of his first target. From less than twenty feet out, the hollowpoints slammed the man down, his chest a bloody ruin. But even as he fired at the second man's head, he felt the mule kick thud into his side.

The breath left his lungs in a whoosh as incredible pain ripped across his rib cage. He went down in a heap, gasping for air and trying to pull his fumbling reflexes together. He'd dropped the Bodyguard, and it lay almost a foot away. As he reached for it, he saw two more gunners break from cover and race toward him, their weapons spitting flames.

Then the water rippled to Turrin's left. He was still reaching for his dropped weapon when Bolan shoved himself up out of the canal, went into a combat crouch and brought a small pistol up.

The small pistol in Bolan's hand coughed twice, cutting the approaching gunners down. Uncoiling with fluid movement, the warrior rushed forward at once, streaking for the nearest of the dead men.

Recovering his weapon, Turrin squeezed off his last two rounds as covering fire while Bolan took up the dead man's gun and slipped two magazines from the guy's shoulder rig. Then he was in motion again, moving toward Turrin, even as enemy guns tried to track him.

"Get them!" the scar-faced man urged. He waved to nearly a dozen gunners who had successfully ringed the area.

Turrin broke his weapon open again and recharged it with his last speedloader.

Bolan dropped into the water again, taking refuge behind the shoreline. "Are you hit?" He checked the magazine in the 9 mm Springfield Model 9, then shoved it back into the butt.

"Vest," Turrin gasped in reply. "I think that's all they got."

"Are you mobile?"

"Only one way to find out, Striker."

Bolan nodded, then his face was illuminated briefly as bullets sparked along the concrete canal wall only inches away. He spun in the direction of the shots and raised the 9 mm weapon.

Turrin was bringing his own gun to bear, grimacing at the pain that tore into him. He lifted the .38, but by the time he had it up, the Executioner had already dropped one of the two gunners left aboard the *vaporetti* and driven the other one into hiding.

"Are you alone?" Bolan asked, wading west along the canal.

"Yeah," Turrin replied, following. "Didn't plan on company." The water was sluggish and dark, not really cold at all. Footing was tricky.

"They were looking for you," Bolan said. "One of them had a picture of you on the water bus."

"Could be," Turrin said. The stitch in his side was fading. The vest had taken most of the impact and stopped the slug cold, but the blunt trauma was going to leave some bruises and sore muscles. "I'm known here."

"What name?" Bolan asked. He scrambled aboard a small motorboat anchored near a gondola stand. Four gondoliers gave ground immediately, waved off by the big warrior's pistol.

"My own." Like Bolan, Turrin had found it necessary to work under other names since his undercover days with the OrgCrime unit in Pittsfield. He was still Leo "the Pussy" Turrin in some circles, and was thought to be a semiretired wiseguy who acted as an advisor to some of the East Coast Families at times. But as Leonard Justice he occupied an office in Washington, D.C., and assisted covert operations from the secret counter-terrorist hardsite called Stony Man Farm in the Blue Ridge Mountains.

"This business?" Bolan asked. He was hunkered over the engine, working quickly.

"Part of my past, guy. Debt of honor that needs repaying. I called you in because I needed help."

A yell went up from shore, indicating that they'd been spotted. Bullets slapped into the water around them as the scar-faced man led his troops in a rush. A siren wailed from the east. Beyond the line of approaching gunners, Turrin saw the blue lights of a patrol boat flash over the canal.

He took aim at the gunners and fired steadily. One of them turned in a sick, twisted spiral as the others went to ground.

An instant later the boat's engine clattered to life. Bolan took the seat in the bow and twisted the throttle. The boat moved in response, surging out toward the center of the canal. Guns blasted behind them, and some of the bullets thudded into the boat.

"There's no way we can outrun that police boat," Turrin said. He emptied the spent brass into the water and thumbed in fresh cartridges. He didn't bother to return fire. Most of the gunners were trying to find other boats, but the pursuit was breaking up with the arrival of the police vessel.

"I know," Bolan said. "The plan is to take the boat to the public gardens and lose ourselves. It's about five hundred yards away. We can make that before we're overtaken." He glanced over his shoulder. "And we should shake the welcome wagon by then."

Turrin nodded. He was cold and hurt, still aching from the bullet.

"What kind of umbrella is over this operation?" Bolan asked.

"*Nada,*" Turrin replied. "I'm here on my own. If you take a look around and decide things are too nasty, I'll understand."

Bolan met his gaze honestly. "Couldn't do that, buddy."

Truth to tell, Turrin already knew that and felt a little guilty. But he also knew that if Bolan had found out what was going on and that he was involved, the big man would have probably come on his own. "Then it's just you and me, amigo."

"We've been there before," Bolan said.

Turrin managed a tired grin. "Yeah, but generally everybody was neatly divided up into two camps—us and them. Things aren't so cut-and-dried here at the moment."

"Then we'll make them that way."

Turrin devoutly hoped so. Because with events balanced on razor edges the way they were, he figured it was going to be everything they could do just to stay alive. And out of the hands of the police, he thought as the police boat siren screamed after them.

BOLAN THROTTLED down and brought the boat around in a sweep toward the steps at the side of the canal fronting the Giardini ex Reali. The police boat was less than a hundred yards behind and closing fast. Searchlights probed the water and occasionally blanked out the whirling blue cherry on top.

"Lay down your weapons and surrender!" a deep voice ordered over a PA system.

"Out," Bolan ordered, steadying the boat.

Turrin managed the leap onto the steps leading up to the public area in front of the park. Rifles barked as Bolan followed him. A few rounds cut leaves from trees over their heads as they ran.

"Which way?" Turrin asked.

"North," Bolan answered. "The park's less than a quarter-mile wide. Then we take to the canal again and fade into the neighborhood." He knew the area from the street and topographical maps he'd studied while on the flight into Rome. Terrain was either a soldier's best friend or his worst enemy.

"You got a plan?" Turrin asked.

"I've got an objective," the warrior replied. He slapped tree branches out of his face and cut through the landscaped brush. "We get clear here and we plan later."

The crash of bodies through the foliage behind them and the scattered flaring of flashlights let them know the police unit had landed.

"Can you make the sprint, Leo?" Bolan asked.

"If I don't," Turrin said, "I'm going to be in a hell of a mess."

Bolan took the lead, scrambling through the trees and across the uneven ground. Turrin held the pace with difficulty. The wet clothes were an extra burden. Along with being cold and heavy, they also restricted movement. In minutes they'd made their way to one of the smaller access canals. The police unit had been left behind, spreading out and trying to pick up the trail.

Slightly winded from the exertion, Bolan dropped the 9 mm pistol into the pocket of his bomber jacket, then thrust the single remaining magazine in the other. He scanned the open area beyond the park and found nothing.

A short swim later, he and Turrin were walking down Ascensione Street, still angling north. A police helicopter swept by slowly overhead, and they didn't flinch away when the searchlight sped toward them. If the chopper crew had infrareds, they'd have already detected their body heat and presence.

Venice didn't have automobiles or streets fit for them. There were pedestrians here and there, but generally they kept to themselves.

"So why are you here?" Bolan asked. There was still no sign of pursuit.

"Long story," Turrin said. "We find a café that's open, I'll stand you to a cup of coffee and tell you."

"Okay."

Turrin seemed occupied with his own thoughts. He turned up the collar of his trench coat against the onslaught of wind, but wet as it was, it only succeeded in curling a little higher. "You know who Pietro Magaddino was?"

"Yeah," Bolan said. "Old-line Mafia. Came out of Palermo in the thirties and clawed his way to a leadership position in the Italian La Cosa Nostra during the forties and fifties."

"With a gun in each hand and a knife between his teeth," Turrin agreed. "And a smile in his heart, the way some of the old guys tell it. The truth was that Magaddino was a tough old son of a bitch. Anyone who crossed him died. In the seventies he moved to Venice, as a sort of retirement, he said.''

"But he didn't retire," Bolan said. From his early war on the Mafia, the big warrior knew about Magaddino, but his sights had never dropped on the man.

"Far from it," Turrin said. "Magaddino established Venice as the seat of his power. He ran a lot of operations behind the scenes. Not so much taking an active part in the more criminal operations, but he handled a lot of the money laundering and helped Mob forces get into legitimate business. When he talked, a lot of people listened."

"Magaddino's dead," Bolan said.

Turrin nodded. "They had the funeral yesterday. Funny thing, I thought about coming, just to see for myself how the power division was going to shake out. There's a lot of people that have been waiting on Magaddino to kick the bucket for years. People were starting to wonder if he wasn't just too mean to die."

"So, if you're not here because of him, what?"

Turrin was silent for a moment, ramming his hands deep in his coat pockets. He matched Bolan stride for stride. "His granddaughter, Julia. Julia Magaddino back then, but Julia DeVincenzo for the last eight years."

"Her husband went down fighting off a bid against Magaddino."

"Right." Turrin nodded. "The old man looked on DeVincenzo as a son. He'd already lost his own.

Magaddino had some guys working a laundering operation here in Venice, tucked in quietly behind some good, solid fronts. It was a cherry operation, almost invisible and dependable as a Swiss watch. Only the two guys running it started to get greedy and took on some side work. Before they knew it, they let some Interpol agents in the back door. If DeVincenzo hadn't moved fast, old man Magaddino would have spent his golden years in prison. DeVincenzo took out the men running the operation one step ahead of Interpol's offensive play, but lost his life in the process."

"But Magaddino was left in the clear?"

"Oh, yeah." Turrin looked up at his friend. "But that was old business. I don't know how much of it applies to what's going on now. I just wanted you to know how Julia stood in this thing."

Bolan kept silent.

"She's alone in this mess," Turrin said. "She doesn't want any part of her grandfather's business, and has already made it known through the proper channels. There's enough money left in the Family holdings that she'll never want for anything. But last night someone kidnapped her five-year-old son. She called me because she trusts me and knows I can network between the Families. And because I owed her." Turrin glanced at Bolan. "All she wants is to get her son back."

Bolan didn't hesitate. "I'm in."

Nodding, Turrin said. "I thought you would be. Thanks."

"Do THE POLICE KNOW about the kidnapping?" Bolan asked a half hour later. They were seated in a small all-night café that handled mostly a domestic crowd. The menus were in Italian only, and the waiters and waitresses spoke English with difficulty.

The decor was green and white checks and plastic tablecloths. The coffee was strong and black. Gondoliers sat in packs, rotating among their group as some went back to work earning the tourist dollar and others came in for a bite to eat or a quick rest.

"Yeah," Turrin replied as he forked up a large bite of lasagna, "but they quashed it. Some of the paparazzi caught wind of it, but they've been warned off by the police and by Julia's people. Julia's something of a celebrity and is even more in the news since her grandfather died." He chewed the lasagna with gusto.

Bolan worked his way through his plate, as well. They'd also managed a stop at a clothing store that hadn't been open until the warrior picked the lock. After taking the clothing they needed, he'd left enough lira to cover the expenses and relocked the door behind them. The bomber jacket and pistol were in a carryon he'd taken from the clothing store. Both would have to be cleaned soon if they were going to remain serviceable.

Now that they were in warm clothes and eating a hot meal, the attack on the water bus seemed as if it had taken place more than just a short hour ago. The slim waitress came by and refilled their coffee cups.

"Does Julia DeVincenzo think the kidnapping's just for ransom?" Bolan asked.

Turrin shrugged. "I didn't get to talk to her long, Sarge. Her grandfather's telephone lines have been bugged by the local police department and the *federales* for years. Not to mention the competition he's been up against all that time. Julia's used to living her life in a fishbowl. She asked me to come, and I did because I owe her."

Bolan finished the last of his meal and pushed the plate aside. He understood debts. There were a number of markers out there with his name on them.

"There's money involved, sure," Turrin said. "The old man left her millions. But I get the feeling she doesn't figure it boils down to something that simple."

"Family business?" Bolan asked.

"Maybe. But Magaddino made sure Julia was kept clean. When she got involved with DeVincenzo behind his back, Magaddino put out a contract on the guy. At the time DeVincenzo was one of his top men, like family. Julia found out about the hit and went to her grandfather. The old man didn't like it, but she made him listen. DeVincenzo hadn't gone after her—she'd gone after him. Of course, I got this all secondhand, so the story could have gotten stretched some in the process."

"How old did you say the boy is?" Bolan asked.

"Five. Just a kid. I got my own, you know, and I can remember how vulnerable they were at that age. Makes me sick to think of how scared he must be."

Bolan silently agreed. "How well do you know Julia DeVincenzo?"

"We were close for a time," Turrin answered. "It was during the early part of my career with the OrgCrime unit in Pittsfield, back when I was with Angie Marinello's group. I was still pretty confused in those days. Just got out of the military, just married and wound up with one foot in Family business and the other in a federal cop shop through genes and my own sense of ethics.

"It was hard," Turrin said in a low voice that still carried the weight of those years. "Everybody was wanting a piece of my day. The Family, the Org-Crime unit, Angie, all of them needed me to prove my loyalty and none of them really believed in me because they knew the load was heavy. Angie was putting pressure on me to get out of the Family business, too. It was like living three different lives."

"When you're in that deep," Bolan said, "it's hard to remember which way is up."

"No shit." Turrin nodded with feeling. "During one of those times when I felt the whole house of cards was about to drop on me, Pietro Magaddino made one of his rare appearances on the East Coast. He preferred life out here because he had control. America had too many hot dogs willing to make their own breaks. He used to tell all the old guys that, but nobody really listened."

Bolan sipped his coffee. Outside the café windows, a gentle rain blurred the velvet spray of night that lay over the city. The police-boat sirens had long since died away.

"I remember the first time I saw Julia. She was in some kind of white party dress. Maybe eighteen years old. Tanned like you wouldn't believe and as slender as a willow. Every guy in the place felt the heat when she walked by. But they knew Magaddino would have killed them where they stood if they made a move on her. And Julia never gave any of them the time of day. Except me.''

''Why?''

"Don't know. Maybe it was because I was a newly made guy and a lot of people were giving me attention. Maybe it was because I was just married and she figured she'd be safe with me. Could be because it was easy to laugh with her. I'd been thinking about quitting, you know, being one or the other—a cop or a wiseguy. Either one had to be easier than trying to live out the lies I had standing between me and the truth. But I spent the evening in a corner talking to her, dropping our conversation when other people came to pay their respects, but talking really deep. I found out she was a lot like me—trapped by the Family ties and trying to make sense of life.''

The stocky little Fed shrugged. "I couldn't tell you today what we talked about that night. But as I looked at this little slip of a girl and realized that she was getting on with her life in spite of everything, I found enough determination in me to keep going.''

"She's never been involved in Family business?'' Bolan asked.

"To my knowledge, no. A lot of businesses Magaddino owned at the end were strictly legit. I made a few phone calls after Julia contacted me. From everything I've been able to find out, she's not involved in anything illegal.''

"If the kidnapping isn't involved with the Family business and it isn't for profit," Bolan asked, "then what's the motive?"

Turrin spread his hands. "I figured we'd ask Julia when we saw her."

Bolan finished his coffee. "Let's go." He dropped money on the table and headed for the door. The air was cool and clean outside. Mist washed across his face. He'd fought the Mafia long and hard after his family had died, and he'd helped bring justice to parts of the organized-crime network. He didn't know if Julia DeVincenzo was an innocent or not. But there was no doubt about her five-year-old son. However it turned out, he knew he was in it for the duration. With an innocent life on the line, he couldn't turn away.

CHAPTER TWO

Standing across the Rio di San Barnaba, Mack Bolan scanned the low-slung transport boat tied up on their side of the canal, presenting a broadside to the Magaddino home. He waved Turrin to the shadows of the bicycle shop beside them.

"It's staked out," the warrior said.

Turrin nodded. "I saw them." A display of three mountain bikes was on the other side of the window behind him. "Any idea who they are?"

"No, but they're well equipped." Bolan noted the antenna and the small satellite dish at one end of the cabin, barely noticeable above the structure's line. "Anybody who goes in or out of that building, they're going to know about it."

"Probably running the phone taps from there, too."

"Yeah."

Turrin grinned. "Julia's got a cell phone, and I've got the number. They can't trace a call through that from either end. And if the conversation's short, chances are no one can get a fix on it fast enough to listen in."

"Then we need only a diversion to get inside." Bolan looked up the side of the building and spotted the electrical lines crossing the canal three stories up above. A blue-and-white card in the window of the bicycle shop advertised the presence of an alarm system in three languages. "Give her a call and let her know to expect company."

Turrin nodded. "Spotted a pay phone back a couple alcoves. Do it now?"

"Yeah." When the Fed left, Bolan turned his attention back to the transport boat and the canal. They were far enough off the beaten path of the city that tourist traffic, especially at this time of night, wasn't going to be a problem. There weren't any streetlights. Pale gold illumination spilled from the porticoes on the ground floor of the buildings and a few of the windows above. He guessed that most of them would have emergency power supplies.

He took the 9 mm from the carryon and threaded the silencer into place. Then he waited.

JULIA DeVINCENZO SAT in the recliner at the foot of her bed and stared through the misty pane of glass facing the canal. To the left Palazzo Rezzonico's basilica thrust up toward the dark clouds.

She was dressed in a dark business suit and felt hollow inside. An untouched glass of sparkling wine had gotten warm and gone flat in her hand. The last time she'd felt that desolate was when Stefan had died in her arms at the hospital. There'd never been another man since her husband. She'd given her life over to Nicky. Her grandfather had never needed anything, it seemed, from anyone. And with the house security as tight as he'd kept it, she'd existed more or less in a vacuum. Now her son was gone, too. Unbidden, the premonition that she'd never see Nicky again stole over her.

Nausea twisted her stomach as she thought about what Nicky might be facing. Unable to sit any longer, she pushed herself out of the recliner, amazed at how cold the room had gotten in the past few hours. She'd made no move to adjust the temperature or turn on the lights. Her hands felt stiff and awkward as she tried to place the wineglass on the small coffee table at the foot of the chair.

The glass fell from her fingers and shattered against the hardwood floor. Instantly Armando forced his way through her bedroom door, his gun in hand.

"Mrs. DeVincenzo," he called out, switching on the small penlight he held.

"I'm all right," she said. "It was just an accident."

The penlight beam dipped to focus on the broken remains of the wineglass. "I'll get the maid in here to clean it up," Armando said.

"I can get it," Julia replied. "I'd rather not see anyone right now."

"Let me." Armando put the gun away and got the small whisk and dustpan from under the sink in her bathroom. He knelt and cleaned up the mess. He looked like hell, too, she realized. Probably he'd been unable to sleep since the kidnapping, either. Armando and Nicky had really liked each other.

She kept back the tears that threatened when she caught herself thinking of her son in the past tense. She *had* to go on believing Nicky was alive.

The phone rang. At first she thought it was the main line to her bedroom. Then she realized it was from the cellular phone beside the recliner.

Armando picked up the phone and activated it. "Hello."

"Can I speak to Julia?" The man's voice sounded tinny from the distance.

"Who may I say is calling?"

"Leo. I'm a friend."

"Let me have it," Julia said. She crossed the room and took the phone when Armando held it out. "I've been waiting for this call." She lifted the handset to her face. "Hello."

"Have you heard anything?" Turrin asked.

"No. Where are you?"

"In town. I can be there in a few minutes."

"I'd heard there was some trouble along the Grand Canal."

There was a brief pause. "I think you've got a leak, Julia. Those people down there were looking for me. They had a picture."

His words chilled Julia. Her first impression had been that Nicky's kidnapping was aided by someone inside her household. Turrin had just confirmed it.

"Are you sure coming here is safe?" she asked.

"I want to look around your house. Maybe get a fix on something you can't see because you're too close to it."

And take a look at the staff, Julia knew. Turrin had lived among people who sold each other out on a regular basis. The American Mafia was still splintered in many areas, still struggling to find a power base. That hadn't happened around her grandfather. Not while he was alive.

"It'll be okay," Turrin said. "But there's a boat out in the canal that's got you under surveillance. We're going to have to do something about that."

"We?"

"I brought a friend. Somebody who's good in the trenches. You just stay loose and keep the back door open."

"I'll be here." Julia listened to the click as the connection broke. Putting the phone down, she walked to the window and looked out. She spotted the transport boat at once and studied it until she was certain it wasn't the same boat that had carried Nicky away. Then she told Armando to get the rear entrance ready because they were expecting visitors.

"WE'RE ON," Turrin said when he returned to Bolan's vantage point.

"You know the way?" Bolan asked, watching a pair of gondolas poling down the canal, away from the immediate vicinity.

"I got a map earlier while I was waiting on you. This place is filled with cul-de-sacs."

Bolan knew that from previous time spent in Venice. He lifted the 9 mm and took aim at the power line above. "This is going to happen quick."

"Go for it," Turrin said.

Bolan stroked the trigger and rode out the recoil. The bullet flew true, striking the thick cable near the center. A shower of sparks ignited, then built into an electrical explosion in a heartbeat. Lights in the neighborhood went dark.

Severed by the final eruption of sparks, the thick power cable flailed through the air and landed in the canal near the transport boat. A fresh cascade of electrical sparks spit over the water as the power cable tried to ground out. It slithered, popped and jumped like a snake on a hot patch of asphalt. Electricity swarmed over the transport boat and shot bright blue veins of current through the water.

In response the muted lights aboard the transport boat went out, as well.

"Go!" Bolan said, breaking into a trot toward the stone bridge that arced over the canal less than ten yards away. He kept the pistol at his side, out of sight. The pavement was slick with precipitation from the mist.

The power cable was still hissing in the water when the crew aboard the transport boat stepped out. Most of them had guns and moved as if they thought they were under attack. Flashlight beams probed the water, then started flicking along the shorelines. Yellow cones picked out the scattered pedestrians.

Bolan crossed the bridge at a dead run. A flashlight beam trailed along behind him, only inches from catching up to Turrin.

"The alcove on the right," the Fed directed. With a burst of renewed effort, he took the lead.

The Executioner followed. He was only a couple of steps behind Turrin when a guy reached out from the shadows of the alcove. The pistol he carried made a hard line in his hand.

Before the aggressor's hand could touch Turrin, the Executioner grabbed his shoulder, then brought a knee up into the man's stomach. The guy's breath left his lungs in an explosion of coughing, and he sagged to the ground.

Bolan kicked the gun away then pressed the barrel into his opponent's neck. "Don't move," he ordered.

The man clutched at his stomach, wheezing with effort. But he didn't try to get up.

Frisking the man expertly, the warrior turned up a wallet. Footsteps sounded outside, and men screamed at residents to call for the power company. Bolan opened the wallet and glanced at the badge and ID inside. He tossed it back onto the man and joined Turrin.

"Local?" Turrin asked.

"Police," Bolan answered. He followed Turrin through the maze of tunnels and out the back. An eight-foot wall enclosed a courtyard around the rear of the Magaddino mansion. Iron spikes lined the top.

"Up," Turrin said.

Bolan laced his fingers together and gave his friend a boost. He managed the jump himself and seized the top as he heard the approach of running feet. He yanked himself up and over, negotiating the spikes with only little difficulty.

Inside the courtyard a dense garden in seasonal half bloom occupied much of the space, leaving just room enough for a circular concrete table and walkways that intersected and made a figure eight. Three armed men were spread out around the trees and bushes, their guns trained on Turrin and Bolan.

"Get down," a thick-set man ordered.

Bolan glanced back the way they'd come. Already the alcove had gathered extra shadows, and some of them carried flashlights. The trail they'd been following through the building continued into a rabbit warren of alleys and other structures and offered no real escape.

He made the drop into the garden. The ground was soft and spongy. Turrin landed beside him.

"On your faces," the man commanded, waving the gun. "Hands behind your head. You're familiar with the drill."

"Armando," a woman's stern voice called out.

Bolan saw her standing in the back door, silhouetted by the soft light coming from inside.

"That's not necessary. These people are friends," she said.

"Mrs. DeVincenzo," the bodyguard said, "I'm supposed to protect you. Your grandfather didn't allow—"

"My grandfather is dead now," she cut in sharply. "And my son is missing. Let them in." Her tone allowed no room for argument.

Reluctantly Armando waved them forward with his pistol. His smile was tight and white. "I'll take the guns, though."

Bolan and Turrin handed over their pistols as they walked to the back of the house. The screened porch was huge, filled with plants and heavy wooden furniture. The waxed hardwood floor gleamed, and overhead two lazy ceiling fans stirred the air.

"You're probably going to have visitors in a few minutes," the warrior told the lady.

"The police?" she asked.

He nodded.

She led the way into the house. The rooms were expensively furnished in Mediterranean style and arranged for intimacy. Bolan knew it was a place for family, not for the business Pietro Magaddino had directed on a daily basis. The old man's hands might not have been clean, but the warrior was willing to bet the home was.

"You could have knocked," Julia said irritably as she led them up the stairs.

"I would have been seen," Bolan said. The room she guided them into was a large den. Watercolors decorated the walls, all of them of different places around Venice. A large inlaid teak desk was to the left, tucked quietly around the corner. The center-piece was obviously the black stone fireplace outfit-ted with shiny brass accoutrements. A pair of plush sofas fronted it, facing each other across an antique coffee table supporting a medieval chess set. Oppo-site the desk the remaining full wall was covered with glass-fronted shelves filled with delicate porcelain figurines.

"What difference would that have made?" Julia demanded.

"They already know me," Turrin said as he walked to one of the windows and peered through the blinds. "And they know your people. We were thinking it might be helpful if there was someone they weren't aware of."

"You're still going to have to get back out of the house," Julia said. "Don't you think they'll be watching then?"

"They'll have to replace their electronics first," Bolan said. Through the blinds he saw an emergency-rescue boat arrive. The spinning red cherries threw light over the surrounding buildings. Knots of men stood around conversing as the cable continued to spit and leap in the water. "I don't intend to stay here long enough for them to get that set up."

Julia crossed her arms over her breasts and met Bolan's gaze levelly. "I don't know who you think you are, mister, but you don't just waltz into my house and disrupt everything going on here."

Bolan gave her a short nod and went back to watching the activity in the canal.

Turrin approached the woman with his hands upraised in a placating gesture. "Julia, we're not the enemy. We're just here to help."

"This isn't what I had in mind for help, Leo," she answered brusquely.

Turrin started to place a hand on the woman's shoulder, but Armando stepped in quickly and slapped it away. "Nobody touches Mrs. DeVincenzo," he warned. "Unless I say it's okay."

Bolan regarded the household staff quietly, reading their body language as they reacted to the situation and their unexpected visitors. With their daily routines around the woman and her son, they were the first ones to be suspect in the kidnapping.

"It's cool," Turrin said, taking a half step back. "I didn't intend any disrespect."

Armando still bristled, insinuating himself between the stocky little Fed and the woman.

"Armando," Julia said, "please go make sure the rest of the staff is ready to admit the police in the next few minutes. I want the living room readied, as well as the den and the kitchen. If they want, the officers who arrive may have the run of the lower floor, but nothing else. Have someone get pastries and a fresh pot of coffee ready for them."

"Of course." When he left, Armando made it clear that he didn't like the idea of leaving the woman alone with them. The other men left with him.

"He seems overly protective," Bolan commented.

Hot spots flared on Julia's cheeks. She faced the warrior squarely her spine stiff and straight. "What's that supposed to mean?"

Bolan gazed at her. She was slim and lovely, even with the lines of tension and anxiety the past twenty-something hours had etched into her face. Her perfume was a delicate hint in the air. But looking at her in the business suit and seeing her so composed, he knew it was only a front, a smoke screen she maintained with effort. The warrior decided not to pull any punches with her. "It means that Armando could just as easily have been the person who set up the kidnapping."

"Yes." She didn't flinch from the possibility. "So that means I'm supposed to be paranoid about all the household staff?"

"No," Bolan replied. "I'm going to do that for you. I just wanted to know if there was any reason for Armando to be so protective."

"It's his job," Julia said. The exasperation was evident in her voice. "So you're thinking maybe I'm screwing my security chief, who—incidentally—was the one who masterminded my son's kidnapping?"

Bolan made no reply. An answer either way would have triggered the anger pent up inside the woman. And he couldn't blame her for it.

"You think I haven't already had the police in here trying to sort through whatever dirty laundry they might find, too?" When Bolan still didn't answer, Julia switched her attention to Turrin. "What's the deal, Leo? I called you here in hopes that you could help me, not undermine the little confidence I have left."

"We're going to, kid. But if he wasn't asking you these questions, I would be." Turrin paused. "Somebody sold you and Nicky out. If we figure out who, it'll put us one step closer to getting him back."

After a moment she broke the eye contact and turned away. "It's okay. I understand. It's just hard." Her voice broke. "I know Nicky's out there somewhere, scared and wondering why I'm not coming to get him, and it drives me crazy."

"You'd have had to think this through yourself," Bolan said.

"I have," she said. "But if I could have figured out who might be responsible for this, I'd already have looked into it. As far as Armando goes, he and

Nicky were kind of close. When I wasn't with Nicky, Armando was."

"I'd say Armando's got some feelings for you," Turrin observed.

She glanced at him. "Probably nothing more than a benign jailer's fondness for his charges. Armando was groomed by my grandfather, handpicked from all the men he knew, to take care of me. Armando's been doing that job for the past eleven years."

"He have family?"

"No. And to answer your question, there's no relationship between us."

"There still hasn't been any contact with the kidnappers?" Bolan asked.

Julia shook her head. "That's not a good sign, is it?"

Bolan felt she deserved the truth. "No, it's not. Usually someone would have been in touch with you by now, given you time to raise the ransom. How much money could you get together in seventy-two hours?"

"I had my accountant look into it," Julia said. "She tells me somewhere between ten and thirteen million, depending how fast some of the paper could roll over."

"The people who took your son would know that," the warrior said. "Have you started getting it together?"

"Yes."

Bolan glanced back out at the canal. Outside, the power company had managed to switch off the electrical line, and workers were already on top of the building disconnecting the damaged cable. Two police boats had joined the emergency-rescue unit, and the crew of the transport boat mixed with them freely. "They'd be aware of that, too."

"I know. The Italians perfected kidnapping, remember?"

Bolan knew it was true. Kidnapping had become an industry in Italy since the 1970s. Safeguards, including hardware, technology and training, had all been beefed up during those years to counterbalance the threat.

"I've lived in the shadow of that all my life as the granddaughter of Pietro Magaddino."

Locking eyes with her, Bolan said, "You don't think your son was taken for money, do you?"

"Leo," Julia said, cold and distant, "it just came to me that I don't even know your friend's name."

"Mike," Turrin answered. "His name is Mike, and he's really good at this sort of thing."

"What sort of thing?" Julia demanded. "Both of you come blasting your way in here, getting the police all stirred up again, and I'm getting grilled. When I asked you here, it was because I figured this was a Family problem. I thought you could negotiate with the people around here and get my son back. Unharmed." Her gaze was dark and intent on Bolan.

"You think one of the Families is behind this?" Turrin asked.

"Like your friend says," Julia replied, "if it was someone who was only interested in the money, I'd have been contacted by now. My grandfather was a very powerful man and he made a lot of enemies. But he's dead now, and it's possible someone wants to make sure this organization falls completely apart."

"Would you care?" Bolan asked.

There was no hesitation. "No. If there's something someone wants and it's within my power to give it to them, I will. The only thing that matters is Nicky. I've never been directly involved in Family business, and I damn sure don't want my son to grow up and die the way his father did." Her voice lowered. "Or to die out there somewhere all alone." Tears misted her eyes.

Bolan gave her a moment to keep herself together. "If there was something to be gotten from this organization of your grandfather's, what could it be?"

"I don't know," Julia said. "My grandfather had a very strict rule about his business. It was hardly ever discussed in this house, and never around me or Nicky. Even he and Stefan stuck to that."

"Leo?"

Turrin shrugged. "I'm pretty much retired these days. Do a few favors for friends, a little politicking between Family members when there's friction, but I don't keep up the way I used to. And Pietro played things pretty close to the vest, especially during his later years."

Bolan knew that also meant nothing had triggered the interest of Aaron Kurtzman, head of Intelligence gathering and analysis, during a computer search at Stony Man Farm. He decided to try another tack. "Have you had anyone look into the shootings at the canal earlier?"

"Yes," Julia said. "The police are still working on identifying the bodies they recovered."

"Did your people see them?"

"Two of them," Julia said. "Neither of them was known to us."

"Do you know someone at the PD who could help us ID them?"

"No. Armando suggested that he knew a policeman who didn't mind...accepting bonuses, but I told him no. The situation is difficult enough without muddying the waters further."

"Leo," Bolan said.

The stocky little Fed nodded. "I think I carry enough weight to get us in that far."

Someone knocked at the door, and Julia told them to enter. Armando stepped into the room. "There's a detective downstairs who'd like to talk to you," the security man said. "Canova."

"The man from last night."

"Yes."

"I'll be right there."

Armando hesitated for a moment, then left.

"Mind if I tag along?" Turrin asked. "I'm going to need to get to know this guy soon anyway."

"Of course." Julia shifted her attention to Bolan. "Will you be joining us?"

"No."

"You don't want to be known by the police, either?"

"No."

"You're a very distrustful man."

Bolan gave her a small smile. "I trust Leo. And for the moment I trust you. That's enough for now."

"Will you be all right up here?"

"Yes."

She turned and left the room, and Bolan watched her go. He didn't know what to make of the woman exactly. She appeared to be intelligent and whip-cord tough, but she was also at her most vulnerable. His gaze wandered the room. He knew what kind of man Magaddino was, knew the kind of things he could do and he knew that the violence Magaddino traded in could wash back over his family without warning, even from beyond the grave.

As he spotted the gold-framed picture on the desk, the warrior had to wonder if that's what the kidnapping was about. Was it some old, unfinished piece of business or was it something totally new. He crossed the room and picked up the picture.

A small boy sat on Magaddino's knee. The picture had been taken probably in the spring, Bolan judged from the blossoming plants in the background of the photos. Magaddino wore a white shirt and slacks and looked totally relaxed. The boy was grinning, his arms around his great-grandfather, pressing his head to the old man's cheek.

The boy's features were a lot like his mother's, bright, sharp eyes, thin nose and dimples in his cheeks. But he evidently got his hair and coloring from his father; both were dark.

No matter what Magaddino had done during his life, the boy didn't deserve to get caught up in it.

Bolan turned his attention from the picture and started studying the rest of the room, trying to find Magaddino's presence so he could get a grip on the dark secrets that threatened to destroy what was left of the family.

"YOUR FRIEND ISN'T Family," Julia DeVincenzo said as she descended the stairs with Leo Turrin beside her. Anger and fear warred within her, all of it triggered anew by the man they'd left behind.

"No," Turrin said. "But he's been around Family business a lot."

"He scares me."

Turrin nodded. "He has that effect on a lot of people." He gripped her elbow and stopped her for a moment. "But he's also one of the kindest and gentlest men I know. Getting Nicky back isn't going to be easy. We don't even know what the stakes are yet. But when push comes to shove, my friend is a good man to have in your corner."

"Maybe. But will he care about what happens to Nicky?"

"Yes. On my father's eyes, I swear that to you, Julia."

Julia tried to believe that, but she kept remembering how the man had acted, sizing everything up as if it was some kind of military engagement. He carried himself straight and tall, with his shoulders drawn back, and he'd shown no fear of Armando at all, who usually intimidated most people. In some ways he reminded her of Stefan. Realizing that made her feel good and more uncomfortable at the same time.

"He is an honorable man," she said.

"You won't find one more so," Turrin promised.

At the foot of the staircase, Armando turned and looked at them impatiently.

Julia started forward again. "My grandfather was feared more than respected in the Family."

"Men of power—"

"Please, Leo," Julia said without looking at him, "don't soft sell me. I know very well what kind of man Pietro Magaddino could be. He was ruthless and violent and remorseless. But he'd made peace for a number of people in this area and prevented several bloodbaths."

"I know."

"Naturally he also made a number of enemies. In several instances, he used blackmail to get what he wanted or needed. He didn't think I knew, but I did."

"Kids learn a lot more than parents think they do," Turrin said. "And your grandfather kept you real close to him."

"You sound like you've had experience with that."

"More than I'd want."

"After my mother and father were killed when I was sixteen, I was with him all the time," Julia said. She stepped off the last step and moved toward the den. "My parents and my husband died as a result of my grandfather's business. I don't want that to happen to Nicky. Whatever debts my grandfather owed or owned, they were buried when we put him in the ground yesterday. My son is not going to pay them.''

THE MEN TRAILING Father Jericho Light became braver as they got a half mile from the train station. He'd spotted them in the passenger car before his arrival in Venice and had monitored their whereabouts as he read. He carried only two books with him, as usual: a favorite Bible presented to him in Tokyo by Father Joseph Cornish, when he'd been still seeking a way out of his old life, and a battered copy of the *Hagakura,* which had helped him to isolate himself from that life and to accept the emptiness he felt as a strength. Neither book had his name inscribed in it.

The idea of accepting death, as taught by the *Hagakura,* had appealed to him then, and the strength he'd gotten from that had made him very effective at what he did. But it paled in comparison to what he received after he accepted the might of salvation. If his old employers could have seen him now, none of them would have believed the man he had become.

He walked through the night without fear, a tall man in comfortable, casual clothes. He carried his spare clothing and the books in his backpack. Silently he prayed that his pursuers would be happy with robbing him, but he didn't think so.

Initially he headed northeast, along the Rio Terra Lista di Spagnia, toward the apartment that had been rented for him. Not wanting to lead them to his residence no matter how things ended up, he wandered left, behind the Labia Palace then along Vergola.

Even after all the years in crowded Tokyo, he still felt closed in by his surroundings. In the night Venice seemed to be nothing more than a collection of very old buildings built upon sinking rocks. The history of the city's efforts to keep from drowning in the Adriatic Sea had been chronicled in most of the tourist pamphlets he'd read while back in Vatican City. Tonight, however, he felt they were doomed to failure.

He found a place in the shadows at the side of the Cannaregio Canal and took off his shoes as if resting. Making himself comfortable, he waited. It didn't take long. His pursuers had already dropped the distance to fifty yards, letting him know they were confident of themselves in spite of his size.

The two men came up on either side of him and stayed just out of reach. They were dark and swarthy, with scars showing a long association with a violent trade.

"I don't want any trouble," Light told them. He dropped his wallet on the ground with the thick stack of lira notes sticking out. Money didn't mean anything to him; if he needed more, the church would send it. "If you've come to rob me, that's everything I have."

"We didn't come to rob you," the man on Light's right said. "But it'll make a nice bonus." He knelt and scooped up the wallet. Stripping the money from it, he quickly leafed through it. A puzzled scowl darkened his beefy features. "Don't you have any ID?"

Light smiled benevolently. "Yes."

"Then let's see it."

Resting his arms on his knees, his body tensely coiled, Light said, "Do you have to know who you're robbing?"

"This is the guy, Solly," the other man said. "From the description, he can't be nobody else. Let's just do him and get the hell out of here." He pulled a small revolver from his pocket and held it at his side.

The only potential witnesses around were dozens of yards away. The men could pull the triggers and disappear before anyone could be the wiser.

"Be quiet." Solly dropped into a squat and faced Light. "Don't mind Lorenzo. He ain't got any manners."

Light didn't reply. Already his reflexes had moved up. It was as if the man were talking in slow motion.

"They say you're a priest," Solly said.

"Yes."

"Past or present?"

"Now," Light answered.

Solly nodded, but his eyes never left Light's. "You figure it's a sin to kill a priest, Father?"

"It's a sin to kill any man. You don't have to look any further than the Fifth Commandment." Light felt the weight of the words as he spoke them.

"But a priest," Solly persisted as if genuinely interested, "a man of the cloth. Wouldn't that be worse?"

Light shook his head, meaning it. "Not any worse than killing any other man."

Solly was quiet for a moment, digesting the information, then he said, "That's good to know." He removed a small automatic from his jacket pocket. "Are you afraid to die, Father?"

"No."

Solly placed the pistol's muzzle against Light's forehead. "Not at all?"

"No."

"Good."

Light waited until Solly's knuckles turned white as he applied pressure to the trigger. His eyes didn't blink, and his senses were moving so quickly he could almost see the beads of sweat form on the man's face.

Then his defense system snapped on, and his body reacted fluidly. Aware that the other man was waiting for his partner to shoot, Light slapped a hand against the inside of Solly's wrist, then wrapped his long fingers around the arm, controlling it with his greater strength.

Light rammed the stiff fingers of his other hand into the base of Solly's throat. The flesh ripped easily from the force he was using.

Solly staggered back, gagging and wheezing. Blood stained his lips.

Lorenzo cursed and aimed his pistol

Even as the man squeezed off the first round, Light pulled his feet under himself and twisted his body in a backward somersault. The bullet whined off the pavement where he'd been.

He saw Lorenzo coming around with his weapon even as he landed and set himself. Before the killer could fire again, Light thrust his leg out in a side kick with all the power of his body. Ribs crunched and folded in on themselves when he made contact. He knew immediately the impact was probably fatal; the man's heart, if not torn by snapped bone, had been ruptured.

Lorenzo sailed over the canal's edge and disappeared into the water.

Moving swiftly, the priest gathered his shoes and his backpack. People were already being drawn by the gunshot. Before he could leave, Solly grabbed his ankle, leaving bloody fingerprints on his socks.

Light looked down at the dying man and saw the word framed silently on Solly's lips: *please.* Drawn by the responsibility, the priest knelt and took the dying man's hand in his, the blood making the skin slick and tacky at the same time.

Light administered the last rites as the man's eyes dimmed, then became opaque with a cold distance. It was a look he'd seen many times before. With his fingertips he closed the man's eyes.

Looking up, he saw that a few of the bystanders were starting to close ranks. He grabbed his things and moved, breaking into a run easily. In seconds he'd left them behind.

Maybe it would have been possible for him to outdistance the two men, rather than have to kill them at all. But he'd had to know how much they had on him in case it compromised his mission. The church had centuries of experience in dealing with secrets, but as with most networks that had been in existence for some time, he'd found, there were those within the ranks who dealt in those secrets.

The secrets he was after himself had been held for over fifty years and had cost a number of people their lives. He'd been given to understand it was still a delicate matter, potentially explosive.

He prayed that the situation wouldn't get out of hand and cost the woman and her son their lives, as well. Personal experience had shown him how few innocents were actually left in the world.

He hoped Julia DeVincenzo would listen to reason.

CHAPTER THREE

Giacomo Canova had been a policeman for over thirty years, and a detective for more than twenty of those. He'd also been in Pietro Magaddino's house during that time, had stood in this very den a number of times. Over the years he'd learned how not to be intimidated by the wealth and grandeur that surrounded him. Being angry also helped, especially when he saw the man who'd accompanied Julia DeVincenzo from upstairs.

Julia looked totally calm as she walked through the double French doors. "Good evening, Detective Canova," she said easily. "I trust you've been taken care of."

"Yes, thank you." Manners dictated the response, not a fear of her or her position. Canova openly studied the man with her. The man didn't appear concerned about it in the least.

"You have some news of my son?" Julia asked, seating herself in one of the plush couches. She waved him to another across from her.

Canova sat, balancing his hat on one knee. He was very aware of the two armed men Armando had left in the room. They stood like bookends on either side of the French doors, their hands clasped before them.

"No," Canova said. "There has been some trouble in front of your home. I thought—"

"Yes," Julia interrupted. "I'd noticed the surveillance boat. I hope your department has warrants for those phone taps and for the right to spy on me."

Canova was a little taken aback. During previous visits to her grandfather, the woman had appeared docile. Last night, after the kidnapping, she hadn't been aggressive at all, just a mother who'd lost her son.

"It wasn't there to spy on you," the detective said.

"You were keeping an eye out for the kidnappers," Julia supplied.

"Yes." There was no other way for Canova to answer. Since they both knew it was only an attractive lie, it made him even more uncomfortable. The man seated on the couch beside her seemed amused.

"Since you have no news of my son, I have to assume that you haven't spotted them."

"No."

"Then your visit here is to make sure we weren't troubled by the inconvenience your men suffered out in front of my house?"

Canova leaned forward, pushing out of his mind the fact that the woman's son had been kidnapped. "Mrs. DeVincenzo, the power cable across the canal was severed by a pistol shot." He held up two fingers. "Two men were spotted running to your home."

"You mean they were running *toward* my home."

"Yes." Canova locked eyes with the man beside her. "They assaulted one of the plainclothes officers assigned to this watch. I came in here to ask you if you know anything about these men."

"No," Julia answered. "I don't. Do you think these men might have something to do with my son's kidnapping?"

"We're investigating that possibility." Canova was surprised at how effortlessly she'd been keeping him on the defensive. But then, he'd known he'd entered her house on a flimsy excuse. Back when Magaddino was still alive, the old man would have handed him his head at the door. "We were wondering if perhaps they'd gotten inside your home. I'd like to take a look around."

"You think my security people wouldn't have noticed?"

Canova tried a smile. "For my peace of mind."

"No," Julia replied. "You've been assigned to find my son. I talked to your superiors this morning and confirmed that. When I spotted the boat loaded with surveillance equipment out front, I was furious but I kept quiet because I wanted your help for Nicky. Now you're asking to snoop around my house on the presumption that I'd let my son's kidnappers inside. I'll be damned if I sit still for any more of this. If you don't have anything more, I'd like you out of my house."

The two security guards took a meaningful step forward.

"I see." Canova stood. "However, I'd like to speak further with your guest."

"I don't think that's possible," Julia replied.

"I do," the detective insisted. He locked eyes with the man. "There's a certain matter of an incident that took place in front of the Palazzo Ducale earlier. I have some questions." He looked at Julia. "And in his case, a warrant *can* be arranged."

"I'll take care of it, Julia," the man said. He stepped forward and offered his hand. "Leo Turrin. If you're the cop in charge of the kidnapping, I need to talk to you anyway."

Canova was totally taken by surprise.

"You want to do this here or downtown?" Turrin asked.

Keeping his composure with difficulty, Canova said, "Outside. For the moment." He tipped his hat at Julia.

Turrin turned to the woman. "I'll be back in a few minutes."

She nodded.

Canova figured they'd have to see about that. It was going to be hard for Turrin to explain why his picture had been recovered at the scene of the gunfight.

MACK BOLAN FOUND the security cameras built into the big desk after only a couple of minutes of working the concealed locks. It was a modular unit, complete with three monitors and state-of-the-art audio equipment. The graphics, resolution and audio were all computer enhanced. He glanced at the leg of the desk and saw the wire running down it and into the floor. A guess told him that the main frame for the system was built on the other side of the wall behind him.

Carefully built into the desk, there was also a keyboard that pulled out under the center drawer. He skipped that for the moment and worked with the trackball beside the monitors. In rapid succession he flipped through several of the rooms in the house. He couldn't remember seeing the cameras, so he knew they were hidden in the walls, as well. Pietro Magaddino had played every move close to the vest.

When he found the downstairs den, he stopped and watched Julia DeVincenzo and Turrin enter the room. Only a couple of minutes later, Armando walked out.

Bolan flicked through the cameras and managed to find Armando again in the spacious kitchen. Turrin could take care of himself, but Armando's behavior intrigued the warrior. The security chief walked to the kitchen phone and lifted it.

Already suspicious of the man, Bolan reached over and flicked the toggle that activated the audio on the phone line, then lifted the earphone to his ear. Record flashed on the screen to let him know it was being taped.

On-screen Armando leaned against the pantry, his attention on the kitchen door, and punched in a local number. He was turned so that Bolan couldn't get it all. He counted the beeps. Three rings later the phone was answered by a long beep. Armando punched in four beeps and was answered by three. Apparently satisfied, the security chief hung up the phone and went to the refrigerator for a glass of tomato juice.

With a little searching, Bolan found the Glass Optical Jukebox drive connected to the computer. When he opened it, he found the carousel of recording units all marked. Two of them were even dated after Pietro Magaddino's death, including the night Nicky DeVincenzo was kidnapped.

He accessed the command menu for the recordings. Using the trackball, he located the disk Armando had been recorded on. He played back the sequence of events involving the security chief, using other modifiers to slow down the action.

The number was still out of his view.

He scooped up the phone and punched in a number he'd been given for Stony Man Farm. A few seconds later, after the signal had been bounced through a series of cutouts, the phone rang.

Aaron Kurtzman answered at the other end.

"Striker," Bolan said, identifying himself. "I need some help."

"Always happy to oblige," the cybernetics genius replied. "You made your connect with Sticker?"

"Yeah. But we're really low on Intel."

"A particular specialty of mine. What do you need?"

"I've got a recording I want you to look at," Bolan said. "It's a man making a phone call. I can't make out the numbers, but I thought maybe you could match up the individual tones the buttons made and get me a location through a crisscross directory."

"You and Sticker are still at your prearranged locale?"

"Right."

"You want me to call?" Kurtzman asked. "Or do you want to call me?"

"I'll call you. Things are complicated here. Until a few minutes ago the phone lines here were compromised. That could happen again at any time."

"Roger, buddy. But right now I'm reading you clean and green. Modem line appears the same."

"Fine. The file's on its way." Bolan hit the Send button and broke the connection. He cradled the phone and turned his attention back to the Glass Optical Jukebox drive menu. It only took the modem a few seconds to kick out the audio and video files he'd sent to Stony Man Farm.

Once the system was clear, he shut off the modem and pulled up the disk on the night Nicky DeVincenzo had been taken. At first the file read easily. He shunted over to the recording that had been made of the boy's room. In the lower right corner, a neon green LED read out the time on a twenty-four-hour clock.

The LED showed 21:09:34 when Julia carried her son to the bedroom and laid him down in the Lamborghini-shaped bed. They talked for only a short time, laughing and taking time for a final hug and a kiss. Then Julia turned down the night-light beside the bed and left. Nicky picked up a Power Ranger action figure from beside his bed and played with it for a few moments, then dropped off to sleep with the action figure beside him.

Bolan sped up the recording, watching the LED flick through the numbers. The boy slept the whole time. Then at 22:37:05 a shadow fell across the window. The blurry shape was vaguely manlike.

Without warning, the transmission came to an end. Gray, fuzzed static filled the screen. When he switched to the other camera views that had been available, Bolan only found more of the static. The sole constant had been the LED readout, which kept marking time. Bolan fast-forwarded. Twenty minutes later the recording resumed, showing Julia in the bedroom with three men down around her.

He froze the picture, watching how Armando was covering her body with his. Then he was aware someone had entered the room and was watching him.

"DO YOU MIND telling me what you're doing here?" Canova asked.

Turrin watched the detective fill his pipe. They stood outside the stoop of the Magaddino house, just sheltered enough to avoid the wind. "I'm a friend of Julia's." He knew the guy had been around the block and could read inferences into anything he said. But living a double life in the Mafia had made lying an art of survival.

"Her grandfather's, too?"

"I knew him."

Canova nodded and lighted the pipe. "How?"

"Some people I knew did business with people he knew."

"So you met at socials, did you?" The detective's grin was knowing and wry.

"I guess you could call them that."

"What kind of business are you in, Mr. Turrin?"

"These days mostly I'm retired."

"You're a Family man." The inflection was deliberate.

"Sure," the stocky little Fed said. "Wife, kids, dog and a mortgage. The whole bit. You ever get to the U.S., call me. We'll invite you to a cookout."

Canova ignored the sarcasm. "Just exactly how is it you're supposed to help Mrs. DeVincenzo?"

Out on the canal a tug had come up and attached itself to the transport boat. The diesel engines sounded loud and throaty as they began pulling. Striped sawhorses lined the canal edge on both sides, keeping back the curious neighbors.

"You're aware that her son's kidnappers haven't called to make demands," Turrin said.

"At least, we don't know of any contact," Canova argued.

"They haven't," Turrin stated flatly. "So Julia's beginning to think her son was taken for other reasons. Possibly revenge or blackmail."

"I see." Canova sucked on the pipe. "From everything I've been able to discern, Mrs. DeVincenzo has never taken any part in her grandfather's business. So why would anyone wish to harm her or her son?"

"I don't know. That's part of what I'm here to find out."

"And how exactly are you the person suited for that? She has a large staff here. Also she has the ear of the upper brass at the police department."

"Negotiations are my strength," Turrin said. "I know a lot of people. She thought by doing some networking, I could find out who'd taken Nicky, then help cut the deal."

"Do you care if the boy makes it out of this alive?" Canova's stare was penetrating.

"Yes."

"Do you think that he will?"

Turrin felt himself turn cold inside at the thought. So many times in his earlier career, he'd been aware of how vulnerable his own family had been. If he'd made the slightest misstep, their lives could have been forfeit at any time. He'd been lucky but he'd been good, too.

"I don't know," Turrin answered honestly. "I hope so."

Canova nodded. "I, too, hope so." He released a lungful of smoke. "About the incident at the Palazzo Ducale..."

"I don't know who those men were," Turrin replied.

"Were you there?" the detective asked.

"You tell me."

Canova's eyes narrowed. "We could do this downtown."

"Be a bigger party," Turrin said. "I'd have to invite all my attorneys along. This late at night they'd charge me extra. I'm going to pay the big bucks, I'll want them to ream everybody they can at the police department for bothering me. Maybe I'll even get the State Department legal eagles involved just for sport. After all, I'm an American citizen."

"True, and as such you can be deported."

"That would also involve my attorneys. And probably a great delay while you tried to prove that case."

Canova looked stressed. "We'll talk here."

"Fine."

"These men had a picture of you," Canova said. "We found it on one of them. They were also roughing up a man who could have easily passed for you."

"Maybe it was him," Turrin suggested, "and I happen to look like him."

"Possibly," Canova said. "Except that they also had your name. And the picture is one I've seen among the ones Mrs. DeVincenzo keeps in her bedroom. I saw it when I was here talking to her about her son's abduction."

"Ah." Turrin filed that away. The theory of an inside man was bearing fruit quickly now. "You must have a very good memory to have remembered one picture among so many."

"I do," Canova said. "Also the crime-scene investigators took many photographs. I looked through their files to confirm my suspicions."

"I don't think Julia would have sent those people after me."

"Nor do I. Unless you pose some kind of threat to her and aren't here to help her at all."

Turrin decided to let that one go.

"But you appear to get along too well for that," Canova said. "She's relaxed with you."

Turrin nodded. "Since we know where we stand concerning the action down by Palazzo Ducale, I'd like to ask you some questions."

"What?"

"Have you identified any of the shooters involved?"

"I'm afraid that's police business," Canova replied.

"I see." Turrin reached under his jacket and took an envelope out of an inside pocket. He handed it across to the detective.

Canova held his hands away from it. "I'm not taking that letter. If you have someone photographing this little chat, which you arranged to be out here, things could look very damaging if the wrong face were to be put on this."

"Like if it were a payoff?"

Canova shrugged.

"It's a letter. Allow me." Turrin opened it and quickly read the missive. It was short and to the point, asking that police assistance be given to Leo Turrin regarding the kidnapping of Nicky DeVincenzo. It was signed by Harold Brognola of the Justice Department, and by a representative of the State Department. Since a Stony Man umbrella couldn't be erected over Turrin's involvement, Brognola had done what he could. Turrin had arranged for the request to the Justice Department to come from one of the capos he knew who had influence on the Hill, so no suspicion would be directed at the stocky little Fed and his cover would remain intact.

"I'll take the letter and forward it to my superiors," Canova said. "Obviously you are a man of many resources."

"Yes."

"But we've not identified any of these men yet."

"When you do—"

"I will let you know. I'd prefer it if I could get the same assurances from you."

Turrin shook his head. "I can't lie to you. I'm only here to help get the boy back. If it's felt that your department will be a liability, I'll have to go by that."

"I understand." Canova turned to go, then stopped. Outside the nimbus of illumination provided by the stoop lights, he looked pale against the darkness. "There's one other thing I need to ask you."

"Sure."

"Do you know how a copy of Mrs. DeVincenzo's picture of you got into the hands of those men?"

"No."

"You might want to keep that in mind."

"I'm growing eyeballs in the back of my head even as we speak," Turrin said.

"Good. Maybe you'll be able to keep it on your shoulders that way."

Turrin watched him go. Provided the picture was a copy of one Julia had, then the house security was definitely compromised. It also meant that their arrival had probably been reported and someone out there already knew about them.

"WHERE IS THE PRIEST?" Alonzo Galvani demanded.

"I don't know, boss," Willy Simonelli answered in a quavering voice. "The police picked up Lorenzo and Solly only a few minutes ago. Both of them were dead."

"What about the priest?" Galvani hated to hear his voice when he got mad. It sounded like an old man's voice. At seventy-four, he figured he still had a lot of years ahead of him, maybe most of them not so good, but he wasn't hanging on by his fingernails. He exercised at the gym regularly and even stayed away from hard liquor as much as he could these days. Women were another matter, a vice he hadn't been able to give up. In spite of all the care, though, his lungs had rebelled against his body, only pumping in part of the air he needed. So when he raised his voice, he could no longer yell the way he could in the old days. There were times back then when he remembered men pissing their pants when he yelled.

"He got away, sir." Simonelli was on his knees on the expansive Oriental rug that covered the floor of the parlor.

"The police didn't see him?" Galvani asked in a more normal tone of voice.

"No, sir."

"The priest killed these two men?"

"Yes."

"How?"

"With his hands."

Galvani glanced at the man as if doubting him.

"Sincerely. He used only his hands and his feet. It was like nothing I'd ever seen. Both of these men already had their guns out, pointed at him. Yet he killed them and remained unhurt. Lorenzo was able only to fire one shot before the priest made his heart stop."

"A priest did this," Galvani said. A chill spread across his shoulders and sent arrows toward his heart. With effort he kept the fear from his face.

"Yes, sir."

"The church doesn't use killers," Galvani said.

"I know only what I saw," Simonelli replied.

Glancing up, Galvani checked with his head bodycock. Gabe Valente hung up the phone and nodded. Valente was six-two and muscular, in his late thirties and in the prime of life. He kept his dark hair in a military-styled cut and never failed to turn the ladies' heads. He was wearing a crimson-and-gold sweat suit and looked ready for a fast game of tennis.

"They're both dead," Valente reported.

Galvani took a deep breath and tried to maintain control. He gazed around the room, reminding himself how much power he wielded. For years men had lived and died by his word, in spite of the hammerlock Magaddino had had on him.

He was tall and thin, more stoop shouldered than he'd like to admit. His hair was gray and wiry, and jutted out if he let it get too long. Tans no longer held, either, with the condition of his skin. He wore a dark blue suit with a white silk scarf. Hawk nosed and angular featured, he no longer had the looks of his youth, but he was a striking man.

The parlor was dark because he liked it that way, and the illumination in the room came from the fireplace and the recessed lighting above it. The big desk was to one side, fronted by a trio of red leather chairs. Beyond them was a wet bar. Adorning the walls were expensive paintings that he never looked at but were held in awe by the wealthier people he entertained.

"You're sure this man was a priest?" Galvani asked.

"He was the guy your people spotted in Vatican City," Simonelli said. "And after he tore out Solly's throat, I saw this guy give him the last rites."

"If you were that close," Galvani said, "why didn't you shoot him yourself?"

"Mr. Galvani, you know I'm no shooter." Simonelli looked panicky. Beads of sweat rolled over his broad face.

Turning on the man, Galvani said, "You knew I wanted this man dead, Willy. You failed me."

"No, sir. Lorenzo and Solly failed you. I tracked the priest and put them onto him, just like I was supposed to."

"Where did he go?" Galvani asked.

"I don't know. It all happened so fast. First it looked like Lorenzo and Solly had him, no problem. Next thing I know, I'm looking at two dead guys, neither of them the guy that's supposed to be dead. Minute after that the priest takes a powder, and the cops are getting there."

"That's not the way I heard it," Valente said. He took a seat on the edge of the massive desk. Of the seven men in the room, he was the only one Galvani would allow to take liberties like that. "My guy tells me it took the police seventeen minutes to get there. He should know, because he wears one of their uniforms."

"I didn't want to get caught, that's all. Please, sir."

"It's okay," Galvani said, waving at the man to calm down. "We found the priest once, we can find him again. This is our city, after all."

"We can," Simonelli said enthusiastically. "I swear, I won't rest until I do."

Galvani wasn't taken in by the lie for even a second. He lifted his wineglass from the desk, his last of the evening even though he wanted more. "That's fine, Willy. Go get a drink while I consider our options."

"Sure, boss." The big man pushed himself to his feet with difficulty and waddled across the Oriental rug. He mopped his face with a handkerchief.

Galvani waited until Simonelli was about to pour himself a drink, then slipped a silenced Colt .45 Government Model from under his jacket. "Willy," he called gently. When the man turned, Galvani shot him five times in the face, the force of the bullets throwing his corpse against the wall.

The old Mafia don crossed the room and looked down. The Oriental rug ended a few feet in front of the wet bar. None of the blood had fallen on it. The rug was a favorite, and he would have disliked having to replace it.

"All in the face," Valente commented at his side. "Not bad."

"You should have seen me in my prime, kid," Galvani said. "Time was when I could have placed those rounds in a playing card with either hand at forty yards."

Valente shrugged. "Dead is dead. I figure you probably wasted four shots. He checked out after the first one."

Galvani glanced at the four other men. None of them seemed surprised by the violence. "You guys get this mess cleaned up. Gabe, come with me. We need to talk." He wiped his prints from the pistol and dropped it onto the dead man's chest. The bullets and magazine had already been wiped before Simonelli had arrived.

Disposing of the corpse would prove no problem. When he'd bought the house thirty years ago, Galvani had paid for a hidden chute in the basement with direct access to one of the old flood drains beneath the city. With everything that had been done for the past hundred years on behalf of land-reclamation projects, no one would be able to trace the corpse back to him when and if it turned up. Especially not after spending the next several hours in the lime pit he also had ready for such emergencies.

Living so close to Magaddino while under the man's thumb had proved difficult. Galvani had adapted.

The old man led the way up to the third-floor balcony and took a seat at the patio table. Drizzling rain made patterns on the glass walls of the balcony. In the distance a helicopter cut a path across the city.

"We must find this priest," Galvani said. He placed his wineglass on the table, laced his fingers before him and peered at Valente.

"If it can be done, I will see it done," the bodycock said. "I know you've disagreed in the past, but give it some thought again—maybe it would help if we, or even only I, knew why this priest is so important."

"No. That's out of the question." Secrets had been kept so long that he'd forgotten how frightening the truth could be until the day he'd learned of Pietro Magaddino's death. So much would change if those secrets became public knowledge.

Valente shrugged and let it pass. "We'll find him. As you pointed out, this is our city. He's just a foreigner. Soon he'll make a mistake, then we'll have him."

"As soon as you do, kill him," Galvani said. "I don't want any chances taken. Those fools probably would have had him tonight if they hadn't gotten so cocky."

"There's something else I need to talk to you about. Rufio called it in about the time Willy showed up."

Galvani nodded.

"That action on the television news about the shooting down at the Palazzo Ducale?"

"Yes."

"Rufio scabbed onto some information that they may be Romanians."

"He knows this for sure?"

"No, but he's working on it. For now it looks solid."

The Romanians had been a thorn in Galvani's side for over a year. With the fall of the Berlin Wall and the abandonment of communism by the USSR and her satellites, Eastern Europe had marched into capitalist ways with a fever. A number of markets dealing in arms, drugs and illicit merchandise had opened up, and the old don had worked hard to get as much of the territory as he could.

Even if Magaddino had known, Galvani doubted the man would have cared. Eastern Europe was given to internal political and religious stresses that had always existed there but had been kept in check by the presence of Russian heavy metal—and by the determination of the Communist governments to crush rebellions.

Galvani circled the rim of his wineglass with a forefinger and listened to the low-pitched hum of the crystal. "Are these men linked to that bastard Mihai Lupu?"

"It wouldn't surprise me," Valente said, "but we haven't found out definitely yet."

"If they were Lupu's men, what were they doing here?"

"They had a picture of a man named Turrin."

The name clicked in Galvani's mind. "Leo Turrin?"

Valente nodded. "Do you know this guy?"

"From the old days. He's American."

"Anybody to be worried about?"

Galvani shook his head. "They called him Leo the Pussy in the old days."

Valente smiled. "He lack a spine or what?"

"No. Leo came up running the girls, then he moved on into the more delicate areas of negotiations between capos. These days he's pretty much retired from what I hear."

"Was he a friend of Magaddino's?"

"His granddaughter's, I think. Where is he now?"

"I don't know. I can find out."

"Do that." Galvani tried to figure out what Turrin's presence had to do with the things that were presently going on in Venice, but he couldn't seem to put it together. He sipped his wine and stared out over the city. Venice could have been his so long ago, and perhaps a great deal more besides. He'd had more guts and more desire than Magaddino. But Magaddino had had him by the balls. Silently he cursed his old foe's memory and hoped his soul rotted in hell. "What of Julia DeVincenzo's brat?"

"Our guys are still looking," Valente answered. "They've checked around, but the teams who usually specialize in hitting the moneyed families aren't involved."

"Then it was someone from outside."

"Probably."

"These people would still need someone inside the house," Galvani said.

"Yeah."

"Have you checked on that?"

"Mrs. DeVincenzo's been keeping that household buttoned up tight since yesterday."

"Find out," Galvani ordered. He didn't like how the pieces were starting to shake out. The Romanians were perhaps in the city, gunning for Leo Turrin, who was known for working things out for the Family heads, and kidnappers who could vanish like ghosts; all that added up to more than he wanted to face. He had to wonder whether his secrets hadn't died with Magaddino. If they were somewhere in that house, waiting to be discovered by someone who wouldn't be content to keep him in check the way Magaddino had, then he was possibly in more trouble than he'd at first imagined. "Let me know when you do."

"I will."

Galvani finished his wine. "And have my boat brought around. I think it's time I went to offer my services to Mrs. DeVincenzo."

THE MACHINED PIECES of the Beeman/Hammerli Model 280 Sport Pistol went together easily in Jericho Light's hands. They gleamed darkly of oil in the weak illumination provided by the small lamp beside the bed.

Sitting cross-legged on the floor in sweatpants and a T-shirt, he slid the first four rounds of .32 ammunition into the magazine, worked the action to chamber the first one, then added the fifth. The target pistol felt natural in his hand. When he was finished, he slid it into a nylon ankle holster. He filled five other magazines and laid them beside the pistol. Those would be hidden in his clothing later.

He leaned forward again and reached into the hole in the wall. His instructions had been explicit, and without them he knew he would have been challenged to find the hiding place.

He took a long gun case from the space left between his apartment and the next when carpenters had remodeled the house more than twenty years earlier. He sat the case across his knees and opened it up. Inside was a Weatherby Vanguard VGX Deluxe bolt-action hunting rifle chambered in .30-06. In minutes he'd broken it down, cleaned it and oiled it and had it reassembled.

Satisfied, he put the rifle in the case and returned it to its hiding place, then fit the paneling back over it. After strapping the Beeman/Hammerli to his ankle, he put away his clothing. None of it was personal and all of it could be left behind at a moment's notice.

He locked up and went downstairs. On his way in, he'd noticed a late-night café with takeout available. He ordered a carton of spaghetti, six pieces of garlic bread, a coffee and went back out.

A fine mist was falling, wrapping oily rainbows around the street lamps and turning the canal water dark. Light sat at one of the outside tables. It was chill but not cold enough to be uncomfortable. He wanted to be alone to deal with the deaths of the two men who'd tried to kill him.

"Do you mind if I sit with you?" a small voice asked in Italian.

He turned and saw a young girl of no more than fourteen standing in the shadows beside the café. The windows beside her held neon tubing advertising lasagna, pizza and pasta, and the bright hues leached all the color from the girl.

"You're young to be out so late," Light commented.

"I've nowhere else to go," she replied.

"Your parents?"

"I haven't seen them in a long time." She stepped forward and reminded him of a cat, all slender and sinewy, languorous, but ready to bolt at a moment's notice.

"Where do you live?"

"Wherever." She waved the question away, and her attention drifted to the spaghetti and bread on the table.

"How do you get by?"

"Sometimes I stay with friends in empty buildings." She looked at him, but her eyes were cold and distant. "Other times I spend the night with men. For money." The invitation was obvious.

"I see." Light opened the bucket of spaghetti. "Have you eaten?"

"No."

"Would you like to eat with me?"

"Do you have enough?"

"If we don't, we can get more. Please, join me."

"Okay." She sat across from him, and he could see she was tense, ready to launch into flight at any sudden move on his part.

"Let me get a paper plate and I'll be back." While he was inside, he also bought her two cartons of milk and a cup to drink it from. He tried to give them to her, but she didn't accept them.

"What do I have to do for dinner?" she asked. "If you want me to go to bed with you, I want money and I want it up front."

"I don't want you to go to bed with me," Light said, dividing the spaghetti into equal portions.

The girl was silent for a moment. "You think I'm dirty or something? Too good for me?"

"No. I just don't feel like a woman's company tonight."

"Oh." She seemed pleased that he considered her a woman. "Then what do you want?"

"Conversation would be nice."

"You're new to Venice."

"Yes." He broke the garlic bread and gave her half of that. She started to fork up the spaghetti. "Wait."

"What?" The lights in her eyes suggested that she was ready to fight for the food she'd been given if she had to.

"I'd like to say grace before we eat, if you don't mind."

"Okay." She put her fork down and clasped her hands before her. Her head was bowed, but Light was sure she didn't close her eyes. That would have made her too vulnerable.

He kept the prayer short. She crossed herself at the same time he did.

"You're a religious man?" she asked through a mouthful of spaghetti. Sauce dripped down her chin.

He nodded.

"Do you really believe in God and all that stuff?"

"Yes. Don't you?"

"I think maybe I used to. Then life got too hard, and nobody seemed to care about me. My dad died of cancer and my mom turned out to be an alcoholic who hated me because I was always in the way. It's easier living in the streets than it was living with her."

"I'm sorry."

"Me, too. But I have to ask myself what kind of god would allow that to happen to a kid, you know?"

"I understand. But I also think you're confused. God doesn't allow things to happen. That choice was made a long time ago. But He does allow salvation for those who believe and trust in Him. It is every person's journey and burden to find a time and a place, and the strength to put his or her life in God's hands. As it is yours."

The girl chewed and swallowed and appeared to consider his words. Light realized he'd been speaking to himself as much as to her, putting the violence in a different perspective. She said, "You make it sound easy."

"It's not," he replied.

"Will you do me a favor?" she asked.

"What?"

"The next time you pray to God, would you tell Him about me and ask Him to watch over me?"

"I'd be glad to."

"Thanks." She turned her attention to a fresh piece of garlic bread.

"Will you tell me your name?" Light asked. "For the prayer?"

"There's no need to," she replied. "He's God. He'll know who I am."

"Of course." And Light knew it was true.

CHAPTER FOUR

"What are you doing?" Julia DeVincenzo demanded.

"Checking over the security system," Bolan replied. He looked at the woman as she came around the desk and stared at the equipment. There was no mistaking the surprise in her eyes.

"How did you know that was there?" Julia asked.

"I didn't," the warrior told her. "I found it. You didn't know this was here?"

Julia shook her head. She folded her arms across her breasts defensively. "My grandfather had many secrets. He didn't want me involved in any of his business, and I didn't exactly approve of it, either." She looked at him. "I've been asked before why I didn't just leave him if I felt that way."

"It wouldn't have mattered," Bolan said. "Anywhere you went, you'd still have been Pietro Magaddino's granddaughter. At least around him, there was protection."

"Not many people realized that."

"Maybe not."

"Leo told me you've been around Family business," Julia said. "But you're not exactly of the Families, are you?"

"No."

"Then what are you?"

Bolan looked at her. "Right now I'm someone trying to help you get your son back."

Her eyes were dark and penetrating. "Leo told me if anyone could do it, it would be you. Is that true?"

"I'm going to try," Bolan said. "But first we're going to have to figure out what these people want. If it was money, they'd have been in touch by now." He tapped the keyboard on the security setup. "Since you didn't know about this, can you guess who might have known about it other than your grandfather? Did he have electricians who regularly worked on the house?"

"There was a company he used." Julia reached for the Rolodex and quickly leafed through it. "I've got the owner's home number here. Is it important?"

Turrin reentered the room and took in the security system at a glance. He walked around to the other side of Bolan.

"Call him," the warrior directed. "See if he knows anything." He checked his watch. It was 12:17 a.m.

After a brief conversation with the electrician, Julia hung up. "Neither he nor his people ever put anything like that in this house."

"He could have had it done by specialists from outside the country," Turrin suggested. "Took a weekend out with the family somewhere, left a key with the installation team and had it done by the time they got back. Nobody had to be the wiser."

"Not my grandfather," Julia said. "He wouldn't have left this house open to anyone without supervision."

"I agree," Bolan said. "Magaddino would have left someone here. What about your husband?"

Julia took a moment to think about it, then shook her head. "I can't remember a time when we went anywhere without him. Grandfather always organized our outings if they were going to last more than a few hours. Security was very strict."

"Who was your grandfather's chief of security?" Bolan asked.

"Joey Tarrintino," Turrin said.

Julia nodded. "After my grandfather's death, Joey came to me and told me he was retiring. I wasn't surprised. He's sixty-six, and his loyalty was to my grandfather more than me." She paused. "When I was growing up, I said a lot of things to my grandfather in front of Joey that Joey would have never let anyone else say and live."

"Can you call him?"

"I can try. Whether he talks to me is another matter." Julia lifted the phone and made the call. She talked briefly to a maid at the house, then scribbled an international number on a piece of paper from the desk. "He's in Switzerland. On vacation, but Rozella gave me the number." She dialed, then put it on speakerphone.

After four rings a deep male voice answered. "Mr. Tarrintino's rooms."

"Denny, this is Julia DeVincenzo."

"Hello, Mrs. DeVincenzo. I was there at your grandfather's funeral, but I never got the chance to speak to you. I'd like to say how sorry I am. Your grandfather was a great man."

"Thank you."

"If there's ever anything I can do—"

"Actually," Julia said, "there is. I need to speak to Joey."

"That may be a little hard to do. Mr. Tarrintino's stomach is bothering him tonight. You know how that is."

Bolan flipped one of the dated Glass Optical Jukebox disks to Turrin. In and around Stony Man Farm a lot himself, the stocky little Fed recognized it even as he caught it. His eyebrows arched up, and he nodded in understanding.

"This has to do with my son's kidnapping," Julia said.

"Yes, ma'am. Well...let me see what I can do." The line was put on hold.

"Why is this important?" Julia asked as she took the disk from Turrin and turned it over for inspection.

"Somebody's still been using the surveillance equipment after your grandfather's death," Bolan said. "This is the disk that was being used last night."

"When Nicky was kidnapped?"

Bolan nodded.

"Then you have the kidnappers taped?"

"No." The warrior played the disk, letting her watch the replay until it fuzzed out to gray static.

"What happened?" she asked.

"Someone deliberately erased it," Bolan answered. "I'm guessing that whoever knew about this surveillance station was also in on your son's kidnapping. We find out who that was, we'll be one step closer to getting him back.''

The speakerphone spit white noise, then an old man's phlegmatic voice came on. ''Julie? This is Joey.''

''Joey, I need you to tell me about the security setup in my grandfather's office.''

''I ain't no brain, kid, you know that. There should be a book there somewhere.'' Tarrintino coughed and hacked. ''Look, I know things was pretty strained between us at times, but if there's anything I can do to help you with Nicky, you let me know. I don't want to step on Armando's toes, though, but I got a few more years in with these things than that kid. He made it pretty clear that me and mine were to butt out where you were concerned once your grandfather was buried, God rest his soul.''

''Who knew about the security system?'' Julia asked.

''Me. Armando. Probably nobody else. The old man didn't like too many people knowing his business, though he sure as hell liked knowing theirs.''

''Thanks, Joey.''

''No problem, kid. But you keep in mind what I said about Nicky. I love that little guy. I've already got some feelers out, guys who owe me favors. I find something out, I'll give you and Armando a ring.'' Tarrintino broke the connection.

''Where's Armando?'' Bolan asked.

"I'll get him." The wrath in Julia's gaze was complete. She called for the security chief over the house intercom.

"Personally I figured we wouldn't have been able to shake him," Turrin said.

Less than a minute later one of the other guards called back over the intercom. "Armando's not here, Mrs. DeVincenzo."

"Then where is he?" Julia demanded.

"He went out. He said to tell you if you asked, that he thinks he has a lead on where Nicky is."

Bolan exchanged looks with Turrin. Neither of them believed it.

"Where did he go?" Julia's voice was harsh.

"I really couldn't say. You know how Armando can be when he chooses to keep things to himself."

"Dammit!" Julia snapped off the intercom, then looked at Bolan and Turrin. "He's a part of this, isn't he?"

"Maybe," Bolan said. He pushed himself up out of the chair behind the desk and started for the door.

"Where are you going?" Julia asked.

"To check on a few things."

"You can't just walk out of here like this, dammit! This is my son we're talking about!" Her voice sounded as though the veneer of self-control was almost worn through. She came across the room at him as if she was ready to do battle.

Bolan paused. "Look, Mrs. DeVincenzo, I understand that you're afraid. All I can do is ask you to trust me and to trust Leo. At the moment your whole security staff could be compromised. Do you want to take a chance on any of them?"

Julia's eyes turned watery, but her chin was firm. "Take me with you."

"I can't," Bolan told her honestly. "If you try to leave, people are going to follow you. And there are policemen still posted outside who'd do the same thing. I can get out of here, but you can't. I'm sorry."

"He's right, Julia," Turrin said.

She wiped her eyes. "I don't have a choice, do I?"

Bolan shook his head. "No."

"What are you going to do?"

"If Armando is going to bring Nicky back? Nothing. If he continues hiding him out, I'm going to bring Nicky back to you."

Visibly steeling herself to turn away from him, Julia said, "Then do that. And get back here as soon as you can."

"I will." Bolan opened the door and left the room. He knew it was hard for the woman to just let him walk away, having no idea what was going to happen but knowing that he wasn't telling her everything. She'd lived in and around lies all her life; she knew how to recognize them.

On the other hand, she also knew how to tell them. He had to keep that in mind, as well.

He left the house by way of the backyard garden. He went over the wall and disappeared into the shadows. His combat senses drew a net around him, and his mind raced. Armando only had a few minutes head start on him. He had to close the distance.

ABOUT A QUARTER MILE from the Magaddino house, sure that no one had followed him, Bolan stopped at a pay phone and again went through the routine to get a secure line to Stony Man Farm. When Kurtzman answered, Bolan said, "Tell me you got it."

"I did," Kurtzman replied. "Number and address that was called."

"Give me the address."

"It's in the Dorsoduro district west of you." Then he gave directions.

Bolan memorized them. "What about armament?"

"There's an antique shop not far from you," the cybernetics expert said. "It's a front for a CIA drop. If you're not looking for anything too exotic, they should be able to fix you up. The password's 'Arctic Dawn.'"

"Cryptic," the warrior commented.

"That's the CIA for you."

Bolan thanked him and hung up. He flagged down a gondolier in the canal and ran to the boat. Money changed hands, and the gondolier adjusted his course, kicking in the outboard motor for the extra cash instead of using the pole. Bolan sat at the front of the boat and went over everything Kurtzman had told him.

The area where the phone call was received was one of the older sections where there was an ongoing battle with rising water. Several buildings in that region had a whole floor underwater, offering the possibility of veritable catacombs. And the clock was ticking.

"So THIS DIDN'T have anything to do with my grandfather after all," Julia DeVincenzo said. "Armando took Nicky because of me."

"You think so?" Turrin asked.

They were still in her grandfather's office. She stood at the window looking out over the city and wondering if she'd ever felt so afraid of it. "He's had...feelings for me a long time. Even before Stefan. Since my husband's death, he'd made it obvious that he was there for me in whatever way I wished. I think my grandfather talked to him at one point and made him see the error of his ways. But now, if he really was part of Nicky's kidnapping, it's become an obsession."

"Yeah," Turrin said. "That's what I'd call it."

"In a way it's ironic," she said.

"What?" Turrin asked.

"I both loved and hated my grandfather at different times, and when Nicky was taken, I was sure it was all somehow his fault."

"That's understandable under the circumstances. You didn't exactly have a normal childhood. Everything revolved around your grandfather. I don't think you were jumping to conclusions, you were just following an established pattern."

"I don't feel guilty."

"I don't think you should. Probably even your grandfather would have understood."

"Maybe. But I don't believe it. My grandfather was a hard, ruthless man. There were a number of attempts on his life after World War II when he started organizing the Families in Italy. He met a lot of resistance. He wouldn't have made it as far as he did if Alonzo Galvani hadn't thrown in with him. A lot of people felt Galvani should have made the climb into power instead of Pietro Magaddino."

"That's ancient history to me," Turrin said, "and another planet besides."

"Not around here," Julia said. "It's still talked about occasionally. Of course, only when the speakers don't think I can hear them."

Someone knocked on the door. Turrin answered it and found one of the housemen standing outside.

"I'm sorry to interrupt," the man apologized, "but Mrs. DeVencenzo has a visitor."

"Who is it?" Julia asked.

"Don Galvani and members of his staff."

"What do they want?"

"To speak with you. I told them I'd see if you were still awake."

Julia looked at Turrin, perplexed.

"Could be the other shoe's about to drop," Turrin said. "I think we should talk to him."

Although a fresh wave of panic had set in, Julia agreed. "Invite them in and tell them that I'll be down in a few minutes."

The houseman nodded and left.

"Maybe there was more to Armando's interest than love," Turrin said. "Could be there's a little greed mixed in there, as well."

"If Galvani's mixed up in this, it could mean more trouble for your friend. And Nicky."

Turrin reached out and took her hand. "He can take care of himself and he's big enough to take care of Nicky, too. In the meantime you're going to need to be strong enough to face Galvani like it's business as usual."

Julia knew Turrin was right. She took a deep breath, held it for just a moment, then let it out. Control, however fleeting it proved to be, returned to her. "Okay. I'm ready." She took Turrin's arm and let him lead her from the room.

BOLAN WENT WITH THE NIGHT. The CIA drop had provided dark clothing and boots, as well as munitions. He wore a Kevlar-lined windbreaker over a black shirt. Black jeans and steel-toed boots completed the ensemble. Camou paint muted his face and hands to the point he would have looked like a patchwork man in the best moonlight.

For his lead weapon, he had an H&K MP-5 SD-3 submachine gun. He carried a SIG-Sauer P-228 Night Stalker on his hip. Extra magazines for both weapons rode in a web belt along with smoke and antipersonnel grenades. A pair of AN/PVS-7 night-vision goggles were inside the windbreaker.

After he'd given the man at the antique store the password, no questions had been asked. Bolan had been in and out in minutes.

He jogged along the canal until he found the pay phone beside a closed glassware shop. A brief flick of his penlight revealed that it was the number Armando had called.

Keeping the subgun under cover of the windbreaker, the warrior scouted the terrain. All the businesses in the area were closed for the night, and most of them had two or three, and sometimes four, stories of apartments above them. Besides being risky, it would take hours to search them all.

Then he felt someone move along his backtrail, triggering his combat senses. Bolan kept walking and checked the reflections in the windows of the buildings beside him.

The guy following him was six feet tall and rangy. He kept his hand in his jacket pocket and his attention riveted on Bolan.

The warrior read his pursuer as a floating sentry, with orders to investigate but to not get involved. However, it wasn't apparent what the guy was safeguarding. Bolan turned right at the next alley, then looked up and saw the wrought iron balcony within leaping range above him.

Letting the submachine gun hang by its shoulder strap, Bolan leaped and snagged the balcony lip. He pulled himself up, then flipped over the edge of the balcony, making hardly any noise. The combat webbing kept his gear secure around him.

A few seconds later the guard turned the corner after him, obviously surprised that Bolan was no longer in sight. Instinctively, he lifted the Beretta pistol from his pocket. Then he reached for a throat mike.

Without hesitation the Executioner dropped to the alley behind the guard. As the man started to spin around, the warrior grabbed the mike from the lapel of his jacket and ripped it loose. He caught the man's gun wrist in his other hand, then lifted a knee into the guy's crotch.

An exhalation of pain that wasn't a scream and wasn't even close to ordinary conversation robbed the man's lungs of air. The pistol dropped from his trapped hand. He tried to fight back, but the Executioner head-butted him in the face. His nose snapped audibly, and blood spilled down to his chin.

Knotting his left hand in the man's jacket, Bolan slammed him up against the building, not letting him draw a breath of air to yell a warning. Before the sentry could recover, Bolan grabbed the H&K MP-5 in his right fist and pushed the blunt silencer under the man's Adam's apple.

"I'm here for the boy," Bolan said. "One word from you that gets him hurt, you die. If you understand, nod."

The man nodded slowly. Blood continued dripping from his nostrils. His nose had taken on definite S lines and was swelling visibly.

"Is the boy all right?"

The man nodded again.

"Is he here?"

Another nod.

"Where?" Bolan dug the submachine gun in meaningfully.

"Underground," the guy croaked. "There's drainpipes. You go in there." He pointed toward a manhole farther down the alley. "Way you were moving, I thought you knew already."

"Walk me through it," Bolan ordered. He felt the man's breath against the back of his hand, ragged and warm. The doomsday numbers spun in his mind, adding up the variables on the play. It was possible the sentries patrolled in pairs.

"Get in," the guy said. "Go north about fifty yards, then turn east. Another thirty, thirty-five yards you'll see some white chalk letters and numbers marked on the wall. They look like the letters and numbers the sanitation crews use along this section, but they're not. CKS411. There's a hidden release built into the wall at the bottom. Slide it over, and a section of the wall swings in. You follow that tunnel and it'll take you to the boy. He's in a room that was used for contraband by smugglers years ago."

"Is Armando here?"

The man nodded.

"You work for him?"

"Yeah."

Bolan took a roll of ordnance tape from his pocket and quickly bound the guy's hands and feet with it. He added a final piece across the man's mouth. When he was finished, he threw the man over his shoulder, carried him down to a large refuse bin, and dropped him in.

"Everything's the way you say it is when I go in," Bolan said, "you live. I find any problems, you're history." He lowered the lid and left the man covered atop a pile of bagged, smelly refuse.

The manhole cover was large and heavy, but he got it moved. It was even harder working it back into place while standing on the narrow rungs of the ladder built into the wall. In complete darkness he followed the ladder down by feel, till he stepped on water-slick pavement.

Taking the NVGs from his pocket, he put them on. The world took on a greenish cast, but he could see. The flood tunnel was twelve feet across and nearly ten feet high. Holes punched through the concrete crust indicated that it had been constructed out of stone, then layered over in brick with a final frosting of concrete poured over that.

Bolan moved out, following the directions. He kept the submachine gun in a loose port arms before him, ready to swing in any direction. The shelf he walked on was less than three feet wide and coated with years of slippery crud, making it difficult to navigate.

The air down in the drain was thicker, loaded with humidity and the strong scent of decay. His hearing was partially obscured by the sound of water running through the heart of the drain and the steady splash of more water dripping down from above.

For a moment Bolan had the strong sensation that the island city had waited until now to curl up and die. He found it hard not to believe that it wasn't sinking a little more with every step he took. Brushing the disturbing images aside, he concentrated on the environment. The boy had to be up ahead of him.

He made the turn to the east and scoped out the new tunnel. It was two feet lower and about a yard narrower. The water slopped up over the sides of the canal lip in most places, inches deep in some areas. He moved on more cautiously, able to hear his own footsteps as he moved through the water, though he doubted the sound carried very far.

A grating noise reached his ears. Immediately he flattened in a crouch against the wall. The NVGs showed a section of the wall ahead of him open inward, and a green rectangle of light flared to life. A man stepped out from the middle of it and turned toward Bolan. The guard held a two-way radio in one hand and an Uzi in the other.

The warrior assumed the man he'd taken out topside had been missed in the security loop.

After sealing the hidden door, the guard came toward him, unaware that death waited less than ten feet away. A crimson, dime-sized ghost raced across his face and startled him. He brought up the Uzi as he came to a stop.

Bolan's finger tightened on the subgun, keeping his target covered but holding his fire. Since the laser sight wasn't his, other intruders were present, and Bolan could use that to his advantage.

Then the dot of the laser sight settled over the guard's left eye. A shot rang out a heartbeat later, thundering along the enclosed space. In response the guard's head snapped back.

The blood on the wall looked like green splatters in the NVGs, but Bolan knew it for what it was. He was already in motion as the corpse dropped into the rushing water and disappeared. Knowing he wasn't alone in the drain, he searched for cover.

LEO TURRIN KNEW that Galvani's arrival wasn't a simple visit. He'd seen the old don a number of times before, back when Galvani had been younger and more aggressive, wanting to back someone in the United States.

Instead, Pietro Magaddino had somehow convinced Galvani he needed to stay close to home. Magaddino had always seemed content to remain small and profitable, gradually easing into more-legitimate enterprises. Alonzo Galvani's ambitions had entailed great risk with the sights constantly on huge payoffs.

Many of the American capos, if not outright afraid of the man, had at least been wary of him. Galvani had a tendency to shoot first and steamroll over the consequences. Turrin knew of at least three probable murder convictions awaiting Galvani in the U.S. covering a period of seventeen years. But no law enforcement agency could get enough international cooperation to pull Galvani back to the trials.

And there was a contract that was presumably still floating around with Galvani's name on it, issued by one of the Chicago Families after Galvani had cut them out of a deal involving black-market goods coming out of Denmark. The first man in had made the money; everyone else had picked up chump change. Magaddino had smoothed it over and forced Galvani to make it right to a degree, but the enmity had run deep. Still, the last attempt to pick up the contract had come three years ago. The would-be assassin had been found scattered over Milan, courtesy of Gabe Valente.

The bodyguard stood behind Galvani and to the right, within easy range of the old man to sweep him out of the recliner and protect him with his own body. Galvani appeared to be very relaxed.

Julia sat on the couch, totally together now, and Turrin stood just to her side. He could feel the tension in the room. He glanced at Valente and saw the small smile playing across the man's thin lips. The .38 Bodyguard at the back of Turrin's belt under his jacket was cold comfort, but the Kevlar weave under his shirt cut him a finer edge.

He wasn't exactly sure why he felt threatened, but the feeling was there just the same.

"To what do I owe this visit?" Julia asked politely.

"To my sense of chivalry, of course," Galvani replied. "With everything you've been through the last few days, I wanted to see how you were."

"I've been better," Julia answered.

"And to offer my assistance."

"At this point," Julia said, "I'm not sure what assistance I might need."

"All the more reason to offer." Galvani held up a cigarette, and when she nodded, he lit it. "This way you know more about what resources you hold."

"Thank you."

"Oh, this isn't entirely selfless, my dear," Galvani said. "When one of us has troubles, if they're not handled correctly and quickly, it simply encourages other street trash to take a swing at us. Maybe next time it could be me. If an example were to be made of these people, it could only benefit all of us."

Diplomatically, Turrin thought, Julia made no reply.

"You believe some of the locals are responsible for Nicky's abduction?" Turrin asked.

Galvani's penetrating black gaze pulled over to Turrin, glacial cold and probing. He took a hit of the cigarette and blew a smoke ring. "You've discovered something to the contrary?"

"No."

"Your question suggests otherwise," Galvani said.

"I didn't think so."

Valente took a step forward, his mouth a hard, thin line. "Mr. Galvani doesn't like to be lied to or made fun of."

The tension was suddenly thick enough in the room to cut. Turrin held up his left hand, keeping the right near the hidden pistol. He didn't think Valente meant to push the issue any further, but with Galvani involved, that wasn't a certain thing. Magaddino had been the only person able to keep him in check.

"No disrespect was intended," Turrin assured them. "But given the kidnappers' abilities to slip into this house in spite of the security and take Nicky away, I don't think the local talent suddenly decided to go big-time overnight and got lucky."

Galvani waved Valente back into place. "I see your point, but it's also possible they had inside help." His eyes moved from Turrin to Julia. "I trust that has crossed your mind by now?"

"Yes," Julia answered, her face betraying nothing.

"And?" Galvani prompted.

"We've considered it. So have the police."

Galvani referred to a small memo pad from inside his jacket. "Represented by Giacomo Canova, I believe."

"You do keep up with things," Julia commented.

Galvani inclined his head. "Thank you, my dear. Gathering information was one of my most important talents to your grandfather, God keep him. Taking that into consideration, where does that leave you?"

"We've found nothing to support that line of thinking."

"Really?" Galvani's tone indicated that he clearly doubted that. "And where is Armando? I'd expected to see him here tonight."

"He's seeing to personal business," Julia said.

"With Nicky missing?"

"He's been putting it off," Julia replied. "I expect him back shortly."

Galvani leaned in. "Listen, if I'm out of place, tell me. But since your grandfather's death, it seems a lot of people have left your fold. Truth to tell, I got kind of nervous for you when Joey the Tyrant left this house. Kind of short on brains, that man, but a strong, loyal heart. God knows, anything was apt to happen after that. I mean, look at the situation now."

Turrin knew the buildup by heart. He'd heard it all the time as he was coming up through the Mafia, and he knew what was coming next.

"If you want, maybe I could take care of this for you," Galvani offered.

"No," Julia said quietly but firmly. "This is my problem. My son. Things are being handled."

"By Armando?" Galvani looked extremely doubtful. "He's not even here now. What kind of protection is that? Next thing you know, somebody's going to be trying to whack you."

Turrin turned the words over in his mind. He couldn't be certain if Galvani was merely pointing out the possible weaknesses or making a threat.

"Your grandfather ever hear of something like that happening in this city," Galvani said, "he'd turn right over in his grave." He reached forward and touched Julia's arm. "All I'm saying is maybe Armando isn't the guy you should be leaning on right now for support. If you'd like, I can send one of my people over till you find somebody who'll be here when you need them. Hell, for that matter, you could take Gabe for a week or two. He'd steer you straight on what's what."

"Thank you," Julia said. "Perhaps if things don't resolve themselves, I'll take you up on that."

Galvani seemed pleased. His smile exposed a lot of white porcelain. Leaning forward again, he patted Julia on the knee as though she were a little girl. Then he looked at Valente. "Gabe, why don't you fix us a couple drinks. You know the way around the bar here. What would you like, Julie?"

"Mineral water." She looked up at Turrin.

Taking the hint, Turrin walked to the bar with Valente. "I'll get it."

Without causing an affront to Galvani, who'd taken control of what was going on in the room, Julia had quietly pushed things on a more equal basis.

"Gabe can get it for you," Galvani said.

As he stood at the wet bar, Turrin watched the mirror in front of him, studying the byplay. Julia was afraid of the old man, but she wasn't backing away from him. He felt proud of her.

"This is my house now," Julia said. "I am supposed to be the hostess."

"Sure, sure. I know that. I'm just used to taking care of things for people, you know. I took care of a lot of things for your grandfather."

"He told me."

Turrin uncapped a bottle of mineral water and poured it into a chilled glass. Then he made himself a screwdriver, heavy on the juice and just a flavoring of vodka, enough to be social without impairing himself.

"So you're Leo Turrin," Valente said as he finished up a bourbon and Coke, then twisted the cap off a bottle of American beer.

"Yeah," Turrin answered. He could hear the competition in the younger man's voice, could see it in the way he carried himself and the set of his jaw. There was no doubt that Valente considered himself a dangerous man. Everything Turrin had heard about him supported that, though, so it wasn't stage dressing.

"Heard a lot about you," Valente said.

"Likewise."

Valente picked up the drinks, and light caught the huge ruby ring on the middle finger of his left hand. The design was baroque, archaic and heavy, making the smooth stone look bloodred. "They say you were something in your day."

Not that many years separated them, and Turrin knew the guy was working on him. The problem was, he didn't know why. A man in Valente's shoes would have been over the ego-stroking days; otherwise, he wouldn't have been much use to Galvani. "Maybe I was," Turrin replied with a disarming smile. "That's a hell of a ring there, Gabe."

Valente turned it over so it caught the light. "Don't I fucking know it. Present from the old man a few months ago. He got it in Romania." The bodycock laughed. "Supposed to have belonged to Dracula or some fucking thing. Before Mr. Galvani got it, the ring was headed for some museum."

Turrin filed the information away and took the mineral water to Julia. Then unobtrusively he checked his watch, wondering what was keeping Bolan.

CHAPTER FIVE

Bullets ripped a line through the canal water to Bolan's side and across the concrete surface above him, letting him know there were at least two gunners tracking him. He sprinted along the narrow shelf of the drain, heading for the hidden door. The sound of the running water had been drowned out by the sudden onslaught of autofire.

He made the hidden door just ahead of a half-dozen bullets that left pockmarks in the wall behind him. A dozen more slammed into the bricks covering the secret entrance and ripped the stone tiles from their moorings.

Painted green by the NVGs, a shadow wheeled toward the Executioner from inside the corridor on the other side of the drain wall. He recognized the blunt L-shape in the shadow's hands as a machine pistol of some type. The action was too fast and the light too uncertain even with the NVGs to be certain which one. He wasn't sure whether it belonged to another of Nicky DeVincenzo's captors or to the gunners who'd taken down the sentry. Either way, Bolan had to act fast.

Lifting the H&K MP-5 into target acquisition, Bolan squeezed off a short burst that caught the gunner in the chest and knocked him off his feet.

Voices echoed through the drain tunnel. The language was vaguely Italian, but there were differences. None of the words reached the warrior's ears and made sense, but the aggressiveness behind them was unmistakable.

Bolan dropped into a crouch and looked back out the door into the main tunnel. Three men dressed in black crossed the shelf after him, less than twenty yards away.

One of them evidently saw him and shouted a warning.

Before the attack team could deploy, Bolan squeezed the trigger. The subsonic parabellum rounds raked the gunmen from the shelf and toppled them into the water. At least one of them was still alive, his head and an arm breaking the surface of the rushing water as he was washed away.

Bolan shook the empty clip free and rammed another one home. His face was clammy, and he rubbed a sleeve along the lenses of the NVGs to clear them. They hadn't been intended for the humidity and flying water that surrounded him.

The powerful blatting of an outboard motor penetrated the cotton that seemed to clot his ears. He glanced back out the door and saw a small boat speeding up the drain tunnel. As he watched, a man stood up with an Uzi slung around his neck and hooked a cable through an eyebolt protruding from the wall.

Bolan figured that with the drainage problems Venice had, it wasn't too much to expect the drain to be used as waterways for maintenance boats. Evidently the hardmen that had arrived had known about the docking areas ahead of time. They'd also known about the hidden door.

The man in the boat began shouting, then fisted his weapon when no one replied.

The hush of the doomsday numbers falling through Bolan's head went unabated, gathering speed. Going forward was suddenly too dangerous without knowing what lay behind. Access from the underground drainage system had to be limited, and so far he only knew of one way out. There'd been no way to do a recon on the strike beforehand.

Bolan stepped around the corner and yelled in Italian for the man to be quiet.

The man said something in an imperative tone.

Gesturing to the door behind him, Bolan said, "It didn't go as planned."

The words were either too far off, or the man realized by Bolan's dress that the Executioner wasn't one of his group. The man raised his Uzi and squeezed off a burst that swept in a half circle.

Two of the rounds hit Bolan in the midsection, but were stopped by the body armor. Rocked by the impacts, he dropped back a step and fired the H&K from the hip. The 9 mm parabellum rounds started low on the man's torso and zipped their way up to his face, knocking the body backward. The dead man sank without a sound into the water.

Moving forward, Bolan listened for other boats that might be approaching, but couldn't hear anything. Similar to the Zodiac rubber boats used by the SEALs, the vessel looked capable of carrying five passengers. Two parallel rubber support struts crossed the center of the boat for added reinforcement. Gear was lashed into place along them.

Four small metal boxes occupied the most forward support strut. Bolan popped the latches on the first one. Inside were blocks of plastic explosive already set up with timers and remote-control detonator backups. The other three held the same thing.

He slipped his combat knife from his boot and sliced through the lashings. There was no time to disarm the explosives. Once they were free, he heaved them into the water. The plastic explosive was light enough, and the containers buoyant enough, that the rushing water would carry them out to sea where they could go off with little or no damage.

He left the boat where it was and returned to the hidden tunnel. Whatever numbers might have been left on the rescue attempt had imploded. He didn't believe the boat he'd found was the only one. The underground drain was rapidly being turned into a death trap. Even when he found the boy, the warrior wasn't sure how he was going to get either of them out alive.

THERE WERE two access routes into the underground room where Nicky DeVincenzo was being held. Thanks to the greed of Danny Franchetti, Mihai Lupu knew them both.

He sat in the bow of the second boat his people were using, having entered the main tunnel through a boat warehouse that had been closed six years earlier and never reopened for business. Four men, one of them Franchetti, sat around him. Everyone but the Mafia man was dressed in black.

"You don't have to go with us," Lupu said to Franchetti.

"No," the Mafia guy said stubbornly. "Armando's got this coming. Fucker tried to stick it in me and break it off a year back. Accused me of hustling some side action in heroin around the city and told the old man."

"Magaddino?" Lupu was very familiar with the Family. He'd been looking toward them as a lever to get to Alonzo Galvani for almost three years.

"Yeah." Franchetti nodded. "The old man didn't put up with any shit like drugs. Everywhere you looked, most of his operations and businesses were strictly legit."

"But they were founded on money he got from several criminal activities."

"No fucking joke. Kinda like the pot calling the kettle black if you ask me." Franchetti was beefy and coarse, and only treated with any kind of respect those things he feared.

Lupu had seen a great deal of difference between himself and the man, but had understood the motivations pushing at him entirely. During his father's tenure in President Nicolae Ceauşescu cabinet's as a national-security adviser, Lupu had seen many men like Franchetti: they thought they were ambitious, but didn't realize their ambition was only a drug that fed on them.

Over the years since Ceauşescu and his wife had been shot down like dogs on that Christmas Day in

1989, Lupu had learned to temper his own ambitions. All of his life, he'd enjoyed the privileges of the party elite in Romania. His father's position had guaranteed that, but that distinction had been swept away by the assassinations and by his father's murder only a few months before.

Lupu was seventeen when his father had been betrayed by friends who'd decided remaining loyal to Ceauşescu wasn't in their best interests. They'd shot him in the back, then tried to cover up their crime by burning the house and making it look like the work of more-militant political dissidents. But the fire hadn't completely consumed the facts.

It had taken Lupu three years to track down the five men responsible for his father's murder, the job made even harder by the lawlessness that had flourished after the assassinations of the president and his wife. But now they were all dead, as well.

The hunt had changed him, though. At twenty-three he stood a little over six feet tall, with powerful arms and shoulders. He kept his dark brown hair cut in a military style, but had grown a beard and kept it short and neat, blocked off low along his jawline. His face was hard and angular, made dangerous looking by a knife scar on his right cheek.

The boat came to a stop near one of the eyebolts marked on the map Lupu had. As they got out of the boat, he asked Franchetti, "So you stayed with Magaddino because you weren't involved?" Actually he was glad the man had suggested accompanying him. If the information turned out to be false, vengeance wasn't that far away. And it lent substance to the belief that he wasn't walking into a trap.

"Hell, yes, I was involved." Franchetti laughed and nearly slipped on the slick shelf they walked along. "One of the sweetest little deals you'd ever want. Heroin had just started making a comeback as the drug of choice, and I had a pipeline into the Triads. We're talking very good China White here." The man rubbed his thumb and forefinger together. "I didn't have to move the H but one time per delivery, and I took my cut right there. Armando was just never able to prove it, so the old man cut me some slack. Otherwise, he'd have cut the balls off me then and there. But it cost me a nice piece of change."

Lupu put on his NVGs. Military hardware was one of the chief items handled by his black-market operation throughout Romania. With the problems the Russians were having these days, plus the efforts of the United States and United Nations to intervene, getting them was not much of a problem. The world reilluminated, and he could feel his pulse quicken.

"So Armando's got this coming," Franchetti said. "He's got a permanent hard-on for Julia DeVincenzo." He shrugged, his face splitting in a wide grin. "Personally I think she's okay, maybe on the skinny side. I like my women with more cushion for the pushing, if you know what I mean."

Lupu smiled thinly, not commenting at all. Instead, he gave orders to his men in Romanian. "Get those charges placed quickly."

Other men who'd been hiding in the shadows joined the three he had with him in the boat.

Studying the lay of the canal, Lupu judged that they'd arrived pretty close to the adjoining drainage canal. He raised his voice above the rush of the water. "Aleksander."

"Yes," a broad man with a Cossack's beard shouted back.

"The boy?"

"This way. We've been waiting for you."

Lupu moved forward. He carried an H&K VP-70 Z butt forward in a military holster on his left hip, and an AK-47 canted across his chest.

The hidden door at this end of the tunnel had been removed. Aleksander stood beside him. "A precaution," the big man said, "in case we're not out by the time the explosives begin. I wouldn't want the door to get jammed by the shifting. This foundation, it doesn't look too steady to these old eyes."

Lupu nodded. "Understood." Aleksander had worked with his father, had taken bullets for him on occasion. Lupu had no doubt the man would die for him when the time came.

Aleksander took the lead, a figure of impressive girth, the chopped-down shotgun in his hands like a toy.

"You run a first-class operation all the way," Franchetti said as he fell in behind Lupu.

"There's no other way for it to be successful," the man replied.

Aleksander said something over his shoulder to Lupu—and Franchetti wanted to know what it was.

"He just said to watch it. The way is very slick from this point on." The tunnel had narrowed to less than three feet, started to incline and grew increasingly treacherous. Just ahead of them, Aleksander walked with his shoulders turned sideways and one hand on the wall.

"No shit," Franchetti said.

"You've been to America."

"Yeah. Born and raised. Been in Venice for the last seven years. Did a favor for Joey the Tyrant once, and he got me hooked up with the old man. Things in Philly had started to turn sour, and relocation seemed like the way to go. Mr. Magaddino fixed it for me."

Lupu kept watching forward, marking the distance in his mind. He'd gotten blueprints on the canal drainage areas, and paid extra for the speed of delivery and the updates that had been tagged with them. He knew they weren't far from the concealed room.

"What?" Franchetti asked.

"Watch your head," Lupu said, dodging beneath a low overhang of rock.

There was a sound of flesh smacking stone, then a lot of colorful cursing from Franchetti.

Lupu stepped through the opening and found himself in another trunk line. This one held primarily stagnant water. At both ends, less than sixty yards apart, the tunnel had collapsed. Lupu was suddenly aware of how much tonnage of rock and brick and mortar they stood beneath. But it all fit in with his plan to blow the tunnels and get out of the city while the emergency-rescue team and police had their hands full.

"Are you sure this kid is going to be okay?" Franchetti asked.

"Yes," Lupu replied without hesitation. Aleksander took the lead again, going to the right. "Do you really care?"

Franchetti scratched the back of his neck. "He's just a kid. He didn't cause any of this."

"He'll be unharmed," Lupu replied. "And treated much better than this, I assure you. The boy's a pawn—a very valuable pawn, to be exact—but leaving him on the board isn't going to alter the game."

"That's what your guy said when he approached me yesterday," Franchetti said.

Lupu had guessed that the kidnapping had been engineered by somebody inside the home. He'd already had information gathered on the Magaddino Family because of the trouble he was having with Alonzo Galvani in Romania, and was trying to figure out how best to use it. Magaddino's death had taken away any chance at finesse. Galvani was a reptile in his thinking, cold and efficient and constantly hungry. The man had sunk his fangs into the opportunities that were forming in Eastern Europe and would refuse to let go—unless his head was chopped off.

Lupu had been intrigued by the relationship between Magaddino and Galvani. The men were not alike in temperament, though both could be ruthless. But Magaddino knew when and how to make the deal to save something for all concerned, while Galvani would fight over the last crumb. Yet somehow Magaddino had kept Galvani in line for fifty years, never bucking Magaddino's wishes even when it cost him money.

"But I also know Alonzo Galvani is interested in Nicky DeVincenzo, too," Franchetti said. "One of his guys also made contact with me yesterday. After your guy did, but we already had a deal."

Lupu swapped looks with Aleksander. The big man hadn't missed the comment. Two more of the Romanians had walked up behind Franchetti, holding their assault weapons loosely.

"Here's the door," Aleksander said in Italian.

An easy grin fit itself to Lupu's face. "I'm glad you honored our agreement."

"Truth to tell, it was better money," Franchetti said with a shrug. "But I'm not one to welsh on a deal."

"I'm sure you're not," Lupu said. He flexed his left arm, and the heavy-bladed throwing knife he kept sheathed there slid smoothly into his palm. "But I'm sure you realize that going to Galvani after we've taken the boy and telling him who we are could be worth a considerable amount, too."

"Hey, look," the Mafia guy said, alarm coloring his voice, "I don't play that. A deal's a deal." His right hand slid down toward the 9 mm pistol at his waistband while he took a step back. He bumped into one of the men standing behind him, who pushed him forward again. "Hey, don't—"

With an economy of motion, Lupu flicked out the blade and slashed the man's throat. Blood streamed out at once as horror filled Franchetti's eyes. The man tried to scream, but couldn't because his vocal cords had been severed, and he was drowning in his own blood.

Lupu grabbed the man's hair with his other hand and yanked him into the pool of stagnant water. Franchetti tried to swim out and crawl up the slimy incline, but he exhausted himself. A final lunge brought him near his killer's feet, then life left him and his body slid soundlessly back into the water till it disappeared.

"We may have a problem," one of the new arrivals said. The rest of the group was falling into formation behind them.

"What?" Lupu cleaned the knife blade and returned it to its sheath.

"We can't make radio contact with the second team."

"Is the signal being jammed by the walls or the water?" Lupu asked. Either had been an expected possibility. He joined Aleksander by the new door. The big man had it open slightly, letting out a narrow band of yellow illumination.

"No. There would be some kind of feedback."

"Maybe they can't respond for other reasons." Peering through the door, Lupu looked down into the room. At one time, the room had been part of a hydro refinement station when the city had still gotten most of its water from underground sources. But when the city planners and engineers had been forced to give up on that and instead built the aqueduct to bring water from the Alps, this refinement station and others had been abandoned.

A staircase that was a narrow webbing of steel led downward from the door to the floor of the room some twenty feet below. The room was nearly one hundred feet by forty. The corner where Nicky DeVincenzo had been kept prisoner was filled with a handful of chairs and a bunk bed. A yellow cable joined a relatively quiet generator in the far end to the junction box that supported a refrigerator, electric stove, lamps, television, VCR and CD player. The rapid *whok-whok-whok* of the generator provided an undercurrent of noise that echoed throughout the room. The diffusion of light made a bubble of illumination that only reached halfway up the stairway. They'd come this far undetected, and the generator could be counted on to help mask their approach.

Armando was standing in the center of the occupied space, listening to a cellular phone as he paced. Four other men were around him seated on the furniture.

"Where's the boy?" Lupu whispered.

"Sleeping bag against the wall," Aleksander answered. "He appears to be sedated."

Lupu looked and saw the small form tucked inside the folds of a full-size sleeping bag. "That's why Armando isn't afraid the boy will tell who really kidnapped him."

Aleksander nodded.

Turning to the two men he'd already assigned to take the boy into their possession, Lupu said, "When we get down there, get some Kevlar on him and leave him inside the sleeping bag. He'll be easier to manage that way."

They nodded.

"Okay," Lupu told Aleksander as he adjusted the AK-47, "let's get it done."

The big man fisted the chopped-down shotgun and led the way down the steps.

HIDDEN IN THE SHADOWS behind the door leading to the room where Nicky DeVincenzo was held, Bolan saw Armando hang up the phone.

"Galvani's at the house," the security chief said. "And that big bastard that arrived with Turrin is missing." He put the phone on the floor. "This is turning out to be a crock of shit."

None of the four men watching him said anything.

A moment more, and the big warrior spotted the boy in a tangle of covers in a sleeping bag on the floor. He appeared to be asleep, his features drawn and sallow, and Bolan guessed that he'd been tranquilized.

Just as Bolan was about to make his opening move, he noticed the action coming down from the stairway behind the men.

The team was smooth, quiet and deadly efficient. The big guy leading them looked like a wall. Armando and his four men weren't aware of their presence until the intruders were almost upon them.

One of the men suddenly let out a yell and went for his gun. Before he could even close his fingers on it, a burst of gunfire blew him backward, toppling him onto the lower bunk bed.

Bolan picked his shots as two more of Armando's men went down without defending themselves. The H&K MP-5 bucked in his hands as he targeted the first man. The big man was partially blocked by Armando's men as they scrambled, and for the moment the Executioner wanted to leave them operational to present a unified front.

The 9 mm rounds caught the outside gunner in the chest and upper arm, spinning him into the rest of the group and causing momentary confusion. Even as the dead man went down, more gunners filled the ranks behind him.'

Armando and his men were dead or dying in moments, their bodies scattered across the small space they'd created to hold the boy captive.

Bolan spun behind the wall as the return fire grew intensive. Bullets chipped wood and brick from the door frame and reduced it to a shambles. Blood trickled from a cut above his eye. His last view of Nicky DeVincenzo had shown two men racing to the boy's side.

A tall scar-faced man shouted orders to the men in Romanian. Bolan recognized the language now.

Knowing there was no way he could hope to rescue the boy, Bolan tried to make the abduction as costly as possible. He kicked out the empty clip from the subgun and smoothly inserted another. He leaned around the door and raked a figure eight that took his attacker high. The 9 mm rounds caught the guy in the throat and shoved him backward.

"Take that bastard down, Aleksander!" the scar-faced man yelled.

Bolan targeted the guy, but the two men carrying Nicky DeVincenzo in the sleeping bag were behind him. As he rolled on around to find the next gunner, he saw the bearded man preparing to launch the FN Bullet-Through grenade affixed to the rifle he carried.

The only option was a strategic retreat. Bolan withdrew inside the door and went flat an instant before the HE round impacted against the door frame and hell came calling. He stayed low, breathing shallowly as the flames rolled over him. Debris dropped from the ceiling, forcing him to drop an arm across the back of his head for protection. Bricks thudded into his body with bruising weight.

The mortar dust and smoke choked him. For a moment he thought the tunnel had collapsed on him. Racked by a fit of coughing, the warrior pushed himself up and located the H&K MP-5. His left shoulder pained him, but he knew from experience that the discomfort would pass.

Warily, he returned to the door. The smoke from the explosion and the accumulated mortar dust had gushed out into the battlezone. Bolan slung the submachine gun over his shoulder, then ripped the lower portion of his shirt away and fashioned a mask over his mouth and nose to filter out the smoke and thick dust.

His eyes blurred, and he squinted as he made for the stairway. No one was on it. His hearing was still affected by the explosion, making it impossible to pick up small, distinctive sounds.

At the top of the stairs, he found the door had been jammed from outside. He hit it with his shoulder twice, but it didn't budge. Then he remembered the explosives the other team had been mining the drain with. Evidently whoever was behind the operation didn't intend for much to be left behind.

He was almost to the door that had received the grenade when movement caught his attention. Instinctively he raked the SIG-Sauer Night Stalker P-228 from its holster, activated the infrared sights built into the pistol's housing and dropped the glowing dot between his target's eyes.

"Hold it right there, you son of a bitch." In a semiprone position on the floor, Armando held his pistol on Bolan. "You aren't going anywhere." The security chief looked badly battered. Blood trickled from the corner of his mouth, and he coughed spasmodically. "Not without me."

"You looked dead," Bolan said, never moving his pistol.

"Maybe I was," Armando said with a pained grimace. "But I'm back now."

"They got the boy," the warrior said.

"I tried to stop them."

"I know." The Executioner didn't elaborate.

Armando squinted up at Bolan, obviously having difficulty seeing, as well. "When did you get here?"

"After they did."

The security man thought that over. "I got a tip that they might be holding him here. I thought maybe I could wrap this piece of business up quick and have Nicky back home in just a little while.''

''You went up against a lot of guns.''

''Yeah. Should have known those Romanians would bring an army when they only needed a couple guys. They don't fight to win over there. They fight to kill you.''

''They've mined the drain,'' Bolan said. ''We don't have much time.''

''How did you get here?'' Armando took a fresh grip on his pistol.

''A tip.'' Bolan let it go at that. Any attempt to dress it up would only have wasted time. With or without decoration, the only thing that mattered was whether Armando wanted to believe the lie.

''Maybe Julia's faith in you guys wasn't over-rated,'' Armando said, ''if you got tied into the network that quickly. You knew about the Romanians, too?''

''Not until I got here.''

''So how come the gun?''

''Lot of people pulling guns in here a minute ago. People that pulled them slow are dead now. You went for yours before I knew you were still alive.''

''My leg's busted,'' Armando said. ''I can feel it.'' He put the pistol away. ''I'm not getting out of here without your help.''

Bolan holstered his own weapon. He didn't believe for a second that Armando meant him no harm. Once they were clear and the security man was on solid ground again, the warrior was sure he'd be in Armando's sights again.

But the situation went both ways. The security man might still be holding valuable information about who the Romanians were and what they wanted.

Bolan walked over to Armando and pulled the guy to his feet. The security man's face blanched and tightened when he put weight on his right leg.

"No time for a splint," Bolan said.

"Just go, dammit. I've been through worse than this."

Bolan began to move, helping to support and dragging Armando at the same time. The partially caved-in tunnel was hardest to navigate. The twisting trail through the other tunnels took only minutes. The soldier was grimly aware of the time slipping away. Still, transporting the boy would have made things difficult, and they'd want to be clear of the area before setting off the charges.

Almost as soon as they'd emerged back into the main canal, Armando made his play. Already staggering under the other man's weight, Bolan was momentarily caught off balance. Armando head-butted him in the face and knocked him down, falling on top of him at once.

"You knew, didn't you, you bastard?" Armando snarled. "You knew it was me who staged Nicky's kidnapping." He threw a heavy-handed punch at the warrior's head.

Bolan slipped the blow and landed a short jab into his opponent's stomach. Armando's breath hissed out. Breaking the other man's hold, the Executioner rolled away and got to his feet.

Armando slipped a small pistol from his pocket and pointed it in Bolan's direction.

Unflinching, the Executioner palmed the P-228 from his hip and squeezed the trigger as soon as the glowing infrared dot touched Armando's forehead. The security man's shot went wild, then his head jerked back from the impact of the bullet.

The rumbling growl of thunder started in the distance, then rolled down the tunnel, gathering intensity. At the corner seventy yards away, Bolan saw the wave of water cascade against the opposite wall, then fold back and charge down the tunnel at him.

He spun and ran for the boat. There was no doubt that the tunnel was going to flood completely. Doubling back through the hidden door would only leave him trapped. He managed to get the pistol strapped into its holster, then launched himself at the rubber boat.

Luckily there was a ledge farther down the side of the channel that allowed him enough purchase to flip the boat over on top of him just as the front of the wave boosted him up before it. He clung to the strut, then felt the jerk as the boat hit the end of its tether.

Water rushed in under the edge of the boat as it flailed like a kite caught in the grip of a tornado. Bolan stripped the useless NVGs away and left them to hang from his neck. Fighting to maintain the precious air bubble left under the overturned boat, the warrior drew the Tanto Cold Steel knife from his boot and slashed it across the restraining rope.

Freed, the boat was violently swept along. Bolan tried to go with its erratic movements, hanging by one arm hooked over the strut. His shoulder was painfully wrenched, and for a moment he thought it was going to dislocate. Then he managed to get his other arm around the strut, too.

He felt the bottom of the boat scrape across the top of the tunnel, letting him know it had completely flooded. He was blind in the blackness, couldn't even see the boat that he clung to. The boat whirled and slammed against the sides of the tunnel like a dervish, losing a little more of the air pocket.

The warrior had no way of knowing how far he'd traveled when the boat suddenly went under. The air pocket shifted. Water covered his head, and he held his breath. At first he thought he'd lost the air pocket entirely, then his elbow broke through the surface. He pulled his head into the small bubble and took a deep breath.

Then the boat swirled in circles. He slammed up against a stone surface, and a deeper blackness enveloped his senses. Still, he clung to the boat, depending on its buoyancy to show him the way up.

Just as his lungs seemed about to burst, the boat coasted to a stop, spinning only slightly. Lazily at first but gaining speed rapidly, it pulled him up in a stream of air bubbles. He saw the pool of light above him. Abandoning the boat, he stroked for the surface.

When he broke through, he floated on his back and drew in great drafts of air. Somewhat recovered, he gazed around and found himself in the Grand Canal. The northern shoreline was only forty yards away. Nearly twice that distance behind him, turbulence continued to knife through the waters of the canal. Bubbles as big as pumpkins erupted across the choppy surface.

On both sides of the canal, crowds were beginning to gather. Gondolas skated across the water and closed in on the site.

Swimming to the shore, Bolan hauled himself out of the water. He stayed in the shadows of buildings. There was no way of knowing if the Romanians were still in the water where big air bubbles erupted across the choppy surface.

He pulled the windbreaker tighter, trying to find warmth in layers even though everything was wet. Armando's motive for kidnapping Nicky DeVincenzo was apparent now, but he had no clue about the Romanians'. There was a storm brewing over Venice and the Magaddino name, and he knew it reached into Eastern Europe. He didn't know how yet, but he was certain Julia DeVincenzo was near the eye of it. And whether she was innocent or guilty, the warrior knew it was going to roll over the woman.

CHAPTER SIX

The phone in the den rang shrilly.

Rising from the couch, Julia DeVincenzo said, "Excuse me. That's my private number."

"Of course," Alonzo Galvani replied. He was working on his second drink. Gabe Valente stood behind him as vigilant as a soldier and seeming to be at ease.

Julia was glad Turrin was there with her. In view of Armando's treachery, if it hadn't been for Turrin, she'd have been alone in the house with the old man, with no one she felt safe with. The realization made her feel cold and helpless, even further separated from Nicky. She'd never lied to herself about Galvani's friendly overtures toward her. She'd known from her grandfather's actions that the two men had remained mortal enemies, even if Galvani hadn't openly opposed Pietro Magaddino in decades.

She lifted the phone on the third ring, thinking it might be Turrin's friend. "Hello?"

"Julia DeVincenzo?"

"Yes." She was certain she didn't recognize the smooth, accented voice.

"You don't know me," the man said, "but my name is Mihai Lupu. I have your son."

Julia glanced at Turrin, knowing the man could read in her gaze that something was wrong. "You're lying."

"No."

"Tell me why I should believe you." Her hand on the phone was so tight it was restricting the blood flow and going numb.

"Because I know Armando kidnapped your son to make himself appear the hero in your eyes. Only moments ago he was killed by my people, and the underground canal where he was holding Nicky was destroyed. It should be on the news very soon."

She made herself stay calm. Nicky was okay. As long as she remained in control, he was going to stay that way. "What do you want?"

"Your grandfather had a working arrangement with Alonzo Galvani. I want to know the specifics of that."

"I've no idea," Julia said. "My grandfather ran his own affairs. He was very firm about that."

"Your grandfather is no longer alive," the smooth voice continued. "He won't be able to stop you from looking for them. There should be papers somewhere, some kind of proof. There always is with blackmail. Find it, and you can have your son back."

Galvani waved Valente to an extension. The old man seemed intent on the conversation.

"Let me speak to Nicky," Julia demanded.

"I'll be in touch in a few hours, Mrs. DeVincenzo. Please don't let Nicky or me down." The phone connection broke.

Moving quietly but quickly, Turrin intercepted Valente's move toward the extension. The hardman gave him a small grin and turned slightly sideways. Turrin didn't back away.

"Stop it," Julia said. "He's already hung up." She cradled the phone and glared at Valente, then Galvani. "You're out of line. This is my house and my son."

"My apologies," Galvani said. "I only thought I could help."

Julia crossed the room and stood in front of the old man. "Do you know someone named Mihai Lupu?"

Galvani leaned back in his chair and swirled his drink. "No."

He was lying and Julia knew it, but she didn't know how to respond. An accusation would only result in Galvani leaving at once, and perhaps Valente going up against Turrin.

"Why?" Galvani asked.

"Because he has my son," Julia answered.

"He kidnapped Nicky?" Galvani asked.

"No. But he says he has him now."

Galvani spread his hands. "Is there any reason you should believe this man?"

"He knows...things," Julia replied. "Details that only someone who had Nicky would know."

"You're sure?"

"Yes."

Galvani sat his drink down and leaned forward. "Would you like me to help you with this, Julia?"

"I wouldn't know where to begin." Julia felt her composure slipping. Turrin came to stand beside her, but he didn't touch her. She was grateful because she thought she would have weakened at that point. More than anything right now, she wanted to be strong.

"For starters," Galvani suggested, "I could find out who this man is."

Maintaining control through an effort of will, Julia sat. "No. Let me handle this. He said he will call. Whatever he wants, it's not worth as much to me as Nicky."

"Whatever?" Galvani echoed. "Then this mook doesn't just want a ransom?"

Noting the predatory gleam in Galvani's cold gaze, Julia replied, "He didn't tell me how much. He said he'd let me know."

"Ah." Galvani leaned back in his chair and steepled his fingers. "The way you handle yourself, Julia, it's important to the Families, you know. We don't want to let out the impression that we can be shaken down by any two-bit rip-off artist that comes along. Bad for business all around."

Julia made her voice hard, meaning every word. "Whoever's responsible for Nicky's kidnapping is going to pay for it. Trust me on that."

Galvani nodded and smiled. "See that, Gabe? That's why she reminds me of her grandfather. Tough as nails beneath that velvet exterior." He glanced up at the bodyguard. "We should be going."

"Yes, Mr. Galvani," Valente said, but his attention never wavered from Turrin.

The old man levered himself up with his cane, took Julia's hand and kissed the back of it. "You need anything, you'll call me, eh?"

Julia nodded. Turrin showed them out, then returned a couple of minutes later. She had the television remote control and was flicking through the local channels. "What about your friend?" she asked.

"I don't know," Turrin answered honestly.

"Do you think he's dead?"

Turrin paused before answering. "I've known him a long time, been through a lot of blowups with him and seen him walk away from things that would have killed most men. I think if anything happened to him, I'd feel it, no matter how far apart we were at the time."

"Then where is he?"

"Looking for your son," Turrin said with conviction.

With effort Julia kept the tears of frustration and rage at bay. She paused on one of the local channels airing a special newsbreak. The location seemed to be somewhere on the Grand Canal, and the focus kept switching from two camera perspectives, showing the turbulence in the center of the waterway and the gaping hole in the shore nearby. Police boats ran searchlights over the area, aided by a helicopter overhead.

"I don't even know a Mihai Lupu," Julia said.

On the television the helicopter dropped altitude and sprayed the searchlight over the canal's surface. Then it fixed on a body floating in the water. Immediately one of the smaller police boats powered over to it.

"We will," Turrin said. He lifted the phone. "I've got to make some calls."

Julia nodded, hypnotized by the action on the screen as two of the police officers dressed in yellow slickers on deck lowered a long hooked pole into the water and levered the corpse up. The body dangled like a speared fish at the end of the pole.

"We'll find Nicky," Turrin said softly. "I promise."

"Can you promise me that it will be in time?" Julia demanded. She knew she was taking some of her anger out on Turrin, but she couldn't hold it in any longer.

"No," he replied. "I won't even try to tell you that." He paused. "What did Lupu want?"

"He wanted to know about the working relationship my grandfather had with Galvani."

"Why?"

"He didn't say."

"Nothing about money?"

"No."

"Lupu doesn't sound Italian," Turrin said.

"His accent didn't sound like he was from here, either." Julia played the strong, smooth voice over in her head, listening to every word. "More guttural, but he spoke very well and very clearly."

"What do you know about any arrangements your grandfather had with Galvani?"

"Nothing."

"Would there be anything in your grandfather's papers?" Turrin held up his hand in a signal as the phone at the other end was answered. He spoke briefly, asking for information on a Mihai Lupu, country of origin unknown.

When Turrin cradled the phone, he looked at her, waiting for an answer. "We could start there."

"Maybe," she said with a tight nod. Julia made herself move, realizing how close she was to becoming frozen by the fear that filled her. She clicked off the television and led the way upstairs.

BOLAN DROPPED CHANGE into the pay phone in front of the closed video store and dialed the number. Beyond the frilled edge of the awning sticking out from the storefront, the police helicopter held its position in the night sky. He was wet and cold, but he'd learned a long time ago to distance himself from those discomforts. Even the ache along his ribs from the bullets striking the body armor had dulled.

The phone was answered quickly, and he was passed along to Turrin.

"I missed the boy," the warrior said without preamble. "There was a third party."

"I know," Turrin said. "He called Julia's private number. We got a name. I've already turned it over to the Bear, but I didn't have a place to tag it to except Venice. He didn't sound local."

"He's not," Bolan said. "Armando said they were Romanian."

"Let me put you on the speakerphone. Julia wants to talk."

Bolan glanced at his watch. Besides a boat, there was only one way out of the city. He figured if Mihai Lupu was going to use it, he still had time to try for an intercept.

"Is my son all right?" the woman asked.

"Yes," Bolan said. "Armando had him drugged, but he looked fine."

"Drugged?"

"Yes."

"Where's Armando?" Julia asked.

"Dead," Bolan stated flatly. "Leo?"

"Yeah?"

"They left bodies behind," Bolan said. "See if you can link up with Canova and turn up anything there."

"I'm on my way."

"What are you going to do?" Julia asked.

"I'm going to try to get your son back before they get out of the country with him," Bolan replied.

"You think that's what they're going to do? Why wouldn't they simply make a deal now?"

"Did they earlier?"

She hesitated before answering. "No."

Bolan studied the flashing lights coasting across the Grand Canal. Quite a crowd had gathered along both shores. "Things are going to be too hot for them to try to settle in here. Did they say what they wanted?''

"Lupu wanted to know about the working arrangements my grandfather had with Alonzo Galvani.''

"Why?"

"He didn't say."

Bolan turned that over in his mind. A military opponent had a lot in common with a criminal once an immediate profit was taken out of the equation. Leverage and positioning were everything. "Is Galvani involved with anyone in Romania?''

"Not that I know of."

"Your grandfather?"

"I don't know."

Bolan had to be on the move. Alone, he could move faster than Lupu and his team, but the clock was still ticking. "Take a look and see what you can find out. I've got to go. If I find out anything, I'll be in touch." He hung up the phone, got his bearings and took off at a jog designed to eat up the distance. It was a little over two miles to the train station, and he knew the odds would be against him.

THE TRAIN STATION was almost deserted at that hour. Mack Bolan was certain he'd arrived before Mihai Lupu and his group. The windbreaker rode low enough to cover the P-228 Night Stalker on his hip, but he carried the pistol in a fist in one of the pockets. During the two-mile run, his clothing had dried out to a degree and he no longer looked as though he'd just climbed out of a canal.

Two young women worked the ticket booth, flanked by a uniformed guard nursing a coffee. A 9 mm pistol rode high and forward on his hip.

Bolan paid for a ticket, then dropped back to the vending machines. He cradled his cup of coffee in his hands, drawing warmth from it, and took up a position where he could watch the ticket sales. According to the postings, the next departure for the mainland was in fifteen minutes.

The way the warrior had it figured, Lupu and his team wouldn't have picked a boat to travel by. It would have put them on the shore and in the open, and it would have been too slow, leaving time for someone to organize an interception. Even though the causeway was available to motorists, it could have been blocked by the Venice police.

That left the train. If any concentrated surveillance had been put on the train, Lupu and his people would detect it. They could lie low until they arranged for another means of transportation.

Bolan knew the only chance he would have at retrieving the boy would have to be fast and dirty.

At two minutes until departure, when most of the other fares had already boarded, Lupu and his hardmen came through the main doors. All of them were dressed in casual clothing. Lupu wore a dark suit.

The big man carried Nicky DeVincenzo over one shoulder, as if the boy were sleeping. A slender woman clung to the man's arm, dressed conservatively to pose as his wife.

Bolan respected the touch. If a group of men had arrived carrying one child, things would have looked suspicious and maybe drawn attention. As it was, the big man and the woman stood apart from the group, even bought tickets by themselves. The ticket sellers ushered them toward the turnstiles.

His hand on the pistol in his pocket, Bolan followed, drifting along in their wake. In the canals the light had been bad and he'd worn the NVGs. His face would be unknown to them.

He showed his ticket and passed through the turnstiles, then headed down the steps leading to the boarding area.

The big man and the woman went forward and boarded one of the more densely crowded cars, third from the end. Lupu and the main body of his crew chose the next car.

Not wanting to draw attention to himself, Bolan made his way to the last car and stepped inside. The doors automatically closed behind him.

Inside the car the lighting was dim, and eight other passengers occupied the seats. A No Smoking sign ran in digital red letters in three different languages across the front of the car. The windows were smeared and turned the points of light inside the station into lances.

Bolan went forward, noting the emergency-exit door that opened up between the cars. Lupu and his group had taken seats near the middle of the car. The warrior sat in the corner at the front where he could view them and take advantage of the blind spot afforded by his own car.

"Everyone, please take your seats," the PA recording addressed them in Italian. "We are pulling out of the station."

With a lurch the train started forward. As it started to gain speed, a warning bell clanged tinnily.

"Warning! Please step inside the door! Keep arms and legs inside the train while we are moving!" The automated voice repeated the message even as three men jogging alongside the train jumped onboard. Most of the car's passengers didn't seem surprised by the move.

Bolan recognized all three as part of Lupu's group. He twisted in his seat and watched them as they took their places at the other end of the car. The pistol in his fist felt reassuring.

The newcomers were expressionless, their weapons hidden by the folds of their raincoats. They remained focused on the Executioner. The eight innocent passengers were suddenly in the no-man's-land between them.

Bolan glanced back at Lupu.

The Romanian was looking at him, a cruel smile curling his lips. He shaped his hand into the form of a pistol, using two fingers for the barrel, then dropped his thumb like a hammer. Raising them to his lips, he acted as if he was blowing smoke away.

Two of the men inside Lupu's car got up and walked back to their emergency door. They sat on either side of it and ignored him.

"What's it going to be?" the biggest of the three men asked in Italian.

"You tell me," Bolan said. He was aware of the growing interest of the other passengers as they realized something was wrong.

"You could walk out of here," the man said. He had long hair and gold hoop earrings in both ears.

"I don't get the impression it's going to be that easy," Bolan said.

"Maybe not," the man said, switching to English. "You're American."

"Cowboy," one of the other men said derisively. "I hate fucking cowboys."

"What's your piece in this?" the first man asked.

"I just want the boy back," Bolan answered. He could feel the tension mounting between them, and he knew that violence was going to spill over at any moment. There was no way to get the eight passengers clear.

The man's eyes narrowed. "Are you working for Alonzo Galvani?"

"No."

The man smiled. "You'd lie if you were, so I guess you're damned anyway if you're telling the truth." He made his move without hesitation, sweeping his raincoat back and bringing up the cut-down Mossberg 500 pump shotgun hanging from a sling underneath it.

Bolan threw himself out of the seat and sprawled along the floor between the aisles of seats. The Night Stalker was in his hand as the shotgun roared, filling the train car with noise.

Passengers cried out in fear, reacting out of instinct and diving to the floor.

The P-228 jumped in the Executioner's hand as he squeezed off three shots. Two rounds took the gunner in the face, and the third took off his left ear and spiderwebbed the window behind him.

Glass showered across Bolan's back as he bracketed the next gunner. The shotgun's tight pattern had blown out the emergency-door window. He fired four shots at the next man, using the red ruby laser sighting to track up the man's chest to his throat. The man dropped to the floor without a word.

The third man grabbed one of the women passengers and hauled her to her feet, holding her as cover. The Uzi in his fist leaped and spit a prolonged muzzle-flash while he screamed in defiance.

Bolan took cover behind the seats. Sparks soared into the air above him, and padding sailed like miniature clouds until they crashed into the rubber-mat floor. The warrior saw the gunner's foot beneath the rows of seats and took aim on it. Triggering a pair of rounds, he saw the foot knocked back by the impacts.

He shoved himself to his feet as the Uzi ripped a ragged line of bullet holes through the train's ceiling. Smoke wreathed the air, and the scent of cordite blotted out everything else.

The screaming woman had taken advantage of the situation to attempt fleeing from her captor. The gunman reached for her, trying to bring the Uzi back to cover Bolan.

The Executioner took a Weaver's stance as 9 mm parabellum rounds from the Uzi cycled through and blew out the train car windows to his left. He fired a single round that caught the gunman between the eyes. Off balance, the dead man fell against the doors, knocking them open and hanging half outside.

"Please keep your arms and legs inside the car at all times!" the automated voice called out. Broken glass littered the floor where frightened people sought cover.

Bolan whirled to deal with the threat at his flank, pulling his pistol before him. The ruby red laser burned through the two windows and spotted the interior of the car ahead of him. Ringing echoes of the gunshots filled his ears, warring with the repeated automated warning. Outside the side windows he saw the dark waters of the Gulf of Venice. Already on the bridge, the train streaked toward the mainland.

Lupu had risen to his feet with his gun in his fist. Around him his men finished taking control of the car they were riding in.

Bolan was sure the Romanian would have sent someone to take over the lead engine and monitor the radio communications. The warrior hunkered in close to the steel wall beside the broken glass of the emergency door. He glanced back at the eight passengers. All were frightened but appeared to be unhurt.

"Stay down," he ordered in Italian.

"Are you a policeman?" one man asked.

Bolan ignored him, wondering how to break the stalemate. Time was on his side. When the train reached the mainland, Lupu wouldn't be able to simply disappear.

Then an explosion of light and sound flared up between the cars. Bolan felt the train car jerk and shudder, setting off a fresh wave of screams from the terrorized passengers. When he looked, flames still clung to the coupling between the cars, letting him know some type of plastic explosive had been used.

The explosion had severed the coupling between the two coaches, and with it went the electrical connections that kept the lights on in the passenger car.

The car ahead was pulling away, and Lupu flipped him a salute.

Bolan watched the train disappear along the track, waiting until the passenger car he'd been stranded in ran out of forward momentum. By the time he'd be able to make it back to the train station, assuming he got someone to listen to him immediately, Lupu would have already reached the mainland.

But staying with the crippled passenger car wasn't an option. After a brief examination of the eight passengers and telling them to stay put until he sent help, Bolan stepped over the corpse in the doorway and went back along the track. He left in his wake the warning lanterns he'd gotten from the emergency compartment aboard the train car. From what he remembered of the train schedule, he'd be back at the station before another train came along, but he didn't want to take any chances with the people he left behind.

His mind worked steadily as he kept his movement up to a jog despite the uneven footing afforded along the track. The wind blowing in from the sea sprayed him with salty ghosts and burned his face where he'd abraded it while diving to the floor of the train car.

Armando's motivation for kidnapping Nicky DeVincenzo had been straightforward. Before he could make an effective countermove against the Romanians, Bolan knew he had to know what prize Mihai Lupu was after. And if Lupu thought he might be working for Alonzo Galvani to take the boy back, he needed to know the reason for that, too.

The campaign was barely hours old, but the Executioner knew from experience that fronts had opened up all around him. For whatever reason, Julia DeVincenzo and her son were at the center of it, standing on deadly ground.

At the moment he didn't know how to get them out of the line of fire. He hoped Turrin was having some luck with the Venice police.

CHAPTER SEVEN

Standing at the edge of the waterway, Turrin cupped his hands and lit a cigarette. Activity at the Grand Canal had slowed in the past few minutes, though the helicopter still hovered overhead. The search-and-rescue boats now dominated the scene, punctuating their movements with hand-held searchlights and blasts of static from their radios. Neoprene-clad divers took to the water and dragged halos of light after them as they descended into the collapsed tunnels around the canal.

The uniformed policeman standing beside Turrin listened to his walkie-talkie intently. Then he motioned Turrin forward to one of the small police boats. The action instantly drew the attention of a small phalanx of reporters who thrust flashing cameras and camcorders his way. Turrin turned up the lapels of his coat and avoided them with moves perfected through years of practice.

He stepped into the boat, keeping his balance with difficulty. The boats out in the canal had made the water choppy. A grizzled patrolman opened the throttle and sent them skimming across the uneven surface to the big police boat that had used a crane arm to scoop the corpses from the water.

"Mr. Turrin," Giacomo Canova said, standing in the bow of the bigger boat. "I was wondering if you would be along." The detective had his pipe going. The searchlights from the other teams whipped across the boat, cutting sharp-edged shadows that moved and disappeared.

Turrin clambered up the hard rubber ladder thrown over the side of the police boat and reached the deck. "You found Armando."

"Yes." Canova studied him intently.

A hard knot of apprehension filled Turrin's belly as he looked at the four canvas-covered figures that rolled loosely on the yawing deck. Water ran away from them in long trickles, evidence that the bodies beneath the canvas were soaked. Even though Bolan had told him Nicky was still alive, he felt relieved that all the bodies were man-size.

"Armando found the kidnappers?" Canova asked.

Turrin looked at the man and went with his instincts. As a policeman Canova was used to getting lied to on a regular basis. He decided to be as honest as he could. It might not gain him any points, but it wouldn't count against him. "No. Armando was the kidnapper."

"I suspected it was an inside job. Does Mrs. DeVincenzo know?"

"Yes."

Canova looked back at him, his face assuming hard lines. "Then we're not looking for the boy's body, too?"

"No. Nicky wasn't in the tunnels when they were blown."

"And Mrs. DeVincenzo knows this, too. Otherwise, she'd be here with you."

Turrin nodded.

"Tell me why I shouldn't take you into custody this moment," the detective said, his voice carrying an edge.

"You couldn't hold me," Turrin replied. "If we can agree on that, I'm going to give you some information you can work on."

"But not everything you know."

With a shrug Turrin said, "Maybe it's going to be more than you'll get on your own. Save you some time, help clean up some of the loose ends."

A pair of divers brought up another body, struggling with it as they rolled it over the side. The corpse hit the deck with a wet smack, its arms and legs splaying wildly.

One of the divers spit out his mouthpiece and looked at Canova. "That was the deepest one we've found yet. There's a maze of tunnels down there. He was in a cul-de-sac. We were lucky to find him at all. If you want any further searching done in there, it'll have to wait until we can get some of those walls shored up. I don't want to take a chance on them collapsing and losing one of my guys."

"Thanks, Tony," Canova said. "I appreciate what you've done tonight."

The diver nodded, then dropped back into the water. Three men on the boat brought out another canvas.

"Wait," Canova said. He reached into the pocket of his rain slicker and took out a flashlight. "I think I know this one."

Turrin followed. He'd felt uneasy about leaving Julia DeVincenzo alone in her house. Armando's betrayal wasn't going to be the end of it. He was certain of that. Magaddino had held the household together, and Julia wasn't going to do that, even if she wanted to.

Canova played the flashlight over the new arrival, whose throat had been slashed. "Danny Franchetti," he said, then looked at Turrin. "Do you know him?"

"No."

"He worked for Magaddino, too, but not lately. Seems he had a falling-out with Armando and was cut loose. But he doesn't fit in with the other men we've found." Canova moved among the covered corpses and pulled the canvas down to reveal their features.

The first one up was Armando, a bullet hole black between his water-filled eyes.

Canova identified the next one as a member of Armando's staff. The remaining two were mysteries; dark, swarthy men with violent pasts etched on them in scar tissue.

"These men have been around," Canova said, "but none of my people recognize them."

"I do." Turrin pointed to one of them, remembering the man with the livid burn scar over his eye who'd tried to ambush him at Palazzo Ducale. "He was one of the guys circulating the picture of me where the *vaporetti* was shot up.''

''You saw him there?''

''Yeah. I remember the scar. Were these guys carrying any ID?''

''No.'' Canova indicated the man's black attire and combat leather. ''These men were outfitted like they were going to war, and one of the factors seemed to be deniability.''

''You got a print guy?'' Turrin asked.

''The crime-scene unit has already been here,'' Canova said. ''The water's too rough, and they can do a better job on land.'' He took a puff on his pipe, then released the smoke and squinted through it. ''For an underworld figure, you seem to know a lot about law enforcement.''

''Long association with the police,'' Turrin said. ''You're hooked into Interpol's terrorist hot line?''

Canova nodded.

''If these guys came in like they were working a mission, loaded this heavy and prepared to blow up anything that got in their way,'' Turrin said, ''I think we can agree that we're not dealing with your common thug here.''

''Agreed. So you believe they may be terrorists?''

''Or they've been around them.'' Turrin borrowed the detective's flashlight, then squatted beside the scar-faced man's body. He took a penknife from his pocket and slit the corpse's shirt open on the side that the scarred eye was on.

The scarred flesh beneath the wet material gleamed waxy yellow in the flashlight's beam. Scarring ran from the dead man's neck to most of the right side of his chest, clumped in tight ridges.

"That's from burns," Turrin said. "I've seen plenty of them. My guess from the pattern and the depth of the burning is that it was some kind of incendiary grenade. Usually they're used on buildings or equipment, but they can be used for antipersonnel, too. A few years ago this guy got lucky and missed the brunt of it."

"He ran out of luck tonight," Canova said.

Turrin nodded. "Since incendiary grenades aren't standard police issue, he'd picked these scars up in some other line of work."

"I've had some experience with the Italian Red Brigades," the detective said. "You think this man belonged to them? Sometimes they've used kidnapping in the past to finance their enterprises."

"No." Turrin decided to come as clean as he could. "I think these guys, like the guys at Palazzo Ducale, are Romanian."

"You know this to be true?"

"Pretty much."

"How?"

"I can't go into it." The silence that descended between them was hard and complete. Turrin had developed a protective shell over the years of living a double life and didn't let any of it touch him.

Canova cursed quietly and knocked the tobacco from his pipe. "What can you tell me?"

"Someone else has Nicky," Turrin said. "We were contacted by a guy named Mihai Lupu. Do you know him?"

Shaking his head, the detective said, "The name means nothing to me."

"He's interested in some old business between Magaddino and Galvani."

"Galvani was at your house," Canova said.

Turrin wasn't surprised the detective still had someone watching the house. "Galvani denies knowing Lupu."

"Is he telling the truth?"

"I don't think so. Neither does Mrs. DeVincenzo." Canova nodded. "Why tell me so much now?"

"I can't keep a surveillance team on Galvani. You can."

"Yes. And if I find out anything, why should I tell you?"

Turrin showed the detective a mirthless smile. "Because you're constrained by the very law you're striving to uphold. I'm not. My only objective here is to get Nicky DeVincenzo back to his mother."

"What about Pietro Magaddino's fallen empire?"

"Let someone else loot that corpse," Turrin said. "My home's in America, and this place isn't even close to my backyard. Once I get Nicky back to Julia and get her situated someplace safe, I'm smoke and this place is just dried ink on my visa."

"How far can I trust you?" Canova asked as if thinking out loud.

"As far as I can trust your department," Turrin said. "It doesn't look like Armando was getting along too well with the Romanians, so I'm not quite as eager to believe he was responsible for the reception committee earlier tonight.'' He paused. ''Which could leave the police department, since they were busy keeping up with Mrs. DeVincenzo's affairs.''

''We'll see how it works out,'' Canova said.

''Let's start with the prints off these guys,'' Turrin suggested. ''If you turn up empty at Interpol, I've got a connection we can reach through the American Embassy on the mainland.'' Stony Man Farm maintained one of the biggest terrorist files in the world. If the dead men had a record of any sort, Turrin was certain Kurtzman and his crew could find them.

MIHAI LUPU USED a cellular phone to arrange the rendezvous on the mainland a few miles out of Mestre, Italy, only minutes after the last passenger car on the train had been blasted free. The original plan had been for the team to debark at the train station in Mestre and drive into Milan for the flight back to Bucharest. Most of that was still possible. But there was no way he could take the train into Mestre.

He gazed out the window and saw the lights flash on the car sitting at the side of the dirt road that crossed the railroad track. ''Here,'' he said into his walkie-talkie.

The engineer put the brakes on and brought the train to a strained stop. Metal grated and sparks shot out below Lupu's window. While his men kept the frightened passengers covered, he debarked and walked to the waiting cars.

Ion Funar sat behind the wheel of the rented Renault and looked totally at ease in a black sport jacket over jeans. His tie hung from the rearview mirror. Though barely twenty-two, Funar had seen his share of battles. He was tall and lanky, with a chiseled face and eyebrows that grew together in a dark, brooding line. Even though it was dark, he wore the Foster Grant sunglasses he'd taken from a CIA agent he'd killed in Bucharest only a few months before.

Lupu opened the door, then made a circle with his arm to the other men on the train. He dropped into the Renault's passenger seat. "Have you had any luck identifying the man who followed us?" he asked.

"Not yet." Funar keyed the ignition, and the car started without hesitation. "Everything in Venice appears to be complicated at the moment."

Lupu noted that the younger man was being polite by not mentioning the fact that he'd killed their primary source of information. "I want him found and neutralized. Quickly. That man is going to be trouble. Gheorghe identified him as American before he was killed."

"The one we were looking for?"

Lupu shook his head. "Another." Franchetti had identified Leo Turrin for them, stressing that the Mafia man might be a problem.

On board the train, Lupu's team departed the passenger cars and dropped smoke grenades behind them. The bilious smoke would cut down the chances that anyone left on the train would be able to identify them or their cars until they got safely out of Italy.

Funar pulled forward and picked up Aleksander and the boy. The call girl they'd hired to accompany the big man and lead observers to think she was his mother had been left on the train, as well. She wouldn't be able to tell the authorities anything helpful, even if she'd been inclined to endanger her own freedom by admitting she was part of the kidnapping.

Staying on the side road, Funar put the accelerator down and led the procession back down the road. He tapped the steering wheel in time to the rock-and-roll station playing on the radio.

Gazing through the rear windshield, Lupu watched the train passengers abandon the cars, driven out by the smoke.

"This man could have been hired by Galvani," Funar said.

Lupu stared through the dusty haze overlaying the road. Something with hard, bright eyes raced across the road just ahead of their headlights. "No. Galvani's response would be to send an army. This was one man, and he didn't back off even when the odds were against him. Not down in the canals, and not on the train. And Galvani doesn't seem to have any support from the Americans."

Funar shrugged. "A day or two at most, and we'll have what we want from the DeVincenzo woman. Then we can send the boy back to her. If all this man wants is the boy, we won't see anything more of him."

"It depends on how the woman handles this," Lupu said. "Whether she believes we'll really turn the boy back over to her when she gives us the information." And there was the possibility they'd have to hurt the boy to make the woman deal. From the man's willingness to fight, Lupu knew he wasn't going to go away easily. "It'll be better if we find this man and kill him."

Funar nodded. "Then we'll get it done."

THE TAVERN HAD originally served dockworkers back in the 1700s. According to the chipped and faded brass plate near the recessed door illuminated by a dim single light, the poets Lord Byron, John Keats and Percy Bysshe Shelley had gathered there upon occasion almost two centuries ago. Over the years it had been constantly reconstructed, and now managed to hang on to a shambling existence of its former self, fitting the rest of the San Croce neighborhood.

Mack Bolan walked through the door and up the narrow stone stairs. A stumbling sailor was coming downstairs, escorting two women who were obviously there to conduct business. Bolan kept the windbreaker open, giving him quick access to the pistol on his hip.

The second floor of the building was divided into a large tavern area and a small kitchen. Dishes were pushed through a rectangular window by two guys wearing sleeveless sweatshirts. Three waitresses worked the floor, evading the advances of the men seated around the plastic tables with a skill born of long practice. American heavy metal blasted from the sound system in the corner. The atmosphere was dark and smoky, filled with the scents of cheeses, beer and simmering sauces.

The short bar was on the right. Large wine casks, already tapped, flanked a cracked mirror that had stained-glass butterflies worked into the design. A thin man with a military stance stood behind the bar smoking a cigar. A bar towel hung over one shoulder.

Bolan walked to the bar. The man he was looking for wasn't in the tavern.

"What can I get for you?" the bartender asked.

"I'm looking for Jules Lippi," Bolan said.

The bartender flicked the ash off his cigar, then refilled two beer glasses a waitress brought to him. "Never heard of him."

The waitress gave Bolan a once-over, then a bold smile before leaving. When she was gone, Bolan dropped money on the scarred bar top. "Maybe you didn't hear me." According to his information, Lippi was an informant often used by the police and CIA.

The bartender flipped through the bills but didn't take them. "You're not a cop, and I own this place, so I don't want any trouble to deal with after you leave. Is Lippi going to be breathing when you're through with him?"

"I plan on it."

"You're American."

"Yes."

"There's a couple Americans helping out Mrs. DeVincenzo. Are you one of them?"

Bolan regarded the man. "And if I am?"

"Pietro Magaddino was a good man. Helped me get established here when I was busted out of the police department for doing him little favors. I was on his payroll, but he didn't have to do that. I wouldn't mind doing his granddaughter a favor."

Bolan nodded. "I'm trying to help her get her son back."

The bartender pushed the money back with a forefinger. "Lippi's upstairs." He pointed to a staircase beside the sound system. A curtain nearly covered it. "There's a game room up there. When he's not snitching, he picks up money hustling pool from the young wannabees."

Bolan bought a draft to blend in so Lippi wouldn't see him and automatically tense up.

"You want to be careful up there," the bartender warned. "Lippi's got his crowd with him, and he's been hitting the hard stuff tonight."

Bolan said thanks, then walked up the stairs. The upper room was smaller and darker. A pool table occupied the center of the room. Overhead a ceiling fan struggled to clear the wreath of blue gray smoke that formed a hazy bubble in the light. A balcony was to the left, the doors thrown open to admit the air.

Seven men stood around the pool table. All of them turned their attention to Bolan when he entered the room.

"This is a private party," a bald giant built like a grizzly said.

Five of the remaining six men were young and dressed primarily in black. The sixth man was of medium height and broad shouldered. He was clean shaved, with a headful of thick brown hair, dressed in slacks and a white dress shirt. Gold chains gleamed around his neck, matched by the earring in his left ear.

"I'm looking for Jules Lippi," Bolan said. He sat the beer on a shelf mounted on the wall above a line of coat hooks.

The bald giant was quick to respond. "He isn't here."

"Yeah, he is," the warrior said, his voice flat and insistent.

The five younger men spread out around the table. Knives gleamed in the fists of two of them.

"Who are you?" asked the well-dressed man.

"I'm just a guy looking to do some business." Bolan took the folded lire notes and tossed them onto the pool table. "If you're Lippi."

"I am." Lippi glanced at the money, then back at Bolan. "What kind of business?"

"I want to know about a guy named Mihai Lupu, and what connection Alonzo Galvani has with him."

Lippi flashed the warrior a nervous grin. "Take your money and get out of here. Talk like that can get a guy killed right now."

"One way or another," Bolan said, "we're going to talk."

Lippi shook his head. "I don't think so." He snapped his fingers at the bald giant. "Giotto, get him out of here."

The big man started forward like an automaton. His huge hands bunched into formidable clubs.

Bolan decided against drawing a weapon for the moment because he wanted Lippi's attention. He set himself as the bald giant kept up his ponderous approach.

Giotto telegraphed his first punch, and the warrior ducked under it easily. He hooked two short jabs to the man's immense midsection but didn't appear to do much more than make him angry. The big man's next blow caught Bolan on the shoulder when he tried to block it. The force behind it sent Bolan reeling backward.

Recovering, he snapped two jabs to the big man's face, scoring both times and breaking his nose. Then he followed up with a right cross to the chin that rocked Giotto back on his heels and left him dazed.

A shadow drifted into Bolan's peripheral vision. Before he could turn to face it, a roundhouse kick caught him in the side, knocking the breath from his lungs. He snared the kicker's foot on the next attempt and twisted viciously. Bone snapped, accompanied by a shrill yell.

Giotto's big fist seemed to come out of nowhere and exploded against the side of the Executioner's head. He tasted blood from a split lip as he dropped to one knee. The other four young men were circling around him, waiting for an opening as the bald giant closed in for the kill.

Maintaining his focus, Bolan slipped one of the pool cues from the rack behind him and held it horizontally in front of him, shoulder-width apart. He used the cue to deflect Giotto's next punch, then grabbed his jacket under the swinging arm and pulled. The big man stumbled off balance, allowing Bolan time and space to move behind him.

The Executioner brought the cue off his shoulder in a line-drive swing. The heavy wooden end crashed into the base of Giotto's skull and snapped off. Wheeling, the warrior used what was left of the cue to whip across the face of one of the other men, sending the guy down with a mouthful of broken teeth. Still in motion, his opponents giving ground before him now, Bolan swung the broken cue and took another guy down.

"Move!" one of the two intact men yelled at the guy standing beside him. He tried to sweep the guy out of his way and draw a small hideout pistol at the same time.

Bolan drew the Night Stalker and fired from the point. The 9 mm round caught the guy in his gun shoulder and spun him. The small Walther dropped to the floor, and the other man dived for it and got clipped by a bullet for his pains.

Bolan kept the P-228 level, covering the group. Giotto was sprawled unconscious on the floor. The other five men he'd taken out were moaning in pain and not making any move at further interference, leaving only one still standing and uninjured.

Blood trickled down Bolan's stubbled chin as he advanced on Lippi. "Playtime's over," he growled. He grabbed the man by the shirt and pushed him backward to the wall.

Lippi held his hands up. "Hey, don't hurt me. You don't have to hurt me. I'll talk."

"Tell me about Mihai Lupu."

"I don't know much. He operates out of Bucharest. His father was some kind of high muckamuck with Ceauşescu's cabinet. Since the fall he's been muscling his way up through the black market operating in Romania. From what I hear, he's the man you want to see in Bucharest if there's anything you need that you can't get legally."

"What's Galvani's interest in him?" Bolan asked.

"I don't know."

Bolan pulled the man from the wall, then slammed him back against it. "Talk."

"I can't. Galvani will kill me."

Yanking the man into motion, the Executioner herded Lippi to the open balcony. He pushed him back against the low railing, then levered his arm under the man's chin and forced him to look at the two-story drop. "That looks like about thirty-five feet to me," Bolan said in a graveyard voice. "If you survive the fall, you're going to have to yell the information back up to me. If you can't do that or you try to run, I'm going to shoot you." He locked eyes with the man. "It'll be even harder to answer if that fall drives some ribs through your lungs."

Lippi clung to Bolan's arm.

"Galvani's been moving into the Eastern European sector," Lippi said. "They're cash poor over there, but trafficking and smuggling are booming. Galvani's setting up connections, cutting himself a little empire over there. Magaddino kept him under his thumb here, wouldn't allow him anything he wasn't willing to give him."

"So Galvani's moving into Lupu's territory," Bolan said.

Lippi nodded, swallowing hard and not relaxing the death grip he had on Bolan's arm. "It's developed into a border war from what I hear. Galvani thought he could just roll over this Romanian, you know? Guy's young. But Lupu plays his cards tight. If Galvani hits one of his operations, Lupu burns two of Galvani's. But it's still costing the Romanian. And now that Magaddino's not around to keep tabs on Galvani, the old guy's not going to be hesitant about stepping up the pace."

"Lupu is looking for leverage to get Galvani off his back."

"Yeah. Everybody knew Magaddino had something on him. But nobody knows what that was." .

Bolan pushed the man farther over the edge of the balcony. "Nobody?"

"I swear on the Blessed Virgin Mary," Lippi said, frantic. "If I knew, I'd have cashed in on it a long time ago."

Bolan believed him. He stepped back and released the guy, letting Lippi drop to the balcony floor and curl up defensively. Turning from the man, keeping the pistol in his fist, the warrior strode from the room. Giotto was still out, and the others scurried down the stairs while he was busy on the balcony.

No one tried to stop him as he left the building. The wind was brisk and cool. Dawn was only a couple of hours away. He felt tired and battered, but the image of the sleeping boy being carried away by Lupu's people helped him keep his edge.

While Magaddino had been alive, all the deadly secrets he'd managed over the years had been kept locked up tight. Now they were threatening to destroy what was left of his family.

As he walked through the dark streets, Bolan also realized that Julia DeVincenzo was a target, as well. If she had something that could damage Alonzo Galvani, or if the man thought she did, Galvani had to view her as a liability. Especially now that Lupu's involvement was out in the open and he had Nicky DeVincenzo. The Executioner knew the play had gone from being strictly offensive to defensive, as well.

Now there were two targets, one to retrieve and one to protect. And they were interconnected in such a manner that Bolan knew there was no way to fully pursue one without sacrificing the other.

"I'VE GOT A MATCH on one of your mystery guys."

Leo Turrin snugged the phone under his jaw a little tighter. "Show me." Aaron Kurtzman was on the other end of the connection, working an untraceable bootlegged communications line through the American Embassy in Milan.

Turrin was sitting on the metal desk in Canova's cramped office in the Venice Police Department. The computer monitor on the desk blinked, then reproduced one of the dead faces Turrin remembered from the police boat.

"Who am I looking at?" Turrin leaned forward and rapped on the glass separating him from the detectives' bull pen.

Outside, Canova was talking to a pair of uniforms and another plainclothes detective. He broke off the conversation when Turrin waved him in and returned to the office.

Turrin punched the speakerphone button, then pointed at the computer monitor. Canova sat behind the desk and started filling his pipe. The exposure to the wind and spray had made him look tired and haggard.

"His name was Avram Suciu," Kurtzman said. "I'm including some hard copy you can go over for a more in-depth read."

"Okay," Turrin said, watching the pages feed through the printer. "I've got a friend with me. Giacomo Canova, of the Venice police." That said, Kurtzman would know not to go to a video feed from Stony Man Farm and would watch what he said. Turrin had told Canova the Intel was coming from a terrorist file kept by the Justice Department through Brognola.

He could tell by Canova's dark glance that the policeman wasn't fooled for a moment that he was getting the full story. His pipe packed, he sucked down the lighter's flame until he had the tobacco going nicely.

"Suciu ended up in jail in 1990 after Ceauşescu's execution," Kurtzman went on. "He was part of Ceauşescu's private militia and had been sentenced to ten years for crimes committed against the state.

An inside black-bag operation broke him out in 1993."

"Lupu?" Turrin asked. He glanced at Canova. The military background could explain the burn scars they'd seen on the other man.

"Possibly," Kurtzman answered. "There was also some supposition that he was freed by Communist sympathizers wanting to use his talents. Suciu was free-lance for a year before beginning a tight association with Lupu."

"Was the other man in the military?" Turrin asked.

"I'm checking on that." The faint clacking of computer keys carried over the line. "A lot of information was lost during the rebellion, and even more has been suppressed since then. I'll get back to you if anything turns up."

"What about Lupu?" Canova asked.

"Rumor and fact since Ceauşescu's fall are running about fifty-fifty," Kurtzman replied. "He's connected with the black markets moving through Romania and has put together an extensive organization, but I haven't found anything between Galvani and him. News reports from Bucharest are sparse. All the good headlines these days are coming out of Bosnia, and the reporters have UN forces covering them while they dish the latest. Of course, with his black market ties, Lupu is unofficially being supported by some of the alphabet crowds that still lurk in the shadows over there."

"So we could be dealing with sensitive territory?" Turrin asked.

"No doubt about it."

Turrin thought about that, knowing Bolan wouldn't back off even if the CIA or Russian military Intelligence were subsidizing Lupu. Until Nicky DeVincenzo was back home, the big warrior wouldn't rest. Turrin didn't plan on it, either, but he hadn't figured on the play going as far from the field as it had. "Thanks, buddy."

"Stay frosty out there, guy." The connection broke with a distinct click. The picture of Suciu remained frozen on the monitor.

"With any kind of luck," Turrin said, "we can contain Lupu and his people here in Venice."

"I'm afraid it's too late for that," Canova said. "I was talking to a couple men out there who were working a train hijacking. I'm getting that file sent to me posthaste. But it sounds like Lupu."

"What happened?"

Quickly Canova explained about the train hijacking and the subsequent shoot-out that had left three dead and several frightened passengers behind. "The dead men left in the car just out of Venice are being taken to the morgue. But one of them has a tattoo like this man's, judging from the description given by the officers." The detective tapped the printed sheets that had spilled out of the printer. The tattoo he indicated had been on the dead man's inner forearm. Kurtzman had tracked it back to a Romanian special-forces contingent that had operated directly under Ceauşescu.

"Was the boy there?" Turrin asked.

"We're not sure," Canova said. "The crime team on the scene is still sorting out the details. The train went on across the Gulf of Venice, stopping short of Mestre. The hijack team got out there and met up with waiting cars. Some witnesses say there was a boy with them. If that's true—"

"Then Nicky may not even be in the city anymore," Turrin said. He used the mouse to change the monitor back to the picture of Mihai Lupu. "You need to keep a lid on this if you can. At least the link between the Romanians."

"Because Galvani may find out and do something rash if he feels threatened." Canova nodded. "I understand. I'll make sure the people I'm using to keep him under surveillance stay on their toes." He reached for the phone.

Turrin downloaded the files Kurtzman had sent over onto three high-density disks and took a copy of the printed matter. The papers were unmarked, carrying no seal, and could have been issued from anywhere.

"I'm going to drift," he said to the detective. "If I find out anything you can use, I'll drop a dime."

"Do that." Canova stood and offered his hand.

Turrin took it, then showed himself the door. His thoughts were dark as he factored in the recent turn of events. Silently he damned the men who'd placed Nicky DeVincenzo in danger and used him so callously.

Galvani and Lupu were both violent men, used to dealing out harsh retribution to people who crossed them. Justice didn't figure into their normal daily agenda.

But they hadn't counted on Mack Bolan, Turrin knew. Justice was coming, and it would be relentless.

CHAPTER EIGHT

Eyes burning from staring at the computer monitor in her grandfather's study, Julia DeVincenzo reached for the television remote control and turned up the volume on the set across the room.

"... no clue why there's been such an outbreak of violence in the city tonight," the reporter said as he faced the camera. He was lean and sincere, wrapped in a dark raincoat. The train station was in the background. "There have been some rumors that this may be terrorist activity, taking into account the bombing of the canal in the Dorsoduro district and now the attack on board the train only a couple hours ago. But nothing has surfaced that makes a link between the two events, other than the presence of automatic weapons."

Offscreen a woman's voice asked, "Have the police said anything about the latest attack on the train?"

Julia watched with interest. She'd been so intent on searching through the computer files that she'd missed the report on the train incident.

"Very little," the reporter on location answered. "Railway officials are keeping the area closed down for the time being, until they can make sure the tracks to the mainland haven't been harmed by the blast used to separate the car from the rest of the train. They don't know for sure when commuter traffic is going to be back to normal today."

A chill ran through Julia unexpectedly. Explosives were another common denominator. She gripped the arms of her chair and pushed herself up. Crossing the room, she refilled her cup from the small electric coffeepot she'd brought in over an hour ago. The brew was black and harsh. She'd had no contact with Turrin or his friend. Despite the rest of the household staff and the security, she felt alone.

"It's a possibility that the train was going to be held for ransom," the reporter said. "One of the passengers on board said the three men who were killed spoke in a foreign language that he couldn't identify. At the time the violence on board broke out, it became readily apparent that there were several more armed people in the other cars. That was confirmed when the engineering crew called from Mestre to let the police and train authorities know that the people who'd hijacked the train had gotten off before reaching city limits."

The reporter went on to describe the actions of the lone man who'd shot the three train hijackers. From the description, Julia was certain it had been Turrin's friend. It also might mean that Nicky wasn't in Venice anymore.

The realization hit her like a physical blow, taking the breath from her lungs and leaving her heart cold. Her hands shook enough to slop coffee over the rim of her cup. Steeling herself, she muted the television and returned to the computer.

"Find that information," she told herself, grasping for focus, "and you can get Nicky back." Tears burned hotly at the backs of her eyes, but she didn't let them go. Crying wouldn't do Nicky any good, and it blurred the words on the monitor.

Columns of file names plastered themselves in neatly arranged boxes as she pulled up another directory tree. She'd never been that far from Nicky. It took an incredible amount of willpower for her to keep at the files instead of smashing the computer system to pieces.

While waiting for one of the programs to load, she glanced at the security monitors. Before last night she hadn't even known they'd existed; now she could fluidly flip through the various perspectives. The house was quiet. The morning cook was preparing an early breakfast, and three of the security guards were drinking coffee in the living room.

She returned her attention to the monitor just as the phone rang. Heart in her throat, not knowing what to expect, she picked up the cellular unit and clicked it on. "Julia DeVincenzo."

"Do you know who this is?"

She recognized the big man's voice at once. "Yes. Have you found Nicky?"

"For a while. I lost him again."

Julia leaned back in the chair. She made herself breathe out, concentrated on the gray dawn lightening the skies outside the bulletproof windows. She'd lived inside the house all her life, had thought of it as a prison, impenetrable. Most of the time she'd resented it. Now she missed that feeling of security. "So what do we do?"

"Regroup," the big man said. "We need to talk."

"Have you contacted Leo?"

"No."

"Where are you?"

"Nearby. I'll be coming in through the back."

"Fine. I'll meet you." Julia switched off the phone, then grabbed the heavy Charter Arms .44 Magnum that Stefan had trained her to use shortly after they'd gotten married. The .380 automatic in the nightstand in her bedroom had always been around her, though she'd never fired it. She'd never wanted to learn to use a gun, but Stefan pointed out that any time they were away from the house together, it wasn't just her life that was in danger, but his, as well.

She'd never seen her husband's assassins until he was dying in her arms. All that training, and she'd never had time to fire even one shot. She walked to the rear of the house and waited.

Only a few minutes later a shadow stepped from the side of the house and stood in front of the door. She hadn't seen him come over the wall.

When she opened the door, the three housemen came running into the room with their guns drawn, alerted by the silent alarm. Julia waved them away as the man stepped into the room.

"Where is Nicky?" she demanded. The room was dark, and she couldn't see him clearly.

"I don't know." The answer was brutally honest.

"Was he on that train?"

"Yes."

"Was he hurt?"

"I don't think so. The car he was in wasn't involved in the shooting."

"What do you think you were doing shooting around my son? You son of a bitch, you could have gotten him killed. They'd been in touch with me. This isn't some cheap western. That's my son they're holding."

Surprisingly his voice was calm. "I know. I was trying to follow them. The more we know about them, the better off we'll be when it comes time to swap the information for Nicky. Just because you give them what they want doesn't mean they're going to give your son back."

His words were harsh, but she knew from the tone of his voice they weren't intended to be. The .44 at the end of her arm felt like an anchor. She nodded, letting him know she understood. She'd known other families over the years who'd had their children kidnapped; a few of the targets had even been Nicky's age. Some of them had been returned unharmed, but others had been killed, their bodies recovered later. And occasionally the children were never seen again.

Julia took a deep breath and let it out. "What do we do?"

"We assemble as much information as we can," the big man said. "Not everything is in the control of these people."

"It feels like it."

"That's how they want you to feel."

"I know."

"There's some other considerations we have to make," he said. "Did you find the information your grandfather had on Galvani?"

"Not yet. It's frustrating because I don't really know where to look."

"Galvani knows Lupu has Nicky, and when I went up against the Romanian's people, they thought I was working for Galvani. A little while ago I talked to a guy who said Galvani has been moving in on Lupu's action in Romania."

The anger surged inside Julia again. "That's what this is about? That's why they took *my* son? Because of some turf war between them?"

The big man nodded. "Your grandfather had something he was blackmailing Galvani with. Lupu wants it to use as leverage to back Galvani off."

"But I don't know what that is," Julia replied.

"We'll find it, and when we do, we'll cut Nicky and ourselves the best deal we can. In the meantime, though, Galvani may take steps to ensure you can't deliver that information."

It took a moment for his words to soak through. "You're saying Galvani may try to kill me."

"Yes. I don't think it's safe here anymore."

Julia hardened her voice. "I'm not leaving. This is where Lupu is expecting to get in touch with me. If I go into hiding, there's no telling what they may do to Nicky."

He said nothing for a tense minute. Then he relaxed. "Okay. We can talk more later, when Leo gets back. Is there someplace I can get cleaned up?"

For the first time she noticed the mud and the blood that stained his windbreaker and clothes. His mouth was puffy, and a shadowy imprint of wiped-off blood trickled down to his chin. Upon closer inspection she noticed the bullet holes that had ripped through the jacket.

Unconsciously she took a step forward and switched on a small lamp nearby. "My God, are you hurt?"

"No. It looks worse than it is." His blue eyes were disarming.

For the first time Julia realized everything the big man had been through for Nicky and her. Pangs of guilt assailed her. He'd been risking his life for them, and she'd never even said a grateful word. Tenderly she touched his face, turning it to one side so she could inspect the damage. "Do you need to see a doctor? I can have one here in just minutes."

"No. Just show me a bathroom. And a first-aid kit if you've got one."

"I've got one. Nicky's always scraping a knee or an elbow." She refused to let herself think about that. She needed her head clear. "I'll show you to a room, then I'll get it." Turning from him, she led him to one of the upstairs guest rooms that had its own bathroom. She left him there, then retrieved the first-aid kit from her bedroom.

When she got back, the water was running in the shower. She started to knock on the door, but decided not to. Instead, she opened the door and walked in. She'd seen naked men before, and she didn't think the big man was the modest sort. And she wanted to know more about him. Leo had said he was good at situations like the one she and Nicky were presently in, but she didn't know much about him. Now, with everything maybe depending so heavily on him, she wanted to know all she could.

He was aware of her the moment she stepped into the room. She knew that. Blurred flesh on the other side of the sliding glass doors of the shower stood under the shower head.

"Just leave it," he said. Steam pooled against the ceiling. He'd folded his clothes neatly and placed them on the vanity, but it didn't surprise her. Somehow she'd known he'd be neat and organized.

"You were in the military," she said, placing the first-aid kit by the sink.

"Yes."

"For a long time?"

"Longer than most."

She knew she should leave, but she didn't want to. "Am I intruding?"

There was a hesitation before he answered. "No."

"I'm scared," she admitted. "I don't even know you, and Nicky and I are depending on you so much. It makes me uncomfortable." She tried not to stare at him, but she couldn't help looking occasionally. The distorted effect of the glass made him even more of an enigma.

"That's understandable."

"I know Mike isn't really your name, and I know you probably won't give me your real name. But Mike sounds too familiar. Isn't there something else I can call you?"

"McKay," the big man said.

Mentally she tried it. The name seemed to fit in an odd way. She touched the ravaged stack of clothing on the vanity, then realized he had no option but to put them back on. Quickly she checked the sizes. "What size shoes do you wear?"

He told her while he was cutting off the water.

Gathering the ruined clothes, she said, "I'm going to bring you something to wear. I'll be back."

She went downstairs and told the security team to find her some clothes that would fit, and a pair of shoes. She specified jeans, joggers and a casual shirt. McKay didn't seem the suit type to her. By the time she'd disposed of the other clothes, the security people had returned with their contributions.

Pausing at the bathroom door, she knocked this time, then entered at the American's invitation. He stood at the sink, a towel wrapped around his midsection. For a moment she just froze, looking at him. Old scars and new ones traced irregular paths across his body. She didn't recognize what had caused them, but she knew it wasn't the same thing. He'd used his body hard, but it still possessed vitality and a rockhewn finish. He was like no one she'd ever known before. A pistol was on a towel beside him, and she realized he'd taken it into the shower with him.

"You can leave them," he said quietly.

Startled, she glanced up at the mirror and saw that he'd caught her staring at him. Their eyes met. Embarrassed and flustered, she put the clothing on the vanity. "Sorry. I'll get you a shaving kit."

"Thanks."

On her way out the door, she noticed the bruises blossoming to full color under his skin along his rib cage and back. "What are the bruises from?"

"Body armor," he said. "Stops the bullet, but doesn't take out all the blunt trauma. It looks worse than it is."

She nodded, wondering if he'd been scared while facing the men who'd shot him. Then she realized that was foolish. He must have been afraid. Only an idiot or a megalomaniac wouldn't have been, and he didn't strike her as either. He'd known what he was going to be facing when he left the house, and he'd gone anyway.

She looked him in the eye. "I don't think I've been very gracious under the circumstances." She kept speaking before he could say anything. "I want to thank you for being here and for everything you're doing to help Nicky."

He nodded. "It's okay."

"I'm going to order some breakfast for you, then I'm going back to my grandfather's study." She closed the door and walked to the intercom, placing an order with the cook for a large breakfast.

In the study once more, she looked out at the second sunrise she'd seen without Nicky since her son had been born. The fear was still with her, thrumming and insistent, but there was something about the big soldier that made the possibility of getting Nicky back seem more probable. None of the men she'd grown up around in her grandfather's house had exhibited the grim resolve and genuine concern that the American had.

Except for Stefan. But her husband, though she had loved him, might not have put his life on the line for someone else's child. She had no doubt that Stefan would have died for Nicky, but McKay didn't even know her son.

It took a very special kind of man to do that. And though she didn't know much about him, she did know he was that kind of man.

THE SUN WAS WARM and crisp as it shone down on Jericho Light, burning off the last vestiges of the cool morning. The traffic along the San Barnaba was intense. Gondoliers shouted at each other over the roar of powerboats as they rushed about to get their fares to their destinations on time. Light was dressed in a dark sport coat, jeans, and loafers, and could have passed as a tourist or a businessman.

He'd had trouble sleeping the previous night. Memories of the men he'd killed came back to haunt him. In the old days he would never have thought of them again, unless there was a potential that their deaths might be traced back to him. After finishing his meal with the young street girl last night, she'd vanished back into the darkness. There'd been no sign of her that morning.

He stopped a block from the house, checking the address against his memory. Part of it was hesitation, he knew. Julia DeVincenzo was an innocent, and she'd already had her son taken from her. Still, he'd been given a mission from the church that he couldn't turn away from. If he didn't act quickly, much could be lost. In fact, it already had been lost for the past fifty years.

As he walked to the front door, Light was aware of the two men watching him from in front of the produce stand across the canal. Sunlight gleamed from a glass surface amid a pile of oranges. He guessed that it came from a pair of binoculars, and that the men were police officers working a stakeout on the Magaddino house.

He walked up to the stoop and punched the button. The sonorous sound of the doorbell echoed inside, letting him know the rooms beyond the door were huge. Patiently he turned, taking in the early morning sights of the city. Many people were walking to work, and shopkeepers were taking Closed signs out of windows, ready for the day.

The door opened behind him and he turned.

"May I help you?" a young woman in a maid's uniform asked politely. Two men stood behind her, and their presence was heavy.

"I would like to speak to Mrs. DeVincenzo," Light replied.

"May I tell her who's calling?"

The priest took one of his cards from his pocket. It was simple, black on white, and announced him as a committee member of the Roman Catholic church in Vatican City. "Father Jericho Light. It's of a personal nature."

The maid seemed confused as to what to do. She glanced back at the two men. One of them shook his head.

"It's okay," Light said, sensing the source of her discomfort. "I understand Mrs. DeVincenzo has had some trouble of late. I don't mind waiting out here."

A relieved smile formed on the maid's face. "Thank you, Father." She closed the door. The locks thunked solidly into place immediately after.

While he waited, Light unobtrusively kept tabs on his surroundings. The two policemen across the street attempted to get photographs of him while keeping their camera hidden. He found it mildly amusing to keep them frustrated, presenting only partial views of his face. With the plastic surgery he'd had less than a year earlier, it was extremely doubtful they'd recognize him even if they had an old picture of the way he used to look.

The door reopened. Julia DeVincenzo resembled the photos he'd seen, but she didn't show the confidence and poise she'd possessed in them. Surprisingly the file on the Magaddino family was extensive. But he'd learned not to be surprised by too many things after being accepted into his order.

"Father Light," she said, making no move to let him into the house. A tall, intense man was at her elbow. The two security men who'd been in the room earlier were gone.

"Yes." He offered his hand, but she didn't take it.

"If you don't mind, I'd like to see some identification."

"Of course." Light took his hand back and reached inside his jacket, noting the fluid ease with which the dark-haired man moved into a ready position. Julia DeVincenzo stayed clear of the line of fire. He opened his wallet and passed it across.

The woman examined the photograph-imprinted identification card briefly, touching the papal seal with a manicured fingernail as if checking the authenticity. Apparently satisfied, she handed the wallet back. "Please, come inside."

Light thanked her and stepped into the room. The dark-haired man moved closer, out of easy reach but immediately available to defend the woman.

"This is Mr. McKay," Julia DeVincenzo said.

Light inclined his head, not bothering to offer his hand. "I just need a few minutes of your time."

"I'm afraid that's all I have. Otherwise, I'd offer you a seat and a coffee." She regarded him frankly. "My family has always maintained a relationship with Father Bob Vasari here in Venice. My grandfather has visited Vatican City twice that I can remember in my whole life. So your showing up on my doorstep has left me unprepared as to how to receive you."

"It's not bad news, I assure you." The calm tones came easily to Light now. Father Donovan's one-sided conversations had drawn him back from near-madness. He'd practiced them in his mind until he knew the cadence and tenor of voice by rote. "First I'd like to offer condolences on behalf of the church at your grandfather's passing."

"Thank you."

Light felt McKay's eyes on him and wondered how much the man could read about him. He didn't scan like hired muscle. There was something more deadly about him. Light recognized the signs easily because he'd gone up against men like McKay before. "My seniors were awaiting some contact from your grandfather's executor regarding some items he'd promised the church on his passing."

"I'm afraid I don't know anything about them," the woman said. "You'd have to talk to his attorney about that."

Light nodded. "These would have been very private things. I'm not sure he would have wanted them to pass through an attorney's hands."

"What were they?"

Light hesitated for a moment. The woman was more blunt than he'd have thought. If she was trying to hide anything, she would have tried to brush the subject aside rather than address it so straightforwardly. "Pictures, jewelry and a few pieces of pottery."

"I know my grandfather was an avid collector of porcelain figurines," Julia said. "And he was somewhat interested in other art forms, but I don't know of any that the church might want."

"I see." Light let a little disappointment show. "We at the church were looking to adding the acquisitions to our museums soon. They've been promised a very long time." He gazed at the paintings on the walls. Most of them were very good and had value, but they weren't the ones he was looking for. He'd committed the images to mind, culled from pictures other priests had been given by Magaddino in the early fifties, and by composite sketches that other priests had made.

"I really don't have time to discuss this further," Julia DeVincenzo said. She opened her purse and took out a card. "This is my grandfather's executor. If you'll talk to him, I'm sure you can get everything straightened out."

"Of course." Light took the card and pocketed it. "I appreciate your time, and I hope your present troubles pass quickly." He exited and walked off the stoop, heading back the way he'd come.

Sparing a glance over at the fruit stand, he saw three men leading the two undercover cops away. Both of them moved stiffly, and the men at their backs were making physical contact. Light guessed that they were being escorted at gunpoint. Most people, though, wouldn't have given the scene a second thought, never suspecting anything.

He walked along the canal, figuring out the options. He felt certain that Julia DeVincenzo was telling the truth when she said she knew nothing about the art pieces. But her troubles were increasing. The television news had hinted at that this morning.

At the end of the block he turned and circled around the back of the house. If he lost her, he lost his lead to the hidden church treasures. He hadn't been sent to fail.

A narrow alley cut between the rows of homes and buildings. Near what he judged to be the rear wall of the Magaddino estate, a man crouched with a toolbox at his side. He was dressed in olive drab coveralls with a stitched insignia on the back advertising a pesticide company.

Light slowed his approach, knowing something wasn't right. The Beeman/Hammerli was strapped to his left ankle. He walked silently.

Less than three yards from the man, he saw the collapsed LAW rocket launcher in the toolbox. He kept walking as if he hadn't noticed anything, but before he'd taken two more steps, a gun barrel was thrust up under his chin.

"Freeze, big man," a harsh voice grated.

The man in the coverall started, whirling with a gun in his fist.

Light came to a stop, automatically spreading his hands out from his body.

"Son of a bitch," the gun wielder said. "Looks like we've picked up a bonus on this run, Henri. Tell me if this isn't that priest everyone's been looking for since last night."

Henri grinned beneath a pair of mirrored sunglasses. "You did good, Taliferro." He looked at Light. "Just happen to be in the neighborhood today, Father?"

Light didn't answer. Glancing around the estate, he saw other men already in position at the top of the wall. Evidently security had already been breached.

Taliferro stepped around in front of Light, still digging the weapon into the priest's neck. He was a solid, broad man with spatulate fingers wrapped around the taped butt of the .45. "You be cool, priest. Dead or alive, you're worth fifty grand to me. I don't know that they want you dead. If you're lucky, they just want you to take a message to the pope or something. But you try anything, you're going to get your halo and wings early. Understand?''

"Sure," Light replied.

"Let's get on with it," Taliferro said.

Light remained stationary, waiting on his chance to act. The man in coveralls lifted the LAW out of the toolbox and pulled the pins to telescope it. With the light antitank weapon settled over his shoulder, the man flipped up the bull's-eye sight ring and took aim at the house through the wrought iron bars.

"Going on three, two, one..." the man said slowly and evenly.

Taliferro's attention wavered as he readied himself for the recoil of the weapon. Light acted immediately. Sweeping his left arm across his body, the priest caught Taliferro's gun wrist in his hand, planted a thumb between his middle knuckles and turned the .45 toward the man's throat. When the gun went off, the round tore the gunman's throat out, spraying blood over his companion.

Still on the move, Light ripped the .45 out of the corpse's hand and launched a kick at Henri just as the rocket rushed from the LAW. Dispassionately the priest put two rounds through the back of Henri's head as he tried to catch himself.

The explosion of the 94 mm warhead striking home was thunderous trapped between the buildings. Flower pots lining nearby fire escapes and balconies dropped and smashed against the concrete floor of the alley.

Bullets whacked the wrought iron bars as Light went to ground. He got a brief impression of the ball of flame that had swelled up inside the hole ripped into the back porch. The LAW rocket had been an incendiary charge. Lining up his first shot, he hoped the treasures he was seeking weren't inside the house because it looked as if the fire was going to spread.

THE EXPLOSION JARRED the whole house. Mack Bolan pushed himself out of the seat behind the desk in Magaddino's study. The Night Stalker filled his hand immediately. On the computer screen in front of him, lines of data chased themselves as they were fed to Kurtzman at Stony Man Farm. So many files had been encrypted without Julia having access to them that she'd agreed to Bolan's suggestion they let someone else look at it. Time was working against them now.

"What the hell was that?" Julia asked. She was standing near the window, a cup of coffee in her hand.

Without answering, the warrior dived for her, bringing her to ground only a heartbeat before a second explosion smashed against the window. The bulletproof glass shattered under the impact, and a pool of fire spread across the floor.

Bolan yanked the woman to her feet, urging her into motion. "Move!" He grabbed his windbreaker from a chair and slipped it on. Three extra magazines for the P-228 were in his pockets.

Bullets hammered through the ruined window, then a shadow dropped across it. A man depending from a line swung into the room holding an assault rifle. He dropped from the line expertly, rolling and searching for position, coming up firing. Five-point-five-six mm tumblers blasted into the wall chest high to Bolan, ripping gouges in the expensive wooden finish as they came around to Bolan and Julia.

The Executioner stepped in front of the woman, offering her the protection of the body armor, and dropped the Night Stalker into target acquisition. He stroked the trigger four times, two in his target's chest, and two in the man's face above the assault rifle's barrel.

The man staggered back as two others swung into the room.

"Go!" Bolan ordered, pushing the woman ahead of him. He pulled the door closed behind him and ducked to the side as bullets punched holes through it.

Julia ran for the stairs meeting Turrin and two of the security guards racing up them. Turrin wrapped an arm around her protectively, his Bodyguard clutched in his fist. He kept her moving down the stairs.

"They're all around the place," Turrin said. "And they've blown a hell of a hole in the back of the house. Way the fire's spreading, we're going to be standing in ash in minutes."

Bolan nodded. "They'll be waiting out front." He took the point at the bottom of the stairs just as the men burst through the door of Magaddino's study. Only one of the shooters moved to the stair railing.

Raising the 9 mm pistol, Bolan fired a half-dozen shots across the man's thighs and lower torso, below the line covered by most concealed body armor. With a shrill cry the man fell back, his weapon falling unfired. The other man kept back but raked the walls above the fleeing party's heads.

Bolan led the way to the great hall at the front of the house. Julia was on his heels, propelled by Turrin and followed by the two security men.

"Where are the other two guards?" the warrior asked as he took up position beside the door leading to the stoop. He kept the Night Stalker in a Weaver's grip in front of him.

"Dead," one of the guards answered. "The back room was hit with some kind of rocket. Those guys never had a chance. Killed the cook, too."

"Is it Galvani's people?" Bolan asked. Out front, traffic along the canal was coming to a stop as confusion spread.

"Don't know," the guard answered.

The other man shook his head.

Bolan examined the possibilities. Everything happening so quickly on the heels of the unexplained visit by the priest was confusing. "Leo?"

"I haven't seen any players I'd know," Turrin growled.

Julia, a small cut oozing blood on her jawline, shook her head. She was holding the Charter Arms Bulldog .44 in her hands, the hammer eared back.

Bolan reached for the pistol, easing the hammer down while it was still in her grip. "Double action," he advised. "Harder to pull and it'll give you a half second more to make sure of your target."

She nodded. "I've got a boat out front."

Bolan moved the curtain and looked at the sleek powerboat. "They'd know about that."

A trio of fast-moving men launched themselves at the front door. The lead man carried a squat, heavy cylinder.

"Down!" Bolan growled, sweeping his arm back to tuck Julia out of the way.

The door cannon roared dully, but the sound of detonation was lost in the crash of the door exploding inward. Splinters and plaster dust rushed into the room.

Spinning around the corner, Bolan lifted the P-228 and caught the first man through the door with three rounds in the face. The blast shield covering his eyes and nose didn't even slow the bullets that crashed into his brain.

Still in motion, Bolan fired the last three rounds from his pistol at the next man through who was slowed by the dead man falling backward. The Night Stalker's slide blew back empty.

The third man shoved the muzzle of his Mossberg Persuader through the door.

Bolan grabbed the shotgun's barrel and shoved it upward. The 12-gauge weapon discharged with a deafening blast, turning the metal hot. Stepping close up, Bolan brought the Night Stalker around in a crashing blow that splintered the man's temple. The shotgun came free in the warrior's hands.

Turrin shoved Julia toward the Executioner as he reloaded the 9 mm pistol and holstered it. "Company," he explained. Turrin took cover and fired back toward the room they'd just vacated. "They firebombed the rest of the house. These guys have to belong to Galvani.''

Bolan nodded as he removed a bandolier of shotgun shells from his last opponent and dropped them over one shoulder. He fed two rounds into the Mossberg, bringing it up to the full capacity of eight again. ''If there's anything damaging inside the house, they're going to get rid of it once and for all.''

One of the house guards suddenly stumbled back, his face ripped away by a burst of submachine-gun fire.

Julia glanced at the dead man nearly at her feet, then up at Bolan. ''Whether they knew about the boat or not, staying here isn't an option. And I damn sure don't intend to die and leave no one to look after Nicky.''

''Okay,'' Bolan said. He glanced out through the smashed door. The canal was twenty-five yards away. A low-slung, hunter-green-and-white private fishing boat with a flying bridge trolled through the water as the pilot tried to see what was happening. Of all the boats out in the canal, it looked like the fastest. ''That boat. Do you see it?'' He pointed.

Turrin, Julia and the surviving security man all said yes.

''When you start for it, don't let up,'' the warrior said. He stepped outside the shattered door and shouldered the Mossberg. Somebody peered around the far corner of the house. Bolan touched the shotgun's trigger, and a tight pattern of double-aught buckshot took the man's head off. ''Go!''

Turrin took Julia by the elbow and hustled her out of the house, streaking for the canal. Bullets danced along the concrete around them, letting Bolan know a shooter was on top of the house.

Pulling the shotgun up, he sighted the gunner on the roof and fired twice in quick succession. He rolled with the recoil, keeping on target. Pieces of the roofing tore loose and dropped like heavy confetti, but he was certain he'd at least gotten a piece of his target.

Then he launched himself in pursuit of the others, pushing himself hard. A bullet hit him between the shoulder blades, knocking him off stride, but was stopped by the PointBlank armor.

The fishing boat was moving almost fast enough that even at a dead run Turrin and Julia were having trouble overtaking it.

Movement in his peripheral vision brought Bolan around to cover his team. As he brought himself to a stop and brought the shotgun down, he recognized the flamethrower only an instant before the man who'd stepped from the side of the house unleashed a blast at him.

A snarling mushroom of orange-and-red flames leaped forward.

CHAPTER NINE

The harsh cracks of gunshots rent the air, but it was a sound Jericho Light had become accustomed to in another life. He was in motion now, rounding the house on the right with the Beeman/Hammerli in his fist. He'd fired the .45 dry and abandoned it.

The stone wall at the side of the house kept his attackers from seeing him. He knew from experience that the aim was to go into the house from the rear and set fire to everything they could, forcing Julia DeVincenzo and her people out through the front.

Near the back of the house, Light jumped up and caught the top of the wall. He hauled himself over easily as bullets chipped stone splinters against his legs. Drawing immediate attention from two gunmen as he landed on the soft ground, he lifted the target pistol smoothly, then squeezed off one round to each man.

The .32 rounds caught both targets squarely in the forehead like small black kisses and knocked them backward.

A man with a backpack-mounted flamethrower moved toward the house, spewing out gouts of fire. Most of the rear of the house was in flames now, and black smoke swirled thick and deadly under the leafy boughs of the trees. The fire spread, climbing upward rapidly.

The staccato roar of autofire to his right sent his reflexes into overdrive. He threw himself to the side, taking advantage of a half-dozen fruit trees. The branches and leaves shook as the bullets cut into them over Light's head. Raising the Model 280, he fired a single round that took out the gunner's right eye above the sights of the assault rifle he carried.

He watched as the flamethrower operator tried to come around. Taking deliberate aim, he punched his last two rounds through the tanks on the man's back. Instantly the man was enveloped by a rush of flame that quenched his final screams.

Light palmed his empty magazine, slipped in a fresh clip, and shoved the old one deep into his pants pockets. It was an old habit, even surer than his fingers on the rosary.

He broke cover and rushed into the back of the house, pulling his jacket over his face as he plunged through the layer of fire wreathing the broken door. Smoky, superheated air seared his lungs for an instant, then he was inside the house. Smoke created a burning fog that filled the interior.

If the art pieces he'd been assigned to recover were in the house, he needed to know. He found the staircase and followed it up. Magaddino wouldn't have left them out where everyone could see them. Their history was tied too closely to the church. Someone would have recognized them.

He took the steps two at a time, pounding upward. At the top of the staircase, he stepped over a dead man and gazed into the burning study. Sparks flew as the fire in the center of the room burned out the computer's electrical connections.

None of the paintings on the walls were what he was looking for. The flames crowded in on him, the heat parching his skin. When he glanced down the staircase, he saw that the whole lower floor was on fire. Stepping inside the study for a moment, he seized one of the assault rifles left by the dead men. From the sound of the gunfire in front of the house, he judged Julia DeVincenzo and the other survivors had made a break for it.

He raced up the stairs to the third floor as the spreading flames rushed after him. Checking the CAR-15's magazine, he found fifteen rounds still available.

In less than twenty seconds on the third floor, he found Pietro Magaddino's bedroom. His breathing rasped in his lungs now, and the smoke was choking him down. None of the art pieces he was looking for was among the collection on the walls and shelves. And the wall safe was much too small to hold any of them, either.

Keeping Julia DeVincenzo alive became a top priority. She was his only connection to the lost art.

He crossed the hall and went to the boy's bedroom overlooking the canal. Newly emplaced bars covered the window. The glass on the other side was safety glass. It took him three tries to knock the window out with the assault rifle's buttstock.

Below he saw three men protecting Julia De-Vincenzo as she made for the canal. Shouldering the

CAR-15, he took aim on one of the men who'd followed them out of the house and was attacking their flank. His finger caressed the trigger. Even as he rode out the slight recoil, he saw his target drop, the back of his head torn away.

Perspiration in response to the intense heat gathering at the top of the house soaked into Light's clothing. He blinked to clear his vision, focusing. More gunfire came from across the street, where he'd seen the policemen taken away.

A man broke cover, streaking for the bridge over the canal. Light settled the CAR-15's sights over the man and squeezed the trigger in a double tap that hit in the center of his chest and flipped him off the bridge.

The priest scanned the field, picking up Julia DeVincenzo again. The dark-haired man was behind the small group, providing covering fire. Then another of the assassins with a backpack-mounted flamethrower stepped into view and unleashed a torrent of fire that leaped for the man.

Light was lining up his shot when the door behind him was broken down and two men stepped into the room.

REFLEXES HONED BY WAR and what seemed like a lifetime spent on the edge of death, Mack Bolan threw himself to the side as the fiery deluge came at him. The flames splashed against the side of a boat tied up out in the canal, setting it on fire instantly.

Almost baked by the intensity of the flames, he rolled on his shoulder and came up on his knees. The

Mossberg floated to his shoulder automatically. Salty perspiration burned his eyes, but he never blinked as he focused on his target. He squeezed the trigger, racked the slide as he rode out the recoil and fired again.

The first charge of buckshot blasted into the man's chest, ripping away his protective jacket and revealing the bulletproof armor beneath. But the impact spun the man halfway around. Before he could recover, the second blast struck the tanks on his back and he exploded.

Bolan bracketed another man wielding an Uzi from behind the stone pier of the bridge. He fired at an exposed leg, ripping him away from his cover. His follow-up round took the gunner out of the play. As he got to his feet, he saw a dead man pitch from the bridge halfway across. The trajectory let him know the shot hadn't come from any of his group.

Glancing over his shoulder, he saw the blond-haired priest standing in the broken remains of Nicky DeVincenzo's bedroom window. Then the priest disappeared, and a heartbeat later a hail of bullets tore out some of the remaining pieces of glass left in the window. The scattered fires inside the home were gutting the building, gathering intensity as they raced to consume the upper stories.

The warrior broke into a run, cutting the distance between himself and the others. Turrin still held Julia, running fast, almost dragging her toward the canal.

A man taking cover at the side of the canal, partially submerged in the water, aimed his pistol at Turrin, who never even saw him.

Bolan fired instinctively, still running. The recoil staggered him for an instant, but he recovered. The tight pattern of double-aught buckshot struck the gunman's hand, knocking the pistol free and spinning him back into the water.

A thunderous explosion ripped along the canal as the Magaddino powerboat in front of the house was turned into kindling and debris. Evidently someone had thought they were making a break for the boat and had set off the planted charges prematurely.

Turrin more or less heaved Julia into the water as fiery splinters and the heavier pieces of the powerboat rained down around them. Then he jumped in himself, followed by the surviving security guard. They surfaced a few yards out, stroking strongly for the fishing boat Bolan had chosen as their escape.

Never breaking stride, with bullets chipping the concrete around him, the Executioner threw himself into the canal in a long dive. Going for distance rather than depth, his body slammed into the water surface with enough force to knock the breath out of him.

He submerged and stayed under as long as his lungs would let him. There was no way he could swim with the shotgun, so he let it go. When he came up, Turrin was reaching for the boat just as the pilot realized he was about to be boarded.

The man reached for his throttle, obviously intending to power out of the situation before getting caught up in it.

Turrin flailed out a hand, caught the side of the fishing boat and hauled himself up. He brandished the .38 in front of him, then fired a warning shot to get the skipper's attention. "Don't!" he shouted as Julia joined him alongside the boat. "Believe it or not, we're the good guys!"

The skipper held his hands up and backed away from the controls.

Bullets slapped against the water, then the gunners found the range and began scoring on the fishing boat.

Turrin helped Julia on board, then clambered up himself. He kept the woman moving, protecting her with his body as he took the bridge.

Grasping the boat coming, Bolan pulled himself out of the water. Gunners lined the side of the canal and the bullets punched holes in the fishing boat relentlessly. Taking cover in the aft section near the fishing chair, he drew the Night Stalker pistol and fired a complete magazine in a thunderous roll, shooting into the gunners nearest the boat. Behind them the mansion was wreathed in flames.

The security guard fell in beside the warrior, adding his firepower. Brass spun and ricocheted off the deck.

Bolan dropped down to eject his empty magazine and shove a fresh one home. He tripped the slide release and stripped the top round into the chamber.

"Shit," the guard said, joining him. He pointed with the magazine he was about to replace.

Glancing behind them, Bolan saw the sleek powerboat coming up fast. Armed men were already taking up positions across the bow. "Leo!"

"I see them." Turrin hit the throttles, and the boat's engines whined in protest. But the propellers spun, twisting the back end of the boat viciously as it leaped forward to gain momentum.

"They're going to overtake us," the guard said. "That boat's a lot faster than this one."

Bolan silently agreed. Autofire slapped into the whitecaps left in their wake, but he knew it wouldn't take the gunners long to get the range. He scanned the back of the boat, looking for options.

JERICHO LIGHT STOOD his ground because there was nowhere to run. Two bullets plucked at his coat as he fired the CAR-15 from the hip, one-handed.

The first few rounds caught the man on the left in the crotch and quickly zipped upward as he allowed the recoil to let the muzzle climb. The last rounds in the clip hit the second man in the chest and face. Both men went backward into the wave of fire that had escalated out in the hall.

Dropping the useless rifle, Light ran into the bathroom. There were only seconds to escape the building. Smoke was already flooding the room and it was growing harder to breathe.

He stood in the shower and turned the water on full force. In seconds he was soaked. It would buy him more time. When he returned to the door, a wall of flame covered most of it, already licking hungrily at the dead men lying there.

Covering his face with his arm, the Beeman/Hammerli drawn, Light leaped through the flame and rebounded from the opposite hallway wall. Flames ate through the ceiling, forcing him to move bent over. The only thing he could hear was the snapping and crackling roar of the fire.

Breathing was difficult. The superheated air was filled with smoke that bonded in his lungs before the oxygen did. A fit of coughing left black spots swirling in front of his eyes.

At the other end of the hallway, another set of stairs led down. The fire hadn't spread that far yet. He went down the steps three at a time, reaching the landing just ahead of the thunderous crash above him as the upper floor's roof collapsed. Gusts of soot, sparks and smoke belched out of the staircase behind him.

He found a window on the second floor that looked out over the garden. Holstering the target pistol, aware of the pool of fire spilling toward him across the floor and that he couldn't hope to cross it without serious damage, he dropped back to the nearest bedroom.

Seizing the door, Light ripped it from its hinges, dizzy now from the lack of oxygen. He turned it sideways, one hand supporting it, with another at the bottom end to provide impetus. Desperately he rammed it into the safety glass of the window. On the second attempt the glass shattered.

His clothes were singed from the trapped heat. Laying the door in the mouth of the window to shield him from the remaining broken shards, Light walked up the door and through the window.

Without hesitation he flung himself outside, not concerned about the story-and-a-half drop. Before he impacted against the soft loam of the garden, the fire evidently reached the gas lines on the second floor.

A massive explosion ripped through the house. Fiery streamers shot out of the window above, then brick and mortar rained over him. He landed off balance, almost twisting his ankle. Sharp stabs of pain resonated up his leg as he forced himself up and into a run for the back of the garden.

Only dead men remained around the house.

Moving lithely in spite of the aching ankle, he grabbed the top of the wrought-iron fence and swung himself up and over. He didn't head toward the canal, because too many people would be gathered there and because the assassins had recognized him, too.

He felt certain Julia DeVincenzo and her group had made the boat they were racing for. Now he needed to concentrate on picking up her trail again.

UNDER THE FLYING BRIDGE, Bolan spotted a Winchester Model 94 lever-action rifle mounted above the cabin door. He made his way back to it as the speedboat behind them closed the distance. Bullets thunked into the flying bridge as he pulled the rifle from the wall and checked the action. The chamber was empty, but the tubular magazine held all six 30.30 rounds.

"Shark gun," the boat's skipper said, clinging to the aluminum ladder leading up to the flying bridge.

"Are there any extra shells?" Bolan maintained his kneeling position with difficulty as Turrin whipped the boat from side to side to avoid other canal traffic and make a harder target.

"Yeah." The skipper fumbled with a metal box mounted on the cabin wall. When it popped open, a first-aid kit spilled across the deck, followed by a flare gun, a dozen flares and a 50-round box of .30-30 ammunition.

Bolan caught the box of ammo first, then stuck the flare gun at the back of his belt and dropped three flares into his jacket pockets.

"Coming around hard!" Turrin yelled in warning. The boat slewed sideways, nearly turning over.

Bolan grabbed the ladder and braced himself. A panorama of colors and shapes paraded by in front of the warrior as they were suddenly less than a yard from the side of the canal.

For a moment there was a respite from the autofire that had been hammering the vessel. As Bolan fed another round into the Winchester to bring it up to full capacity, he saw the pursuing speedboat swing wildly around the corner. The backwash it created capsized three gondolas.

Julia descended the ladder, her face white and grim. "How can I help?"

The speedboat was starting to gain on them again. One of the men took a squat, bulky shape from a man behind him, then shouldered it.

Bolan pointed to the large, built-in storage space along the side of the boat. The top was padded for seating. "Get the extra gas cans and pour them in that. And whatever cans of oil you can find." He reached out for the fishing net coiled neatly on the other side of the boat and dropped it into the chest, as well.

"What are you doing?" the skipper asked.

"Trying to save our lives," Bolan growled.

"I'd have been safe if you people hadn't climbed onto my boat," the man said.

Bolan didn't bother to argue. "Help her get that net soaked." He slid back to the stern of the boat. The speedboat had drawn to within fifty yards, hammering the white wake left by the fishing boat.

"Incoming!" the security man yelled. "Go left! Go left!"

Turrin responded, pulling the boat hard left. Julia dropped the gas can, and it went skidding across the deck, catching up against the fishing chair.

A moment later an explosion erupted in the water to the right, throwing a wave of water across the fishing boat.

"Grenade launcher," the security man said, grimly fisting his pistol and firing at their pursuers.

Bolan already knew that. Shouldering the Winchester, he gazed down the open sights, bracketing the man who was trying to blow them out of the water.

The guy broke open the grenade launcher and loaded another 40 mm grenade.

The Executioner took up the trigger slack as the man rolled over on his stomach. The warrior squeezed off a round, jolted by the recoil, but noticed the bullet went right and slightly in front of his target, throwing up a long splinter from the speedboat's prow.

The grenade launcher fired another round, and the explosive landed just behind the fishing boat. Water splashed down over Bolan as he worked the lever action and jacked a fresh bullet into the chamber. He corrected for the deviation on the sights, took up trigger slack and waited.

When the man had reloaded and rolled onto his stomach again, Bolan squeezed the trigger. The man slumped forward, his weapon sliding from his nerveless fingers and over the side. The warrior scattered the remaining five shots from the .30-30 over the prow of the speedboat as it roared forward. He managed to take out one other man and shoot a sizable hole in the Plexiglas windshield.

"The net?" he asked as he rolled back to shove more rounds into the Winchester.

"Ready," Julia called out.

Bolan joined her at the storage chest. The liquid was dark and oily and smelled strongly of gasoline.

"You've turned this boat into a floating bomb," the skipper accused.

"Drain it," Bolan ordered, noticing the drain hole through the murky depths. He handed Julia the rifle, then slipped one of the flares into the flare gun's breech. Snapping the stubby pistol closed, he shoved it into the front of his waistband.

The skipper bent to let out the chest's contents.

Hooking his fingers into the net, Bolan made sure of its folds, then carried it over to the left side of the fishing boat.

The speedboat was within twenty yards and closing fast. Turrin was still juking at the wheel, weaving side to side.

"Leo," Bolan called.

"Yeah."

"Let them come alongside."

Bullets hammered the fishing boat, but the gunners on the prow of the speedboat suddenly realized their vulnerability. Most of them were trying to retreat toward better cover.

Through the windshield, Bolan saw that three men were inside the steering section. One of them was manning a Browning .50-caliber machine gun that had been mounted on the side.

When the boat was less than twenty feet away, Bolan whipped the net up and out, casting it full and hard. For a moment it looked like a spiderweb in full flight. Then it wrapped around the prow of the speedboat like a huge octopus.

The big .50-caliber machine gun hammered into life suddenly, raking the fishing boat's stern.

Driven to cover during the machine gun's first pass, Bolan drew the flare gun and readied it. When he had clearance, he raised the gun and fired at the gasoline-and-oil-soaked net.

The flare sped true, leaving a burning scarlet contrail in the air separating the two vessels. Then it slammed into the net and ignited the combustible liquids. Spurred on by the wind rushing over the boat, the flames spread out tentacles and embraced the speedboat's prow. In seconds it was aflame.

Some of the flaming fuel mixture had splattered back on the machine gunner, and he deserted his position.

Taking up the Winchester, Bolan fired into the boat, concentrating on the pilot. At least two of his three shots hit the man in the chest and drove him backward.

Out of control, the speedboat caromed over an unoccupied gondola, came up out of the water slightly and smashed against the supports for the arched bridge in front of the Palazzo del Camerlenghi. The resulting explosion turned the speedboat into wreckage.

There were no more signs of pursuit, but Bolan knew the Venice police would arrive soon. The police station was only a fast mile away. He reloaded the Winchester and joined Turrin at the bridge.

"Suggestions?" the stocky little Fed asked.

"We go to Lido and regroup."

"Sun, sand and lose ourselves among the visiting royalty?" Turrin asked.

"That's the plan," Bolan replied. "First let's lose this boat."

WHEN HE'D FIRST acquired the paintings and sculptures, Alonzo Galvani had thought he was getting a good deal. Now, with fifty years of hiding them on his conscience and fifty years of fears that Magaddino might reveal how the items had come into Galvani's possession, he knew they were only ornate nails in his coffin.

He sat in the small, windowless room beneath his home and looked at them. The paintings and sculptures were done by masters from the fourteenth and fifteenth centuries, during the peak of the Italian Renaissance, and had been given to various churches over the intervening years.

Many times after Magaddino had revealed that he knew Galvani had them, Galvani had thought to simply flood the room and destroy all evidence that he'd ever had them.

But he hadn't been able to do that, either. They were worth too much, and he'd paid too high a price for them. There was a parable Magaddino had told him back in the fifties. He could still hear the old bastard's mocking words.

"There was once a monkey who found a banana at the bottom of a ceramic jug. The monkey—being a monkey and hungry, as well—decided he wanted this banana. So he reached in and tried to get it out. Unfortunately, with his hand around the banana, it would no longer come out of the jug. Only a few feet away were trees burdened with bananas. Still, the monkey refused to release the banana he held, so he was trapped by his own desires. You, Alonzo, are a monkey just like that." And Magaddino had laughed.

The old bastard was in the ground now, and probably still laughing.

For a time Galvani had thought his secret had died with Magaddino. But now he knew it would always be out there and he'd always be working to keep it hidden. Unless he could destroy it for all time.

The cellular phone sitting in his lap rang. He answered it. "Galvani."

"It's Gabe Valente, sir."

"How are things there?" Galvani kept his voice tightly controlled.

Valente sighed. "We missed, Mr. Galvani."

Bile rose in the back of Galvani's throat. "How?"

"These guys are good, sir. And they got lucky. Also the priest was here. He helped them."

"They're working with the priest?" Galvani's anger crystallized into cold fear.

"I don't think so, but he definitely took their side."

"And where is he?"

"Gone, too."

"Do you know where they are?"

"No, sir. But I've got people out looking for them. The police are all over the place right now, so we're going to have to lay low for a while. But so are they."

"What about the house?" Galvani asked.

"It's history."

"Did they get out with anything?"

"Nothing I could see," Valente replied. "But things were pretty confusing."

"Try to find them, Gabe. And the priest, too. Also arrange a flight for us to Bucharest. It won't take

Lupu long to realize holding the DeVincenzo boy is going to prove worthless for him. I don't want that upstart little son of a bitch in my face again. When we go over there, we're putting an end to him once and for all."

"With all due respect," Valente said, "making a move like that right now could be pretty costly. We don't know for sure who Lupu has got backing him over there."

"Gabe, you're like a son to me, so I'm going to pretend I didn't hear you question my judgment. But never make that mistake again. I think for this organization, for now and for always."

"Yes, sir."

Galvani broke the connection, took a last look at the treasures that had cost him so much, then left the vault. There was much left to be planned, a lot of markers to be called in.

"ONCE LUPU FINDS OUT the house was burned down, along with everything in it, he's not going to have a reason to keep Nicky alive." Julia DeVincenzo's eyes were misted over, but she kept her voice level. "I don't really think he's the type to simply return Nicky."

"Neither do I," Bolan replied honestly. "So we're going to have to give him a reason to trade with us."

"We don't even know how to contact him."

"Someone does," Bolan said.

They were in an elegant suite of rooms at the Excelsior Palace on Lido, checked in under an alias Bolan had arranged through Stony Man Farm. Less than an hour earlier, Turrin had undertaken the fifteen-minute trip back to the north to see what could be arranged as far as damage control concerning the Venice police.

Room service had brought up packages of clothing only a short time ago. Enough cash had changed hands that no questions were asked. The Lido was Venice's equivalent of the French Riviera, Waikiki Beach or the Gold Coast of Florida. The moneyed and the famous went there to play in the sun.

"How are you going to find Lupu?" Julia asked. She was wearing a simple white cotton dress that showed off her figure much more than she appeared aware.

"By making it too costly for him to ignore me," the warrior replied. There was a knock on the door, and he went to answer it.

A slim, well-dressed young man stood in the hall with an expensive-looking shopping bag. "I have a phone delivery for Mr. McKay."

"That's me," Bolan said. He'd already wired money to the phone service almost two hours ago. After folding a generous amount of liras in half as a tip, he slipped the man the money and took the phone bag.

"How do you plan to do that?" Julia asked.

Bolan extended the antenna on one of the two phones from the bag and punched in one of the safe numbers for Stony Man Farm. An answering machine advised that James Keith Charters was busy at the moment, but would be glad to return a call if a number was left.

"Call me if this line is clear," the warrior said, then added the number he found on the sales slip for the first phone. After repeating the procedure with the second phone, he turned his attention to Julia. "If Lupu has been planning some action against Galvani, he's got people in the city. They'll be connected with every dirty deal that goes down, weighing and measuring Galvani's strengths and weaknesses. If I rattle some cages, I'll find them."

"What am I supposed to do?"

"Stay here," Bolan said. "I know it's hard, but there's nothing else you can do."

"I could go with you."

Bolan eyed her levelly. "No."

She turned away from him and walked to the double French doors leading out onto the balcony.

"Julia." Bolan stopped, not knowing what to say for a moment. "Look, I can't say that I understand your feelings right now, but I do know this—every person, at one point or another, feels the need to fight back. Whether it's against injustice or an oppressor, that need to fight is what gives a person the strength to go on even when the odds are stacked against them. But there's also a time to lie low, and you've got to allow for it."

"And what time is this?"

"It's time for me to fight," the warrior stated simply. "I know how to define a battlefield and I know how to raise the stakes on an operation."

"You know what scares me the most?" she asked suddenly, turning on her heel to confront him.

Bolan remained silent.

"What scares me most is that I have to depend on you, and I don't even know you. My grandfather paid men all his life to do things he wanted them to, to protect him, and some of them even died for him. I could understand why they did the things they did—they wanted the money. But why are you here? What's going to keep you from running and not even telling me?"

"The kind of man I am is going to keep me here," Bolan said. "You and Leo hadn't seen each other in a couple years. Yet you called him when Nicky was taken. You knew he would come."

"Yes."

"Why?"

Julia folded her arms across her breasts. "Because I knew he would. But he's a friend. You'd never even seen me before yesterday, and you're laying your life on the line for a boy you've never seen at all."

"Someone has to lay their lives on the line for the innocents," Bolan said. "It's the only thing that keeps this world civilized. And there's more people out there who would do it than you think. Every time a soldier takes the field, he might consider the people he's protecting to be like the family he left back home, but he knows it's bigger than that."

"You're talking about duty," she said. "It's not the same thing."

"No," Bolan quietly corrected. "I'm talking about honor. Laws aren't what hold good people in check. It's the code of ethics they've adopted." He paused. "It's the same thing that's kept you from getting involved in your grandfather's business."

"That was a personal choice."

Bolan nodded. "They all are."

She looked at him. "You don't approve of my grandfather."

"No."

"Leo said you'd been around Family business a lot."

"Yes."

"But you're not connected with it, are you?"

Bolan shook his head.

"Then why don't you disapprove of Leo?" she asked.

"That's a long and complicated story," the warrior replied. "Let's just say I probably know more about Leo than you do. And whatever else Leo may be, I know he's my friend."

The phone rang and Bolan answered it.

"It's me," Aaron Kurtzman said. "Your lines are clean. I caught a newsbreak on one of the locals and saw the fire. Are you people okay?"

"So far," Bolan said. "We may need a back door out of here, though."

"You, Sticker and the lady?"

"Yeah."

"What about the boy?"

"He's not here anymore. I'm trying to catch up. Did you get all of those files we transmitted?"

"All of them," Kurtzman replied. "I've got Akira sorting through them now. He's the best hacker I've got. Give him time—no matter how encrypted those files are, we'll have whatever's in them."

"I get a call soon as you do."

"Right. On this line?"

"If it changes, I'll let you know. I appreciate the help."

"No prob. One other thing—Farmer Brown and the lady are working on a cover for you in Bucharest. Barb was thinking in light of Mihai Lupu's involvement you might end up there."

"She's probably right." Bolan knew that Barbara Price, working from Stony Man Farm, could arrange logistical support anywhere in the world.

"She worked a deal with the CIA and got a package on Lupu that had been buried for the past few years."

"He is working for the CIA?"

The sound of computer keys tapping carried over the connection. "Strictly contract work. They used him as a pipeline because of his black-market connections and for in-country Intel on the Eastern European problems."

"Is he still active?"

"Officially no. But unofficially I'd have to say he's probably not without resources. When you go in after him, if he investigates you, he'll more than likely have someone who can run your name. But I've got your cover, guy, and no one's going to find out more than I want to tell them."

"What will the CIA say if he goes down?"

"Some of the cowboy section chiefs doing wet work over there and operating out of left field may piss and moan about it, but there won't be any repercussions once you clear the area."

Bolan glanced out the window to where a coed volleyball game was shaping up. "One other thing."

"Name it."

"There's a Catholic priest who appeared on Julia DeVincenzo's doorstep this morning only minutes before the attack. He claimed that Magaddino had donated some art pieces to the church. His name is Gerald Light. Father Gerald Light. The ID had a papal seal on it. When Akira goes through those files, see if his name, Vatican City or those art pieces are mentioned."

Kurtzman agreed.

After switching off the phone, Bolan searched for another box that had been among the earlier deliveries, finding it easily. "Leo's going to call," he said, opening the box to reveal a notebook computer. "When he does, give him the number to both the cell phones." He finished setting up the notebook computer on the glass-topped breakfast table in a corner of the room. After he pressed the power button, the machine came on with a beep. The software they needed had already been loaded. "In the meantime, hook your cell phone into this computer's modem, call this number—" he scribbled a safe number for the Farm on a yellow sticker "—and they'll download the unencrypted files to you."

"Won't they already have looked at them?" Julia asked.

"Sure. But they're not familiar with your grandfather as much as you are. They may miss something that you'll see."

She nodded, then put her hands on the notebook computer and started familiarizing herself with the keyboard.

"I've got to go," he said.

"I know. Just don't wait too long to call, okay?"

"We're going to get Nicky back," Bolan said. "Just hang on to that thought. And we'll also get whatever secret Galvani is hiding out there, too. And if we have to sacrifice him to get Nicky, then that's how it's going to be. But we're going to make sure Lupu plays fair with us. I need you to be focused and help out."

"Okay." Her voice was small, but her eyes met his defiantly. Without a word she stepped across the distance separating them and hugged Bolan fiercely. For a moment he held her silently. When she broke it off, she went back to the computer. "That wasn't for you. It was for me."

"I know." Bolan turned and let himself out of the room. By the time he reached the elevator at the end of the hall, he was reviewing what he knew of Lupu's probable business interests in Venice. The list was slim, but he knew he could build on it.

The city was tense, ready to explode at the seams. Magaddino's passing had left things uncertain, and last night's events and the burn-out this morning would put a lot more pressure on the people who made their life between the cracks of society. The Executioner intended to exploit that to the fullest. Nightfall was coming, and so was retribution.

CHAPTER TEN

"My superiors are thinking very seriously about contacting the State Department and canceling your visa."

Leo Turrin looked up from the black-and-white photos scattered across the desk and at Giacoma Canova. "I appreciate your telling me that."

"I exaggerated your contributions on the De-Vincenzo kidnapping," the detective said, sitting heavily in a chair across from Turrin. They were in a borrowed office because Canova's captain didn't want Turrin inside the detectives' bull pen. "But it did no good. They feel that perhaps you're a magnet for trouble more than a help. It's been suggested that I may be acting a little too sympathetic toward your stated cause here."

"I can understand that." Turrin pushed away the latest batch of pictures and took a sip of cold coffee from the Styrofoam cup he'd been using. He was tired and worn from staying up all night. When he tried to remember the last time he'd called his wife to tell her he was all right, he couldn't. She was used to late nights and secrets, though, but it had been a while since they'd been this extended.

"They also want to know the name of your accomplice."

Turrin shook his head.

"And they want to talk to Mrs. DeVincenzo."

"That's a maybe." Taking out a pack of cigarettes, Turrin shook one out and fired it up.

"Primarily I believe they just want to know that she's well."

"Give me a name and a number she can contact." When the detective did, Turrin wrote it down, then returned his pad to his pocket. "She's not going to be making any public appearances, though."

"That's understandable."

Turrin tapped the pictures with his pencil eraser. They had all been taken after the fire that destroyed the Magaddino household. Several of the shots were of corpses. He'd already separated the ones that he identified as the maid and the security people who worked at the mansion. "Who're these guys?"

"Street thugs," Canova answered.

"Local talent?"

"Mostly. A few are from elsewhere. France. Spain. They're all killers. I can get their files."

Turrin shook his head. He was sure Kurtzman had already riffed his cybernetic fingers through the police files in Venice. If there was anything worth knowing, Stony Man Farm would let them know during the next contact. "Are they affiliated with anyone?"

"On a regular basis? No. The word I get from my sources is that they were employed by Alonzo Galvani. But you already knew that."

"No, but it was a strong suspicion. With Lupu in the picture and in possession of Nicky DeVincenzo,

Galvani's going to want to keep his ass covered. Can you make anything stick?''

"Unfortunately no. We had no survivors taken into custody. The ones who lived through the attack fled before police could arrive.''

Turrin shifted in the straight-backed chair, trying to find a comfortable position. He failed and resigned himself to it for a while longer. "Is anyone watching Galvani?''

"Loosely." Canova fired up his pipe. "With nothing solid to connect him to this, my department can't touch him. In fact, we've been ordered to stay away from him. Galvani has considerable influence in this city." Smoke wreathed his head as he puffed contentedly.

"So what's on the agenda?''

Canova regarded him. "I've been assigned to watch you and make sure you stay out of trouble.''

"Terrific." Turrin gazed out the window at the church steeple in the distance. "I'm thinking Galvani needs the heat turned up a notch. And maybe I can get a message sent back to Lupu. The guy's got to have a snitch somewhere in Galvani's household." He got up. "Are you coming?''

"Of course.''

"We can take the same boat," Turrin suggested. "Save on fare.''

"What if Galvani overreacts?" the detective asked.

"Then you get to work my murder, and at least Galvani is out of the way," Turrin answered laconically.

MACK BOLAN WALKED through the small club scanning faces. In seconds he found the one he wanted at the back of the room. Heads turned as he approached the man, and two guys fell onto his backtrail, letting him know his quarry wasn't alone.

The man at the table was obese, had slicked-back red hair and wore an expensive suit that didn't go with the bar's cheap decor. Freckles spotted his face and arms and made him look soft, but his gray green eyes were as hard and bright and as devoid of emotion as ball bearings. His smile was practiced and easy. A notebook computer glowed softly beside him. As Bolan approached, he hit the Escape key and blanked the screen.

Bolan stopped six feet from the table, throwing off the bodyguards who dogged his steps. The warrior was dressed in a long black duster, black jeans and a black turtleneck. He carried the SIG-Sauer P-228 Night Stalker in shoulder leather.

"Enrico Cabrini," the warrior said in a graveyard voice.

Cabrini put his hands together in front of him. "Do I know you?"

"No. We need to talk."

The man laughed and spread his hands wide, indicating everyone in the bar. "My time is money. Ask anyone here."

With a casual flip Bolan spun the playing card he'd had palmed since entering the building onto the tabletop in front of Cabrini. It landed face-up beside the fat man's drink—an ace of spades.

"Do you know what that is?" Bolan demanded, his voice harsh.

Cabrini's reply was hesitant. Self-conscious, he glanced around the bar. "I've seen a few."

"Then get these monkeys off my back so we can talk," Bolan ordered. "My time pays in blood."

"Sure." Cabrini waved the bodyguards back to the bar. "We got no problems, right?"

"If we did," Bolan said, "you'd be wearing a bullet hole between your eyes now." He played his role to the hilt. A Black Ace was the enforcement arm of the Mafia's La Commissione, and owned a franchise in death. An Ace operated strictly according to the orders handed down by La Commissione, and had the power to deal out a capo in front of his own security and walk away without being touched.

"You want to talk here?"

"No." Bolan remained standing, his hands in his pockets, knowing the man was scared of him and what he represented.

"Someplace else?" Cabrini didn't seem comfortable with the prospect.

"The office will be fine." The Intel that Kurtzman had given Bolan regarding Cabrini revealed that the fat man owned forty percent of the bar. It was also where Cabrini did most of his loan sharking, making enough money to lay out six figures to a film company the previous year.

"The office," Cabrini repeated. "Sure." He got up with effort, then snapped his fingers at one of the waitresses and pointed to the notebook computer.

Bolan followed the man to the back of the tavern, through the small kitchen, where a limited menu was prepared, and into a lavishly furnished office.

"Have a seat." Cabrini indicated the office chair on the other side of the desk.

"I'll stand," Bolan said.

"What do I call you?"

"Omega."

"What kind of name is that?" Knowing he wasn't the object of a Black Ace's mission had made Cabrini arrogant.

"I didn't come here to be asked questions. You might want to remember that."

"Just trying to be social."

"Shut up." Bolan stared the man down as color suffused Cabrini's cheeks. "Tell me about the Romanians operating in Venice."

"What do you want to know?"

"How much business are you doing with them?"

The man spread his hands, palms up. "A little. Not so much that it's going to hurt me if I have to quit."

"Tell me about it."

"The docks, mostly. Common stiffs, they like to bet. Soccer's pretty big over here. Almost like the Super Bowl in the States. The movers and the shakers in the heroin trade bet a little, but they got their own jones they're working out by slipping through the DEA and every other narc cop strung out to catch them. I front a little money sometimes to cover a buy-in on a heroin shipment. H is coming back, and we got it. Finally getting back some of our own from the Colombians and Rastafarians. You want, I can set you up with some people can get you prime price for any investment you want to make trafficking heroin through Europe and on into the States. No risk to you." Cabrini's smile looked as reassuring as a weatherman's.

"You know a guy named Mihai Lupu?" Bolan asked.

"Sure. One of the big guys working the rackets out of Bucharest. He and Galvani are having a little dispute over some territory over there."

"What are Lupu's prime money-makers in Venice?" Bolan asked.

Cabrini's eyes narrowed, and he appeared about to ask questions, then reconsidered. "He does some smuggling along the docks, has it shipped to a clearinghouse down near Ca' d'Oro."

"Give me the address."

Cabrini did. "He also provides cheap labor through a temporary employment business near the Arsenale. After smuggling Romanians and other Eastern Europeans into the area, Lupu farms them out to manufacturing plants, domestic services and textile industries. Places where cheap help is always welcome. Somebody has a problem with the job or the employer, Lupu sends an enforcer in to bust his or her head, then replaces the worker."

Bolan committed that address to memory, as well, then the information the man had on the people who ran the business.

"For a young bastard," the loan shark said, "Lupu is pretty savvy."

There was no surprise in that for Bolan. Lupu had seen Ceaușescu's political machine in operation for years.

"The heroin and the labor service net him a pretty good chunk, and he can use it to watch other people," Cabrini said, "but he's also making millions off a black market ring for American and European movies. He's got a warehouse that makes weekly deliveries. People over there are starving for that kind of stuff, want to be just like the West. Figure out what kind of clothes to wear, how to talk, what to want out of life."

"Give me the address," Bolan said.

After Cabrini complied, the fat man asked, "Are you working off Galvani's payroll?"

"No." Bolan gave the man a cool stare.

"Hey, no foul intended here. I was just figuring, you know. Galvani and Lupu are at each other's throats. Wouldn't surprise me if Galvani wanted to trump the man's play with an Ace."

"I'm not here for Galvani," Bolan said, playing another angle to stir up the pot. "I'm here for Magaddino. His granddaughter was nearly killed this morning, and his great-grandson was kidnapped two days ago. The old man still has a lot of friends on La Commissione. Somebody's going to pay. For both."

A tic flickered Cabrini's right eye. "You know who arranged the hit on Mrs. DeVincenzo this morning?"

"I know." Without another word Bolan turned and left the room. He was aware of eyes on him as he walked out of the tavern, but no one followed.

Galvani would get the message, and he'd know a Black Ace was there to balance the books. Already exposed to the police, due to his suspected involvement in the assassination attempt, there weren't many places the man could turn. And Mihai Lupu was waiting in the wings.

The sun was touching the tops of the tallest buildings to the west. Bolan put more force in his steps. The clock was ticking, and the boy's life was hanging in the balance. He began assembling his strikes mentally. Lupu was about to get his baptism of hellfire.

JERICHO LIGHT WAS on his knees and deep in prayer when the phone rang. He finished his prayer, knowing the caller would wait, then forced himself to his feet. Through the smudged window, he could see darkness consuming the city.

He scooped up the phone and said, "Hello."

"Is Luigi there?" the cultured voice asked.

"No. You must have the wrong room." Light hung up, then retrieved his shoes and put them on. He'd changed hotels after the episode that morning and had watched the television for any sign of the woman's whereabouts. Reporters were still looking for her, as were the police. No one was saying who the assassins were or why they had gone there.

He left the hotel and walked three blocks to a pay phone near a jewelry shop specializing in gold necklaces and chains. SOP required that he call in to Vatican City and leave the phone number as soon as he'd relocated.

Punching in the number he'd been given, he put the call on the charge card out of Vatican City, using another long-distance carrier so the call wouldn't be easily traced through billing information.

"Hello," the cultured voice said. "You are well, my son?"

"A little more wear and tear," Light replied, "but nothing that can keep me from my mission."

"Good, good. I understand the woman has gone into hiding."

"Yes. No one seems to know where she is."

"We've not been able to find out, either. However, our agents have turned up other information that might be helpful. Apparently Mrs. DeVincenzo's son has been taken by someone new. A man named Mihai Lupu, who is high up in Romanian crime circles. We believe he's taken the boy and fled to Bucharest."

"So Mrs. DeVincenzo will have to go there to get him back?" The boy's involvement was a sore point for Light. In all the war-torn countries he'd seen before being taken in by the church and given his new life, children were always among the first victims. They were either unexpected casualties or they were perverted and sacrificed as cannon fodder.

"It seems likely. Even in the event that Lupu brings the boy back to Venice, you could arrange to be there by following him."

A flock of gulls descended on the canal and skimmed the surface for food. "She doesn't know where the artwork is."

There was a pause. When the voice started speaking again, there was a strain in the words. "Jericho, we've not been led this far to fail. You said the art pieces were not in the Magaddino household. So they have to be elsewhere. The woman may not know where, but she does know where Magaddino's properties are. Perhaps even ones his lawyers don't know about."

Light understood that. "The boy is in danger."

"That isn't our affair," the cultured voice said.

"Perhaps I could help." There'd been a number of victims he hadn't been able to help.

"Your mission is clear, Jericho. Don't confuse it. God will take care of that boy."

Light remained silent, watching the lights come on in the various shops around him.

"When we found you," the voice at the other end went on, "and you had a willingness in you to come into the church and do God's work, we considered you a blessing. You've worked hard, and we've worked hard, to understand how you could best serve the church. You've been shaped and molded by everything that has happened to you to make you the best that you can be now. Don't lose sight of that."

"I won't," Light said in a hoarse voice.

"Go to Bucharest and find this man, Lupu. Locate the art pieces and bring them back. Don't let us down."

Light said he wouldn't, then listened to the short prayer that followed, asking a blessing for the Lord's work, and cradled the phone. Fighting the confusion that threatened to tear at the foundation he'd laid since entering the church, he walked back toward the hotel.

Then he noticed the church steeple to his left, a few blocks down. Full dark had fallen, broken only by the pools of light given off by the street lamps. The city had become dangerous to him, although he didn't know the identity of the men who hunted him. Getting out of it was a good idea.

Drawn to the church, he paused outside the door. The exterior was faced with softly colored marble. Two stories above, the rounded roof thrust up yet another story, flanked on both sides and crowned with three figures. The church was a work of art, filled with stained-glass windows and a stained-glass cross worked into the wall above the kneeling Virgin figure over the main door.

Walking up the three steps, he went inside, at once astounded by the intricacy of the sculptures filling the church. The ceiling held dozens of painted panels of saints and prophets.

"Your first time in the church?"

Light hadn't even heard the older man walk up on him. "Yes. What's the name of this place?"

"Santa Maria dei Miracoli," the old priest said. He was easily in his seventies. His hair and beard were a matching silver. "Built in 1489 by Pietro Lombardo and his two sons." He gestured to a pew. "You're Catholic?"

Candles burned near the podium, and a scattered handful of parishioners prayed either alone or in small groups.

"Yes," Light replied, sitting.

"I thought you might be, but we get a number of tourists in here, as well." The priest also sat. "I'm Father Doyle."

Light acted as if he simply missed the opportunity to give his own name. He clasped his hands together in front of him and looked at the church in open wonderment. "Everything is so beautiful."

"Thank you. But the Lord provided all of this, just as He provided the church."

"Have you been here long?" Light asked.

"Since I was an altar boy. Don't let the name fool you. I was born here."

Light nodded. He listened to the low rumble of voices around him as the parishioners continued praying. The tone was fervent but hopeful.

"If you don't mind me saying so, you seem troubled," Doyle observed.

"I am."

"Can I be of assistance?"

"I don't know." Light looked at him. "I've got a strong faith but I struggle with it."

"As do we all, my son."

"Until today I think I was okay. But after this morning, I'm not sure."

"What happened?"

"I'm here on church business," Light said. "I was sent to recover some artifacts for the Vatican that have been missing since World War II."

Doyle nodded. "So you're the one. I'd heard about you, but it was never confirmed. What do you find confusing?"

"You know about the events that transpired at the Magaddino house?"

The priest nodded.

"I was a part of that."

"I see."

Light shook his head. "No, I don't think you can." He took a deep breath, only briefly wondering if he was breaking any confidences by telling so much. Then he decided he wasn't. His life wasn't a secret to the church, and neither was his mission here. "A few years ago I lived in a world of violence. I was a warrior, trained to kill and to forget that I had. The killing came easily. I was good at it. Then I met a priest who changed my life. After talking with him off and on for a few months, I walked away from that violent world and took up the teachings of the church."

"Now you find that your life has once more turned to the violence," Doyle said, "and that leaves you unsettled."

"Yes. I have to ask myself how much has really changed."

The priest was silent for a moment. "I don't know that I have any answers for you, my son, but I can tell you some things that I have seen."

"Please."

"This is a violent, carnal world. You can't change it. You can only try to save it. Sometimes in order to do that, good men have to do things they wouldn't otherwise do. A few months ago a young policeman came to me, very distraught. He'd had to shoot a man to save a woman who was being stabbed to death. Although he saved the woman, he took a life, and he wondered where that left him in the eyes of God. He hadn't been sleeping well since that time, and needed answers, too. I could only suggest that God had put him there, at that time, because he could save the woman. We seek salvation in our lives, and you must believe it is given. What God lays on your heart, only you can know, and He is the only reckoning of whether you've obeyed. King David took lives during his service with God. So have others. In time you'll know the answer to your questions."

Light nodded, then pushed himself to his feet. "I've got to go, but I appreciate your time."

"If I could have your name," Doyle said, offering his hand, "I'll remember you in my prayers tonight."

Light smiled. "Just think of me. He'll know who I am." He turned and walked away. His words reminded him of the girl he'd had dinner with last night, and he wondered how she was. Then he let the night take him and turned his attention to getting to Bucharest. Maybe the answers would come.

"GOING SOMEWHERE, Alonzo?" Leo Turrin called out as he stepped from the water taxi onto shore. Around him street lights cast bright spots against the dark water.

Galvani and his entourage were getting into a large motor sailor in front of his home. Gabe Valente and four men with him instantly dropped into protective positions around the man.

"What do you want?" Valente demanded. His hand was inside his jacket.

Turrin kept walking, a cocky grin pasted to his face even though he knew he was burying the needle on taking chances with Galvani. The old man had been pushed almost as far as he could go. "Just to talk to Galvani for a moment." He turned up a hand at Canova. "You know Detective Canova, of course."

"*Mr.* Galvani," Valente corrected him. Keeping his hand where it was, the bodyguard looked back toward the old man.

Turrin stopped just out of reach for the bodyguards, locking eyes with Galvani. "Vacation? Or are you taking a powder?"

"You son of a bitch!" Valente roared, going for his gun.

Eyes hard, his voice tight, Turrin whipped the .38 Bodyguard from his jacket pocket a half second before Valente. He'd had an edge because he already had the revolver in his hand. Valente's speed was incredible. The stocky little Fed pointed the .38 at Galvani. "It's your call, Gabe, but I think I can take him even after you get me. Anybody else move, I'm pulling the trigger anyway."

"Stop!" Galvani ordered. With his hat pulled low and his collar turned up, the old man looked like a vulture wrapped in an expensive suit. "Gabe, put that gun away."

For a tense moment Valente didn't react. Then he lifted the weapon and lowered the hammer. It vanished back inside his jacket. "Some other time, ass-hole."

"You're small potatoes, Gabe, and you always will be. You take orders from a guy who orders a hit on a woman." Turrin made no move to put his weapon away. The sights remained fixed on Galvani's fore-head.

"You won't be surprised when I tell you I don't know what you're talking about," Galvani said. Even staring down the muzzle of a gun, the old man didn't look scared, just angry.

Out of the corner of his eye, Turrin noticed that Canova had his pistol out, as well, though it was pointed at the ground.

"Is this some form of attempted entrapment, De-tective?" Galvani asked. "Are either one of you wearing a wire, hoping I'll say something you can use to incriminate myself?"

"No," Canova said. "I'm just here to see to it that Mr. Turrin doesn't get into any trouble."

A thin smile curled Galvani's lips. "I see. You're doing an admirable job."

"Until this morning," Turrin said, "Julia didn't know she had a problem with you. She thought you were her grandfather's friend."

Galvani spit at Turrin's feet. "I've never been that bastard's friend. It's just my ill fortune that Magad-dino lived as long as he did."

"And all that time you've been afraid of what he would tell people," Turrin said. "How does it feel to have that kind of fear eating away at you? What's that old saying, something like a brave man dies but one death, while a coward dies thousands?"

"I'm leaving." Galvani stepped onto the boat.

"There were backup computer files," Turrin stated. "You burned the house and everything in it, but there's another set of files. Julia's going through them, and when she finds what she's looking for, she's going to make the deal with Lupu."

Walking to the cabin, Galvani refused to acknowledge Turrin's words. Valente followed him, never turning his back to the stocky little Fed.

"You're going to be right back in the same position you were in," Turrin promised. He lowered the gun but didn't put it away as the boat powered away from the side of the canal out into open water, leaving whitecaps on the water.

"I thought you were going to get yourself killed," Canova said. "I've never seen anyone talk to Galvani like that. Especially with Valente around."

Feeling some of the tension inside his stomach loosen, Turrin mopped the cold sweat from the back of his neck. "Stick around. It could still happen."

"True. Do you think Galvani's running?"

"From the shit that hit the fan this morning?" Turrin shook his head. "Nah. That guy's trying to get some distance on a ghost that's been chasing him for a long time. He's pretty certain you're not going to be able to tie this morning's assassination attempt to him. And even if you did, it seems to be the least of his worries." He watched the boat disappear around a bend in the canal. "He had a lot of luggage aboard. Do you think we can find out where he's headed?''

"I can call the airports and make some inquiries," Canova said.

"Let's do that." Turrin pulled a small flashlight from his pocket. He switched it on and tried to wave down a water taxi.

THE BLITZ WAS ON, and Bolan made the night his domain. He'd arranged another stop at the CIA supplier Stony Man Farm had linked him with, gathering new supplies. Dressed in a blacksuit, with his face darkened by combat cosmetics, he looked like some mythological wraith, a hybrid of shadow and man. The SIG-Sauer P-228 Night Stalker rode in shoulder leather, while a brand-new Israeli Desert Eagle .44 Magnum was on his hip. His lead weapon was a Neostead 2000 combat shotgun. Extra magazines and incendiaries were secured to the combat harness over his body armor. The black duster covered it all.

His watch showed 7:03, and he was right on schedule.

The first target stood between a motorboat-repair shop and a leather-goods outlet. He'd already done a brief recon from atop a building across the street.

A Closed sign occupied the lower right corner of the glass door, and the knob was locked when he tried it. The ground floor held no lights, but the window directly overhead glowed against the shutters. To the public eye, the business catered to exotic spices and coffees. Racks and shelves lined the space inside, filled with bottles, bags and canisters.

Bolan picked the lock easily. Despite the warning about an alarm system, there were no contact wires lining the windows. He pushed the door open slightly, but it caught on a security chain.

Stepping back, the warrior kicked the door. With a screech and several snaps, the chain ripped out of its moorings. The door slammed back against the wall.

Bolan strode across the threshold, his combat senses alert. He brought up the shotgun to cover the stairs directly in front of him.

A man carrying a mini-Uzi started down, probably expecting nothing more than a smash-and-grab artist. When he saw Bolan, he yelled out in Romanian and started to fire the machine pistol.

Canisters jumped and bottles exploded into pieces on the shelves to the warrior's left. Stroking the shotgun's trigger, the Executioner placed a load of double-aught buckshot in the center mass of his target, knocking the Romanian backward. He racked the slide and pumped a fresh round into the chamber.

More yelling came from upstairs, followed by the sounds of movement.

A flash of streetlight on metal in the warrior's peripheral vision sent him to cover. Glass jars shattered overhead. He caught sight of two gunners, and he brought the shotgun to bear.

Seeing that their gunfire hadn't brought down their opponent, the two men behind the cash register ducked for cover.

Bolan triggered a round that turned the cash register into a mangled piece of metal and kicked it off the counter. Before working the slide, he flipped the shotgun's magazine selector to cycle rounds from the right. The South African riot gun held twelve shells in two tubes, and could be set to feed off either one or both. He pumped the action and brought up one of the solid slugs.

When he fired it, the one-ounce bullet punched a massive hole in the counter front. He fired two more rounds, searching for his targets. Then they broke cover and raced for the back of the shop.

The Executioner rose with the Neostead at his shoulder, following his prey. "Stop," he ordered.

One of the men tried to come around, firing blindly.

Bolan stroked the trigger, and the heavy round punched the man down. The other gunner threw himself prone against a freestanding wall that separated the counter area from the rest of the shop. He brought his pistol into target acquisition and fired as fast as he could.

Two of the bullets cut the air just over the Executioner's head. Knowing the wall wasn't built to withstand much impact, Bolan switched the magazine selector back to feed the double-aught buckshot. He chambered the round while on the move, and fired from less than twelve feet away.

The pellets tore through the wall and found the flesh and blood beyond. Hammered away from the wall, the corpse dropped to the ground.

"Vlad! Matthew!" A silhouette paused at the top of the stairs, taking advantage of the corner of the wall that protruded. The stubby muzzle of a submachine gun poked out from the corner, and most of the lower calves and feet were visible.

Bolan aimed at the exposed feet and fired. The buckshot charge threw the man off balance and he rolled down the stairs, yelling incoherently and firing the submachine gun. Bullets sparked off the metal railing along the stairs. Another round put the man down for good.

Feeding more shells into the riot shotgun, Bolan walked toward the stairs. He stepped over the dead man and clicked the double breech closed.

Palming the preset firebomb he'd readied for the shop, he tossed it into the center of the room. The radio detonator was attached to the combat harness.

He could hear more voices, coming from the top of the stairs. There was a window at the back of the room on the second floor, but his recon had revealed the strong iron bars covered it. He unlimbered an M-45C grenade, nicknamed the Comboball because it had a dose of CS gas mixed in with numerous marble-sized soft-rubber balls.

Priming the grenade, the warrior edged to the door, then whipped it inside. Instantly bullets ripped into the door facing, tearing it to pieces. The grenade went off a heartbeat later, sounding like a thunderclap in the enclosed space. White smoke laced with pepper gas, and the rubber balls, filled the air.

Panic hit the people inside the room, followed by coughing and retching sounds.

A man raced by Bolan, blinded by the burning effects of the gas, wiping his hand over his face. The gun in his hand bucked and jumped as he fired continuously at empty air in front of him.

The Executioner stepped in behind the guy and brought the shotgun down hard. When the barrel connected, there was a meaty thunk, and the man went down in an unconscious heap.

Another man tried to make the break, as well, looking like a twisted specter wrapped in the CS gas.

Bolan cut him down with a blast from the shotgun, flinging the corpse back inside. A brief inspection of the room revealed two other men who were at the window, pushing shards of broken glass out of the way. They pulled their guns up to fire, but two blasts from the combat shotgun put them down.

Starting to feel the effects of the gas himself, Bolan retreated. With the shotgun gripped in one hand, he fisted the front of the unconscious man's shirt and dragged him down the stairs.

Once on the bottom floor, he patted down his prisoner and threw away a hideout gun and two knives. He didn't bother with the ID because he didn't need it. All he wanted was to get a message to Lupu.

He dragged the man out of the shop and to the canal's edge. Draping the man over the side, he grabbed the back of his shirt and lowered his head into the brine. A few seconds went by and a few bubbles came up, then the guy was spluttering and in a frenzy to push himself out of the water.

Hauling his captive back in, the Executioner jerked him over onto his back, then shoved the ugly snout of the shotgun into his face. The guy's eyes widened, and he struggled not to cough as he kept his hands at the sides of his head.

"English," Bolan said in a graveyard whisper. A crowd was starting to gather around them, but others warned of the man with the gun and kept the circle loose.

"I speak it," the man said. He was in his early twenties and built big, used to making his way with his fists, judging from the scars on his knuckles and above his eyes.

"You know Mihai Lupu," Bolan stated.

The man hesitated.

"I'm not a cop, and you don't have to live."

"I know him."

"You work for him."

The man nodded.

"I want you to call him and give him a message. You tell him a man came by and said Julia DeVincenzo is ready to make the deal—the information on Alonzo Galvani for her son. But her son had better be in one piece. If he's not, then Lupu deals with me, and I'm not going to back off. Understand?"

"Yeah. I understand." Blood leaked down the guy's neck from the wound at the back of his head.

"You get him that message, or I'll come back looking for you."

"Sure, no problem."

"Tell him I left a calling card." Bolan dropped an ace of spades on the man's chest, then turned and walked away. From his position he could see that the crowd was clear of the shop. The man he'd left alive scrambled to his feet. When Bolan dropped a thumb over the button on the remote control detonator, the guy was knocked flat by the concussion of the firebomb.

Flames licked hungrily at the building, leaping out of the shattered remains of the big display windows and destroying everything inside. The shrill whine of sirens in the distance let the warrior know rescue vessels were already underway and closing fast. Before the fire spread to the other buildings, the fire department would have it under control.

Bolan broke into a jog. The opening round had been fired, but he wanted to make sure he left an impression with Mihai Lupu that couldn't be ignored.

CHAPTER ELEVEN

Standing near the midpoint of the bridge, Mack Bolan unlimbered a pair of light-amplifying binoculars and stared back up the Rio Dell' Arco toward the warehouse. The canal was narrow and gently curved, bordered on both sides by residences and businesses. A cool wind from the San Marco Canal behind him rustled through the black duster.

Few pedestrians were around, nor were there many other boats along the canal. The Arsenale stood proud and tall to the east of the warrior's position, a testament to the city's past as a naval force.

The stone warehouse was small and blended in easily with the other structures around it. In front a large motor sailer waited, its running lights already lit. A phone call to Stony Man had given the warrior the boat's name, *Silver Dipper,* a manifest and a crew list, as listed with the Italian Maritime Port Authorities.

Through the binoculars Bolan watched as the crew made the boat ready. It was riding low in the water, deeper than its normal draw would have indicated. There was no question that the boat was carrying a lot of freight. The warrior had gotten to the scene in time to see some of the men and women hustled aboard.

From the earliest days the predators had traded in flesh because of the profits. Like land, there was only so much of it, and there was a need to own it. It wasn't called slavery these days. It was called illegal immigration. But the end result was the same. People who were brought over had to pay the price of passage through whatever means they could find: sweat-shop labor, extortion, fraud or prostitution.

The last of the lines were cast off, and the vessel got underway.

The boat was a hundred yards out, moving smoothly.

Pocketing the binoculars, Bolan unsnapped the sling on the British Lee-Enfield L-42 A-1 bolt-action sniper rifle. Chambered in 7.62 mm, the rifle guaranteed knockdown power, and the magazine held ten rounds. The Kahles ZF69 telescopic sight, graduated out to 875 yards, made the distance to the *Silver Dipper* like shooting fish in a barrel.

He wrapped the sling around his arm and brought the rifle butt to his shoulder. Flicking off the safety, he peered through the light-amplifying scope and ran through the succession of targets in his mind.

Taking up slack on the trigger, he fired the first round, then worked the action quickly and smoothly enough that his second round was on its way as the first bullet pierced the heart of the vessel's pilot. The man flew backward in a tumble, blood soaking through his shirt. The follow-up round caught him in the face and bounced him off the bulkhead.

The sizzling crackle of the rifle fire echoed over the flat surface of the water in the canal.

Bolan worked the bolt again, throwing gleaming brass to his right. Round three crashed through the boat's Plexiglas windshield and caught another man in the throat.

Both eyes open so he could track the wide movement on the motor sailer, as well as the view through the sniper scope, the Executioner opted out on his planned fourth shot because he couldn't confirm the kill. He switched to one of the outside men and squeezed the trigger.

The round took the man high in the chest as he was turning to see what was going on in steering. Hammered by the impact, the man fell into the canal.

Moving steadily, breathing between each shot, the Executioner picked off another man on the prow. The body tumbled over the side. They still hadn't figured out where he was.

Inside the bridge a crewman was pulling at the wheel, trying to bring the boat around. The motor sailer was seventy yards out and closing.

Bolan's sixth round crashed through the man's temple, shoving him away from the wheel. Out of control, the boat listed to the right but kept coming toward his position on the bridge.

The four remaining men had his position now. Autofire lighted up the prow of the *Silver Dipper* as they launched an offense of their own. Bullets chipped into the bridge, drawing sparks from the metal and rock surfaces.

Abandoning his position, the Executioner went to ground and took up a prone stance five yards away, knowing his opponents would have a hard time sky-lining him against the murky dark hovering over the bridge. He slipped the rifle barrel through the railing and dropped the cross hairs over a guy sprinting back for the steering section. Squeezing the trigger, he watched the man spin and drop to the deck. Another round put him out of it entirely.

Shouts filled the air, both from the boat and the residences around the battlezone.

Bolan lined up a final shot and squeezed the trigger. Sliding through the recoil, the warrior got to his feet while the *Silver Dipper* powered under the bridge, the prow scraping along the side of the canal as it passed. He dropped the rifle and raced toward the motor sailer, getting to the opposite side of the bridge as it floated by.

He placed his hands on the railing and vaulted over, aware that the gunmen had seen him. Flailing his arms, he controlled the fifteen-foot drop, landing hard in the aft section and rolling. He pushed up with one hand and drew the Desert Eagle with the other.

A man came around on the right, firing his pistol, then trying to duck back for cover.

The Executioner leveled the big Magnum and sent a pair of 240-grain boattails winging toward the gunner. The rounds punched the guy in the chest, knocking him back against the cabin structure. Lifeless, the man slid down to a sitting position, rocking with the pitch of the boat.

Bolan went left, listening to the slap of running feet coming toward him. Frightened faces peered out at him from the partially open cabin door leading belowdecks.

"Get back inside," the warrior ordered.

The faces disappeared.

A bullet burned along the Executioner's shoulder as he broke cover. Instinctively he raised the .44 pistol and put two rounds into the man's face from less than eight feet away. When the *Silver Dipper* slammed against the side of the canal, the corpse toppled over the side, already on its way down.

A warning blast from a big horn sounded sonorous trapped between the walls of the canal. Glancing up, the warrior saw a luxury yacht coming around the bend. The motor sailer was drifting into the middle of the canal, leaving the bigger boat nowhere to go. If they collided, the warrior knew the immigrants trapped in the belly of the *Silver Dipper* wouldn't have a chance.

He grabbed the aluminum ladder that led to the steering section and pulled himself up, leathering the Desert Eagle as he took the wheel. He cut the rudder sharply, then added power to the big diesels driving the vessel. At first he didn't think the boat was going to respond. Then slowly the *Silver Dipper* came about. The prow missed the yacht by inches, but the sides rubbed in passing with enough force to pitch the motor sailer to a near-thirty-degree list.

Past the yacht, the vessel came back on an even keel, sending waves over the canal.

Bolan cut the engines and tripped the switch to let out the electronic anchor. He let the line play out even after he was sure the anchor had bottomed, taking up slack every so often to break the momentum.

A shadow leaned in the door, alerting the warrior that he wasn't alone. He moved a split second before a bullet ripped through a cracked section of the windshield and spilled it over the motor sailer's prow. Thinking quickly, he tapped the anchor control with a finger and locked up the cable brakes.

Suddenly caught by the anchor, the motor sailer jerked to a stop hard enough to slam the gunman against the bulkhead.

Bolan moved at once, throwing himself across the intervening distance. Grabbing the gunner's wrist, he kept the gun pointed away from anything vital. The pistol cracked twice, jumping in the man's hand and firing harmlessly into the air before the Executioner knocked it from his grip.

Releasing the man's wrist, Bolan slammed his open palm into his opponent's face, breaking his nose. The guy let out a shrill cry of pain.

Bolan slid his Night Stalker pistol free of shoulder leather and jammed it into the guy's throat. "You don't have to die," he said.

Trembling, the man restrained his efforts to free himself.

"You work for Mihai Lupu," Bolan stated.

The man nodded.

"Get up," Bolan ordered, motioning with the pistol. He half yanked his prisoner to his feet. "We're going to get the people off this boat."

They walked aft as curious people lined the shore on both sides. Others were crossing the bridge ahead to get to the side the motor sailer was up against.

"Do they speak English?" Bolan asked, pointing to the immigrants in the hold. A half-dozen faces were staring out at him, silently imploring, some of them anguished.

"A few," his prisoner replied.

"Then you tell them to climb out of the boat. Tell them that I'm not going to hurt them." Bolan watched as the man spoke rapidly.

In response the immigrant crowd came on deck. Two of the men seized the belaying lines and tossed them to people standing at the side of the canal. In a couple of minutes the *Silver Dipper* was pulled close enough to the pilings that the immigrants could step off.

When the last person had debarked and the belowdecks had been checked, Bolan left a shaped charge in the middle of the cabin floor and dragged his prisoner off the vessel. The crowd along the canal moved back at his direction. Keeping the Romanian covered, the warrior tagged the remote-control detonator on his combat harness.

In response an explosion ripped through the *Silver Dipper,* causing her to shudder. The cabin top burst free and fluttered through the air, breaking into a thousand pieces. Then a geyser of water shot up from the boat's bottom, and she began listing to the left, sinking rapidly.

"You call Lupu as soon as I clear the area," Bolan commanded. "You tell him that as long as the boy lives, we can deal. Julia DeVincenzo has the information he wants about Alonzo Galvani. If anything happens to the boy, I'm going to make this business personal. Do you understand?''

"Yes. I got it.''

"And you tell him you got this.'' Bolan flipped an ace of spades at the man, who grabbed it out of the air. Then the big warrior was in motion, seeking the shadows. He was still at ground zero, but he was sure the message was going out loud and clear.

Bucharest, Romania

THE CHAUFFEUR PULLED the limousine to the curb in front of the club, then came back and opened the door for his boss. Mihai Lupu got out of the car, dressed in one of his finest Italian suits, his shoes so polished that he could see his reflection.

Aleksander got out on the other side, flanked by Funar.

They were on Calea Victoriei, not far from the Muzuel de Istorie. Across the street was the savings bank. Lupu had gotten used to the French architecture that so many tourists found fascinating. The tourists came expecting to see only the Gothic architecture made famous in the Dracula movies.

He walked across the cobblestoned street to the tavern, where two guards stood in front of the heavy double oak doors. A striped canopy covered the walkway between two lengths of flowering gardens.

During the riots and unrest after Ceaușescu's execution and the expulsion of the Communist military forces afterward, the area had suffered some and hadn't quite regained its former glory. But capitalism flourished there now.

"Good evening, Mr. Lupu," one of the bouncers said, opening the door.

"Good evening. How's the crowd?"

"Big," the bouncer replied.

"Pavel's probably out counting his money now, eh?" Lupu said with a smile.

The bouncer shrugged.

Pavel Antonescu's greed was legendary. But his love of the club took a lot of those profits and plowed them back into his biggest investment: the club itself. Lupu knew for a fact that if Antonescu hadn't been as deeply involved in prostitution and extortion as he was, and trafficking in illegal immigrants, the man would have never been able to afford the nightclub.

He walked through the open door and into the anteroom Antonescu had designed to announce the real atmosphere of the club. Vandalism and petty theft were on the increase. In his last years in office, Ceauşescu had outlawed contraception and abortion. His intent had been to increase the population of his country to try to become a bigger player in Eastern Europe. Instead, the policy had created a generation of unwanted children that were left in alleys. For a while after Ceauşescu's assassination, Western governments had come in and freely adopted the children. But a number of them had been left. Now they were teenagers, forcibly taking back from the society that abandoned them.

When Antonescu had first opened the nightclub, he and his clientele were targeted for robbery and other acts of violence. Windows had been smashed nightly until the club owner put up the outer wall and added the bodyguards, giving them a bonus for every teen vandal they shot and killed.

Inside the anteroom the lights were dim and the temperature left a bit cool for the people who had to wait for tables. A scrawl of lime-green neon tubing announced Rick's in giant letters along the wall.

A line had already formed between the red velvet sashes leading to the ornate brass-and-glass door with tinted windows that showed the expensive foyer beyond. A PA system in the ceiling played the sounds of the big-band era, and a woman's voice sang a haunting melody.

"Mr. Lupu," the black-liveried maître d' said with a smile, "please go on in. Mr. Antonescu is waiting for you." He opened the door with a white-gloved hand.

Lupu entered and followed the foyer around to the right with Funar and Aleksander at his heels. No expense had been spared on the club. A white-jacketed band played on both sides of the oval-shaped stage at the front. The tables and chairs were at a discreet distance apart, allowing for a semblance of privacy. Live plants ran in aisles between the sections and at different points along the outer wall, filling the air with scents.

Antonescu waited for him. The club owner wore a dark suit, his hair carefully styled and his pencil mustache elegantly trimmed. He was broad and heavy, and more than a few people had made the mistake of thinking it was all fat. He held a thick cigar in his hand. "Ah, Mihai, my friend. You have returned from your trip. You are well, I hope?"

"Yes, Pavel."

Taking the lead, Antonescu led the way down to the tables in front of the stage, which were always off-limits to the paying customers. A waitress in a gauzy gold dress had drinks waiting for them by the time they sat.

"So," Antonescu said, "how did things go? Did you get the boy?"

Lupu leaned back in his chair, regarding the man. It didn't surprise him that Antonescu hadn't followed the news coming out of Venice. "We took the boy and we have him now, but there have been complications."

"What?" Antonescu's easy demeanor leaked out of him with the next breath of smoke.

Lupu told him about the assassination attempt on Julia DeVincenzo and how the house had been burned down.

"This is very bad news," Antonescu said when he finished. "Our arrangement hinged on being able to tell the others that Alonzo Galvani would no longer be a threat."

"One way or another," Lupu said, "Galvani will cease being a threat."

Antonescu waved a hand through the gray cigar smoke. "You speak with the impetuousness of youth, my friend." Then he looked quickly at Lupu. "That was not said to offend."

"I know." But Lupu felt the tightness in his voice.

"If, as I suggested, Magaddino really had something on Galvani," the club owner said, "knowledge of that could have worked out to benefit us all. His connections to activities in the Western world are worth a small fortune."

"But we are making inroads into those places ourselves," Lupu argued.

"Again you're taking the long view, which is an aspect of youth. Also, I might add, that ability on your part is what helps you stand head and shoulders above your peers." Antonescu shifted in his seat as the waitress came back bearing an appetizer.

The huge plate held stuffed artichoke hearts, lobster and shrimp. Stainless-steel tumblers offered a variety of sauces. After dealing a stack of individual saucers out like a faro dealer working a full table, the waitress left, promising coffee in a few minutes.

Antonescu took his napkin and spread it over his lap, then helped himself to the appetizers. "Come," he admonished Lupu, "eat."

Lupu ate only because if he didn't it seemed to distress the club owner and draw his mind from focusing on the conversation. "We can replace whatever avenues cooperation on Galvani's part would give us."

Nodding, Antonescu said, "In time, yes. But remember that Michael Borsatti, Viktor Petrescu and myself are no longer young men. Our time is limited, and we're keenly aware of this. Also we've labored at our trade for many more years than you."

Lupu knew that. His father had worked with some of them in an effort to shore up Ceauşescu's weakening regime.

"During many of those years, crime did not pay nearly so well as it now does," Antonescu continued. "The three of us, we think we've paid our dues. This unification of forces and resources that you champion so much, hinged on your ability to deliver Galvani. Or at the very least remove him from a threatening position."

Lupu knew that.

"We don't think such a unification will be of as much benefit to us as you believe." Antonescu carved up an artichoke heart with deceptive ease, plopped it into a hot sauce and chewed it.

"Then you've not been listening to what I was saying," Lupu said boldly. He noticed the flame of anger blush under the older man's skin. "If not Galvani, then someone else will try to take over our territory here. Eastern Europe is a growing marketplace for the Mafia, Yakuza and Triads. They *will* come. And if we're not ready to repel them, they'll take everything we have."

"Not without a fight," the club owner growled.

"Dammit, Pavel!" Lupu tossed his napkin on the table. "That's a waste of resources. Of course it would take considerable effort for them to take over these territories by force. But what's to keep them from sending an assassin over here to slip a knife between your ribs some night?"

"I am well guarded."

"For now maybe. But what if one of those men you prize so highly becomes more greedy than you're willing to admit? One night, one bullet, and everything you control is up for grabs."

"And you, Mihai? Would you be so quick to take what I have worked my life for?"

Lupu smiled, knowing he was making his point clear. "Of course. I have seen what your operation takes in."

Antonescu sighed and placed his folded napkin on the table, as well. Only Aleksander and Funar continued to eat. "You spoil a delightful meal, my friend. However, you have a point. If you could deliver Galvani, the others you've proposed this union to would be able to see what they were going to realize out of it. Galvani's organization, coupled with what he's sure to take over of Magaddino's, would be a crown jewel. Without it we are going to be hard-pressed to make them see."

"I understand that. But I need to know if you are with me."

Antonescu raised his glass with a small smile. "A toast then, to that understanding."

Lifting his glass, Lupu drank. Even if Galvani was now out of reach, he felt confident that the syndicate he was trying to assemble would possibly come about.

"I shall talk to the others on your behalf," Antonescu said. "As you have pointed out, you've already laid a foundation in Venice and in Bosnia that we had not tried to do. Neither did we have the CIA or Russian military Intelligence contacts that you possess."

Lupu's father had done business with a number of clandestine agencies while serving in Ceauşescu's cabinet. He'd introduced many of them to his son, and Lupu hadn't been hesitant about renewing those business relationships when he had something to offer—and to gain.

"In truth," Antonescu said, "you've placed us all in a unique position. They won't forget that easily."

"Thank you."

"What are you doing about the situation in Venice?" the club owner asked.

On stage the singer finished her set and took a bow as the baby spot dimmed to the size of a dime and disappeared.

"I've got some people out looking for the DeVincenzo woman. If they find her, I'll know."

"You think Galvani really tried to assassinate her?"

"Yes."

"He was taking a big chance, considering she's the granddaughter of Magaddino. The old man had a number of friends."

"He may have had friends," Lupu admitted, "but none who would want to avenge his granddaughter's death. She's not going to try to fill her grandfather's shoes, so they have nothing to fear from her. Perhaps it would be even better for some of them if she was out of the way. In that respect some of the loyalties among her grandfather's constituents might not be so confused."

The waitress returned with coffee and quickly poured it out.

"There's something else you need to take into consideration," Antonescu said. "That fire may have been set by the woman or her friends in an effort to buy time."

"For what reason?"

"You've let them know you have the boy," Antonescu said. "It could be that Galvani is assembling some form of retribution even as we speak."

"I think it was just Galvani's effort to wipe out any evidence of the blackmail Magaddino had on him."

"I hope it's so," the club owner said. The band had swung into a medley of Glenn Miller instrumental hits that the audience greeted with enthusiasm. "But keep an open—and suspicious—mind."

Lupu nodded as the waitress walked up with a phone and told him he had a call. He took it at the table, wanting to show Antonescu there were no secrets. "Lupu."

The man on the other end was tense and nervous. His story came out slightly garbled, but Lupu followed it, learning how the smuggling operation had just been attacked and exposed. "He killed everybody there except me, Mr. Lupu. He told me he wanted to get a message to you about the boy. He said as long as the boy's alive, you can deal for the information concerning Galvani. Then he gave me a card. An ace of spades."

"One man did all that?"

"Yes. The son of a bitch walked in and just started shooting. No questions, no warnings, nothing. Like some kind of commando or something. He had grenades and explosives and wore some kind of paint on his face that made him look like something you'd see in Hell."

"What did this man look like?" Lupu listened intently, knowing the description fit the man they'd encountered in the canal tunnels and on the train. "How badly compromised is the operation there?"

"It burnt to the ground with everything in it. We'd just taken in that shipment of heroin."

That brought the tally of lost goods up another two and a half million. Lupu let out his breath angrily.

"I tried to call you earlier," the man said, "but no one knew where you were."

"It's okay. Stick around and let me know what you can find out." Lupu hung up the phone. Not only had he lost the heroin and the other contraband at the site—including a shipment of guns headed for a German terrorist group in Ravenburg that was going to be the start of new business—but the front he'd managed the company under was also compromised. It would take months to set up another supply line.

"Bad news?" Antonescu asked.

"Yes and no," Lupu replied. He explained about Julia DeVincenzo still being alive and willing to deal for the information on Galvani, but the loss of the shipping station, as well.

"One man?" the club owner asked in perplexion. "How could one man do all that?"

Lupu gazed at the smoky haze over the table, remembering the tall, dark-haired man's chiseled face and blue eyes. "Obviously this is no ordinary man. But he's a dead man all the same."

"Where are you keeping the boy?" Antonescu asked.

"At my apartment here in the city."

"Does anyone know?"

Lupu shook his head. "Just my people who were with me when I arrived."

"Can you trust them?"

Lupu nodded.

"Do you know the significance of the ace of spades?" Antonescu asked.

"No."

"I've heard stories," the club owner said, "of men in the Mafia, who work directly for La Commissione, the ruling body. These men are known as Black Aces, and their power is complete. These are hard men, Mihai, so you should be careful when dealing with him."

"Maybe," Lupu said, "this man should take care in dealing with me. He has cost me and he's going to pay for that."

Then the waitress came back to tell him there was another call. In minutes Lupu learned of the loss of the illegal-immigration warehouse and the *Silver Dipper*. His voice rose as he spoke with the survivor of the attack. "Listen to me. You get your ass back out there and you find out who this bastard is. I want to hear from you soon." He hung up the phone forcefully.

"What?" Antonescu asked.

Lupu didn't want to go into it. He stood and excused himself, motioning to Funar and Aleksander. "Talk with the others," he told the club owner. "Tell them I need a decision by tomorrow afternoon or I'll pursue my own interests in the matter."

"I will." Antonescu's eyes were bleak and hard. "Just make sure your own house is in order before you overtax your resources throwing such a gauntlet before these men."

"I can handle this," Lupu said as he walked away. "And if I have to, I can handle them, as well. Let them know that."

Venice

AS THE MAN STEPPED from the warehouse and started to lock the door behind him, Mack Bolan emerged from the shadows with his pistol in his fist, a silencer jutting from its barrel.

"Don't lock it," the Executioner said in a wintry voice.

The man looked up, startled. Then he went for the pistol holstered at the front of his waistband.

Bolan didn't hesitate. The SIG-Sauer *phutted* twice as both rounds drilled into the man's face and bounced him off the wall behind him. The pistol bounced free of the corpse's hand without firing.

Moving forward, the Executioner caught the door before it could close. The only sounds around him were the screams of sirens far in the distance and the slap of the water in the canal behind him. Reaching back, he grabbed the handle of the canister he'd brought with him and walked into the warehouse.

He kept the pistol in his fist as he walked. Voices drifted to him from the other end of the warehouse. Pallets covered with cardboard boxes were all around him, and yellow lines marked the walk-through areas. No lights were on, but there was a soft glow in the direction the voices came from.

Using a Ka-bar knife, he opened some of the boxes nearest him. Inside were other boxes that contained videotapes of pirated movies. The covers were black-and-white reproductions of the original films. Still other boxes held American-made jeans, which were also a big seller in Eastern Europe in the black-market arena.

He worked with grim efficiency as he slung the canister over his shoulder, then started spraying with the attached hose and nozzle. It was an ordinary pesticide rig used for industrial jobs, holding five gallons of liquid. After borrowing the spray rig, he'd filled the tank with a mixture of gasoline and laundry detergent, making a cheap napalm, then adjusted the flow to put out a heavy mist. Trapped inside the warehouse, the fumes would become combustible, too.

In only a couple of minutes, he was at the small office in the back. It was about thirty feet square, with doors on two sides. Through the lighted windows, Bolan counted a dozen people manning video-duplicating equipment. Only three men were armed.

The warrior guessed that the other men and women were part of the illegal immigrant trade, pressed into service here.

Using the last of the canister's contents, he laid down a solid line to the corner of the building, moving only when he was certain he wouldn't be seen by anyone inside.

He'd glanced up overhead and found the fire-suppression lines leading to outlets along the naked beams of the ceiling. All of the dull gray lines dovetailed back to a main tank standing against the wall near the small office.

Taking a small penlight from his pocket, Bolan played it over the fire-suppression supply tank, then saw the red toolbox on a shelf above it. He opened the box, found a crescent wrench that would fit the valve, then shut it off. Even when the fire-suppression system sensed the fire and tried to activate, nothing would go through the lines.

Satisfied, he shifted the pistol to his left hand and drew the Desert Eagle with his right. He walked toward the office and kicked open the door.

The three men were caught flat-footed, but they didn't waste any time trying to catch up. Guns filled their hands as they dived for cover.

Bolan stood his ground, knowing he had the element of surprise on his side. Some of the women operating the duplicating equipment screamed in terror, and a few of the men grabbed them and dropped to the floor.

Bullets crashed through the glass windows to Bolan's left. Picking up the targets, the Executioner aimed the Desert Eagle from the point and fired two shots. Both 240-grain boattails caught the man in the chest and punched him backward, knocking over a table holding a pile of videotapes and a duplicator. The machine smashed to pieces when it hit the floor, and the black videotapes rained over the dead man with a crash.

The second man produced a mini-Uzi from under his jacket and opened fire, hosing the inside of the office.

Ducking behind the door frame, Bolan waited until the gunner fired dry, then whipped back around the corner with the pistol leveled before him. While the shooter was attempting to ram home another magazine, the Executioner put a 9 mm sizzler through his temple.

He scanned for the remaining man, catching him from the corner of his eye as the guy grabbed one of the women and pulled her in front of him to use as a shield.

"Hey, man!" the Romanian yelled in English. "They called us. They said you might be coming. Well, you aren't getting out of here alive. We have people waiting for you."

Sounds of running feet sounded behind the warrior. A quick glance showed him seven or eight men spreading out among the crates. They started firing at once. Bullets chipped the glass out of the windows and knocked holes in the wooden exterior of the office.

"Still think you're so smart?" the Romanian challenged. He shoved the pistol barrel into his hostage's ear, drawing screams from her. "You drop your guns, or I put a bullet through her brain."

"Okay," Bolan said. "Don't hurt the woman." Perspiration trickled down his back from the heat trapped inside the room. The warrior stepped into the open, his guns up, pointed away from the man.

The Romanian hunkered down behind his hostage, presenting a small target. "Put them down."

The first man Bolan had killed was only a few feet away. The .45 Government Model he'd carried was in the open inches from his fingers. Keeping his eyes on the man, Bolan put his guns on the table in front of him.

"It's okay!" the Romanian yelled. "I've got him!" Yanking his pistol away from the woman's head, he snapped off a couple rounds in Bolan's direction.

But the Executioner was a blur of movement, diving for the .45. He landed on one knee, grabbed the pistol and rolled, coming up again with the .45 in a Weaver's grip.

The Romanian's head and arm were in the clear as he swept his gun around, still firing and yelling while he struggled to hold on to the woman.

Bolan focused on the gunsight, let out a half breath and squeezed the trigger.

The heavy round slammed into the Romanian's shoulder with enough force to jar him. Shaken free by the impact, his pistol dropped to the floor.

Changing targets, wanting to keep the man alive, Bolan fired between the woman's legs and hit the man a second time in the knee.

Staggered by the bullet, the Romanian forgot about his hostage and grabbed for his knee. When the woman pushed against him to get away, he toppled, blood spurting between his fingers.

A head was framed in the broken window, the hard barrel of a pistol beside the man's cheek.

Bolan pulled the .45 on-target and fired a round that took the man in the left eye and knocked the head back. The pistol's slide blew back and locked, empty. Moving swiftly, the Executioner freed a spherical grenade from his webbing. Yanking the pin, he lobbed the bomb underhanded through the window into the middle area of the crowd.

He recovered the Night Stalker and the Desert Eagle just before the grenade went off. Dropping into cover beside the window, he closed his eyes when he heard the first explosion.

The grenade he'd chosen was designed to stun and disorient. For a full two seconds, detonations came in a rapid-fire sequence, sounding like a drum solo and accompanied by white-hot flashes and burning sparks. The Romanian gunners caught in the blast area yelped and cursed.

Whirling around the door frame, the Executioner saw that the sparks had also ignited the line of gasoline. Flames burned blue and yellow, rushing back to the crates the warrior had hosed down after entering the warehouse.

Return fire was subdued and less than accurate as the gunners fought the spotty vision left over from the blast. Bolan fired relentlessly, knocking down the gunners where they stood or tried to run. When he ejected the empty magazines, there was no one left alive to challenge him.

He holstered the Night Stalker and kept the Desert Eagle in his hand as he walked toward the man he'd shot in the shoulder and knee.

"Does anyone in here speak English?" the warrior asked.

"I do," said the woman who'd been used as a hostage. All the duplication workers stayed on the ground, trying to make themselves fit behind whatever defense they'd found. Many of them were praying, their eyes locked on Bolan.

"Tell them to get out of here," Bolan advised. "The warehouse is going to go up in minutes."

The woman got to her feet and spoke rapidly to the other eight workers. Slowly, conscious of the gun in Bolan's fist and that it might be a trick designed to get them out into the open, they got to their feet. The initial movement toward the door was hesitant, but after the first man slipped outside, it became a rush. The woman was the last one out, helping a girl who couldn't have been much more than eighteen.

"Help me," the Romanian croaked. "I'm bleeding to death and I can't walk."

Outside, the flames had crawled up the stacks of boxes, gaining intensity. Thick black smoke coiled like a tangle of pythons against the ceiling, oblivious to the naked support beams.

Bolan squatted beside the man, staying just out of reach. He pointed the big .44 at the man's face, causing the guy to blink. "Give me a number where I can get hold of Lupu."

"I don't know anyone named Lupu." The man held his wounded leg, pulling it up into him tightly, clamping down hard.

Bolan shifted the Desert Eagle. He gave the man a cold smile. The pop and crackle of the fire sounded closer now, like some hungry monster gnawing at the door. "Then I shoot you in the other leg, and you die in the fire."

The man said the number so fast that Bolan had to make him repeat it. Once he had it memorized, the warrior hooked his fingers in the back of the Romanian's shirt and dragged him out of the burning warehouse.

Alarms were closing in as Bolan let the Romanian drop on the ground. He fished a card out of his pocket and spun it at the man. "When you call Lupu," he said, "tell him the guy who did this left you one of these."

Clutching the ace of spades in a bloody hand, the man nodded.

Bolan sheathed the Desert Eagle and raced for the shadows just as the first police boat came into view around the bend of the canal. Blue lights cut jagged silhouettes out of the surrounding night. The warrior was gone before the first of those lights touched on the burning warehouse.

CHAPTER TWELVE

Bolan glanced at his watch as he waited for the phone connection to be made. It was eight-thirty. He'd made good time on the hit-and-git strikes.

Above him the moon was a pale lemon yellow, almost three-quarters full. A flock of a dozen or so bats unlimbered their wings from the belfry of a nearby church and took off, skating on silent wings through the night in search of prey. The brine smell of the canal water only a few yards away was sharp and bitter, underscoring the cool air that drifted in from the Venetian Lagoon.

A man's voice answered in Romanian.

"I want to speak with Lupu," Bolan said. Tired and bruised, he was running on no sleep for almost thirty hours, and the chill wore heavily on him.

"Who should I say is calling?"

"The Ace of Spades." Bolan answered. He could tell by the way the sound was abruptly cut off that the mouthpiece at the other end had been covered up. There was a click, letting him know at least one other extension had been picked up.

"This is Mihai Lupu."

"I just wanted to call to let you know you're out of the movie business, too," Bolan said.

"One thing I must commend you on is your thoroughness. I've not heard from my people there yet."

"You will. I just left the warehouse burning."

"I see." The anger in the words couldn't be concealed completely.

"How's the boy?" Bolan asked.

"He's fine. What do you want?"

"I want the boy back. Safe and unharmed."

"You've destroyed a lot of my holdings in Venice to be brave enough to call and make demands," Lupu said.

"If I've missed one, let me know."

"And cost me millions of dollars," Lupu went on, ignoring the statement. "You want to explain to me why I shouldn't send the boy back to his mother a piece at a time?"

"Because if you do that, you won't get the information you want on Galvani," Bolan replied in an even voice. "And you'll have me devoting all my attention to you. I can get a lot more expensive."

"Who are you working for?"

"Myself." Bolan glanced around, making sure no one was paying attention to him. The duster covered his equipment, but he didn't know how much of the night's activities had ended up on the television, or if any descriptions had been given of him.

"Not Galvani?"

"I've got a score to settle with him, as well, after this morning," Bolan replied truthfully. "But I'm working on one project at a time. Once I get the boy back, then we'll see about evening that up."

"How do I know that you'll back off me if I let the boy go?" Lupu asked.

"I can guarantee you that you won't get me to back off as long as you have him or if you've harmed him. Anything more than that, you'll have to accept on faith."

"Mrs. DeVincenzo has the information?" Lupu asked. "I thought everything in the house was destroyed."

"It was. But there were backup records she had access to."

"Magaddino was blackmailing Galvani?"

"Yes."

"With what?"

"We'll talk about that when I get the boy back."

"When can we meet?" Lupu asked.

"I'll let you know the time and the place," Bolan responded. He hung up the phone, then waited a moment. It started ringing almost immediately, letting him know Lupu had access to a phone tracing system. Ignoring the phone and walking toward the canal, he flagged down a passing water taxi. With the pressure he'd put on this night, certain that Lupu was ready to make the trade, he had to compare notes with Turrin and Julia. The next moves they made were going to be critical. Even more so if Kurtzman hadn't found the hidden information Magaddino had on Galvani.

Bucharest

LUPU STARED at the dead phone in his fist, then angrily depressed the disconnect plunger and punched in the automatic dial-back feature. All he received was a plaintive ringing. He made himself relax enough to put the receiver on the phone gently.

The suite he kept in the city was elegant and furnished with the best money could buy. Through black-market channels he'd even managed to acquire some Louis XIV pieces. His father had always loved wood and had made some of the pieces for their home himself, but those had all been lost after the executions. Brass sconces hung on the walls, filled with electrical wiring these days instead of oil or kerosene.

Lupu kept himself under control with effort. He walked to the window and stared down the four stories to C. A. Rosetti Street. A few blocks farther, he could see the top of the National Art Museum and the Athenaeum concert hall. His mother had taken him there to listen to the Romanian philharmonic, while his father had taken him to the nearby central-committee headquarters to meet important figures in the Communist Party.

He'd been staying in the Athenee Palace Hotel with his mother as Ceauşescu's guest the day the riots broke out in the streets. Intending to demonstrate to the world how much his country appreciated him, Ceauşescu had called together a mass rally. Instead, cries of ''assassin'' had broken from the crowd. The live broadcast had been ended, and hundreds of demonstrators had been shot down in the streets, the Western world not learning of it until much later.

Lupu had been there to offer evidence about the men who'd killed his father, hoping Ceauşescu could avenge the murder. But those hopes had been dashed the next day, when huge crowds stormed the central-committee building and Ceauşescu and his wife had to be airlifted by helicopter out of the city.

It was then that Lupu had realized that Bucharest offered no life to a man who wasn't prepared to fight for it and kill for it. Success was only measured in how many bodies a man could stand on top of at the end of every day.

"I had the operator trace the call," Funar said as he entered the room.

"Yes," Lupu said, turning to the man.

"It was from Venice. A pay phone."

"Has there been any contact from the people we have over there?"

"As to where this man in black might be?" Funar shook his head. "No."

Lupu walked to the wet bar in the corner of the room and made a vodka and tonic. "He's destroyed every operation I had going over there."

"I know."

"Are Antonescu and the others aware?" Lupu looked back at the Athenee Palace Hotel. His father had thought the place was amusing. All the foreign dignitaries were put up there, and even the ashtrays were bugged. The funny part was, the Western world had known it.

"Yes."

Lupu nodded. It wasn't surprising. Like himself, the others kept spies on their payroll, never quite trusting one another. "What about the boy?"

"He's asleep."

"And in good health?" Suddenly the boy's worth had increased. Not just because his kidnapping could leverage Alonzo Galvani, but because possessing the boy would bring the man in black to him.

"Yes. He was fed earlier, then mildly sedated to get him to sleep."

"Fine." Lupu walked to the back of the suite, to the bedroom where the boy was being kept.

Aleksander leaned back in a chair beside the door to the bedroom, his big hand holding open a Louis L'Amour novel. The big man's lips moved as he struggled with the foreign language. A shotgun was propped against the wall beside him. The book was part of a black-market deal from the closing of an American military base in Europe, and Aleksander had wanted it and others like it to practice his read-ing in English.

Putting the book down on the floor before him, Aleksander instinctively closed his free hand around the shotgun's grip. When he saw who it was, he re-laxed but took up the weapon anyway.

Lupu let himself into the bedroom and switched on the bedside lamp. Nicky DeVincenzo had dark hair like his mother, and a face with clean lines. He slept with his fists under his chin. A purple teddy bear lay trapped in his arms.

Freeing the bear from the boy's grip, Lupu held it up and looked at Aleksander.

"To calm him," the big man said with a shrug.

"You're getting attached," Lupu said.

"Not so very much. He's a good boy. I thought it would be no harm."

Placing the bear back on the bed, Lupu asked, "When the time comes to kill him, will you have any problems?"

"No." Aleksander's tone was flat.

Knowing the man as he did, Lupu knew it was the truth. "Good. Because when his mother and this man in black show up to deal, none of them are walking away alive." He pulled the cover over the boy. "Until then, take care of him."

Venice

LEO TURRIN WAS WAITING with Julia DeVincenzo when Bolan returned to the motel room. They were at the dining-room table, poring over papers and laser-printed black-and-white pictures. The time was 9:41. It had taken longer than the Executioner had guessed to get back to the Lido. The men and women of the Venice Police Department were out in force, combing the neighborhoods for him.

"The Bear found it," Turrin said, then gestured to the pot of coffee sitting on a room-service tray beside the table. "Coffee's fresh."

"A minute," Bolan replied, heading for the bathroom. He wanted to strip out of the combat gear before sitting beside Julia. It would all serve to remind her that her son was in enemy hands.

"Need help?" Turrin asked.

Bolan knew it was a way of asking if they needed to be alone, or if the warrior had wounds that needed dressing. Bolan said no, then grabbed a quick shower and a change of clothes. He kept the Night Stalker in shoulder leather over a baseball-styled jersey, then dumped the rest of his gear in a big suitcase he'd gotten for that purpose. On the way out of Venice, he'd toss the suitcase and equipment in the lagoon, leaving the local law enforcement nothing to trail.

Once back in the main room, Bolan scanned the papers as he poured a cup of coffee and helped himself to a Danish. "What did you find?"

"It was in one of the encrypted files," Julia answered. "Alonzo Galvani worked with the Nazis during World War II, and my grandfather found out."

Bolan knew that most of the Mafia Families had worked with the Western powers during the war to end Hitler's threat and get Mussolini out of power. U.S. military forces had even used black-market routes the Mafia had set up to get men and equipment inside Nazi-occupied territories. The downside to the involvement was that the Mafia was in even better position to set up newer and more-productive routes by the end of the war, one of the more famous being the French Connection.

"Nothing like a truly great evil to unite opposing forces," Turrin said.

Bolan glanced at one of the laser-printed black-and-white photographs. It depicted an armored car with swastikas sitting beside an open touring car with German officers in it. A footnote at the bottom of the page read, "Cefalu, Sicily—1942." In the background was a harbor ringed by mountains.

"And the fact that fascism hurts the idea of a capitalist society," the warrior said. "The Families were getting as hard-pressed as the common populace under Il Duce.''

Julia tapped the picture. "These were digitized on my grandfather's computer. Your friend found them. When they're blown up, you can clearly see who the people are." She moved to the notebook computer and brought it on-line.

Bolan trailed after her, noting that she seemed more together now that she had something to do.

The computer screen cleared, and she tapped a few keys. It blinked while the hard disk buzzed, accessing the files. The same black-and-white picture came on, much more clearly defined now. Julia worked the built-in mouse and drew a square around one of the men's heads in the touring car. She hit another key sequence.

Easy to recognize now, with only a little fuzziness from the magnification process, Benito Mussolini gave the appearance of listening intently.

Julia repeated the process with the other man in the back seat of the touring car. A much younger, though recognizable, version of Alonzo Galvani filled the screen, his shoulders hunched as he spoke.

"My grandfather's files document the whole story," Julia said. "Galvani worked with Mussolini and the Germans against his own countrymen. When Mussolini was ousted and jailed in 1943 after the partisan groups in Milan and other places actively fought against the Nazis, and Sicily fell to American and British troops in July of that year, Galvani set up relations with high-ranking German officers in Italy. He was even part of Mussolini's rescue by the Germans in September. Acting like he was working with the other Families and the partisan movement, Galvani repeatedly sold them out to the Germans.''

"According to the paperwork Magaddino found," Turrin said, "after the war Galvani was going to be issued large tracts of land in Sicily and be granted political powers from Berlin."

"His own empire," Bolan said.

Turrin nodded. "Yeah. I can see it. Galvani's always been motivated by power."

"So Magaddino found this out and held it over Galvani's head," Bolan said. He sipped his coffee, letting all the pieces fall neatly into place.

"My grandfather had suspected Galvani of treasonous behavior for some time," Julia said. "It caused bad blood between them. After the war Galvani managed to avoid detection, but my grandfather didn't give up the search." She waved at the table and the computer. "He spent considerable time and money to find these records."

"Where did they come from?"

"A church," Turrin said.

"Catholic," Bolan said.

"Yeah," the stocky little fed replied. "There's your tie to this Father Gerald Light. Evidently at some point after the Allied invasion, Galvani found out the priest at the church had taken pictures of him and Mussolini. The priest, Father Crispin, left a diary. Crispin had intended to send the pictures and information he'd gathered to the Vatican, so they could be disseminated as the pope saw fit. Instead,

Galvani arrived first, killed the priest after naming him as a Nazi spy and burned the church.''

"My grandfather had Cefalu searched," Julia said. "Even the rubble of the church. He encountered a group from the Vatican, as well, led by a young priest named Uccello. The church had sent Uccello to recover some paintings and sculptures Crispin had been given to hide from the Nazis. In those days Hitler was taking everything of religious symbolism he could locate."

"But Uccello couldn't find the paintings or sculptures," Bolan said.

"No," Julia said. "Galvani had taken them. But grandfather's people found the priest's diary and pictures in a marketplace. A lot of people were taking what they could get and starting their lives anew. It's possible the people who sold the diary to my grandfather's representatives didn't even know what they had."

"And once your grandfather had the information, he leaned on Galvani to bring him in line."

Julia nodded. Fatigue stained her eyes, and she still looked pale. "Not only did he threaten to tell the other Family members who'd lost so much during the war, but my grandfather also promised to turn the files over to the Israeli Nazi hunters."

"Even if the Families had given up on a chase after Galvani," Turrin said, "the Israelis wouldn't have."

"How did the church find out that Magaddino knew where the lost artwork was?" Bolan asked.

"He contacted Father Uccello at the Vatican a few months ago," Julia said. "He knew he was dying, and he wanted to make things right with the church. Letters between them are included in the files. Through his hand, the artwork has stayed lost for another fifty years than it might have." She paused. "Maybe he was seeking a final blessing before he passed."

"Only he died before he told Uccello who had it."

She nodded.

Bolan stood and got another cup of coffee. He turned to face Turrin and the woman. "Lupu wants the information on Galvani. If we give it to him, he's going to be able to use it against Galvani to get him in league with him. But he and Galvani are going to know that you know his secret, too."

Pain showed in Julia's eyes, and she clasped her hands before her. "What you're telling me is that even after we give this information to Lupu for my son, Nicky and I still aren't going to be safe."

Bolan didn't try to soften it. Her life depended on facing the situation squarely. "No. Chances are that Galvani or Lupu will still try to have you murdered at a later date. Galvani will want to cover up his secret. He's protected it for decades and been constrained because of it. And Lupu will want the knowledge to himself because it puts him in a better position to blackmail Galvani."

"All I want," Julia said in a tightly controlled voice, "is for my son and me to be out of this."

Bolan nodded. "To do that, there's going to be considerable risk."

"Anything we do is going to involve some risk, isn't it?" the woman asked.

"Yes. Tonight I closed down three operations Lupu had going in Venice. They were outlets for the black-market trade he's had coming out of Romania. I made sure he needs Galvani's involvement more than ever. But a guy like Lupu is going to want his pound of flesh."

"You think he's going to try to double-cross us."

"No doubt about it," Bolan said.

"What about Nicky?"

"I was told a little while ago that he was okay. I believe Lupu was telling the truth. Also he knows you have the information he wants on Galvani."

"But you didn't know that then."

"Lupu didn't know that, either. But as long as we have it, your son is going to be okay."

Turrin shifted in his chair. "There's a wrinkle."

Bolan glanced at his friend.

"Canova and I found out Galvani and a group of his hard corps took a plane out of Milan for Bucharest a little while ago. I told him Julia had the information and was setting up a deal with Lupu. I figured a little confusion would buy us some time and maybe a little maneuvering room."

"Yeah," the warrior said. "I think so, too." He glanced at his watch and saw that it was 10:13. Moonlight dappled the lagoon beyond the beach outside the window. "What about Gerald Light?" The priest was a wild card on the play.

"Not much," Turrin admitted. He passed across a single sheet of paper. "The Bear got into some of the Vatican's files to dig up even this much. Guy seems to have come out of nowhere, even though there's a bio on him. Pretty bland reading, with no highlights. He's a Jesuit, has traveled Europe and Asia pretty extensively, but there's nothing there that explains the guy you saw in action. He's also known as Jericho Light.''

Bolan knew the Jesuits were the warrior section of the church. Under Ignatius Loyola, the Society of Jesus made forcible converts to the church and withstood encroachments from other religions and empires seeking to extend their holdings. A nation unto itself, the Vatican, he was sure, used some of these people as protectors and defenders, and possibly more.

''Gerald Light isn't his real name,'' Bolan said.

Turrin grinned. ''Birth certificate's issued by the Vatican. Can't come much more pedigreed than that.''

''Not much,'' the warrior agreed. He glanced back at Julia. ''One other decision you need to make.''

''Yes.''

''We know what your grandfather was using against Galvani, but it's not worth much without the proof in those computer files. When we make the trade with Lupu, do you want to give him those files?''

''No. Even if everything goes right, I don't want him to have them.''

''I agree.'' Bolan sat by the computer and made a call to Stony Man Farm. When Kurtzman came on, he told the cybernetics specialist what he wanted, then placed the phone on the modem. In five minutes they were ready, leaving everything behind that wasn't immediately portable.

Last of all, the warrior removed the diskette from the computer and tucked it in his pocket. The front had moved out of country, and the sides were lining up. By the time their plane touched down in Bucharest, he knew there'd be a hell of a war zone.

Bucharest

JERICHO LIGHT GOT out of the battered Dacia taxicab he'd taken into the city. The airport was some twelve miles north of Bucharest proper, and he'd had time to take in some of the war-torn sights. He paid the driver and walked to the door of the modest rectory squatting in the shadows of the turreted church only a few yards away.

After knocking, Light looked over the neighborhood, noticing its shabby hopelessness. He wondered how anyone could maintain a church in such surroundings. Some of the homes were burned patches of rubble, and others looked like fortresses in the making. Gutted remains of small, scarred cars looked like road kill scattered across the street and sitting in yards. A cold front had blown in from the Black Sea and marshaled an army of fogs that skated through the city.

Hinges squeaked as the door opened. A small bald man with a bushy mustache and round-lensed glasses stood in the space left by the security chain. "Father Light?"

"Yes."

"A moment, please." The door closed again, followed by the rattle of the chain as it was taken from the latch. "Please come in."

Light stepped into the rectory foyer and felt the warmth of the place soak into him.

The priest spent some time making sure the door was fortified again, then looked Light up and down. "You weren't prepared for the cold snap, were you?"

"No."

"You should have listened to the weather-advisory messages."

"There wasn't time." Light looked around the hallway and saw a few pictures lining the walls, but the illumination was so dim the details were indistinct.

"Well, come on. It's enough that I've been forced from my bed at such an hour without wasting more time." The priest led the way down the hall and to a small kitchen. "I think we can find a suitable coat for you. Have you eaten?"

"No."

The kitchen was homey in a way that Light could only barely remember. Maybe it touched some distant chord in his childhood, but he couldn't be sure. He sat in a straight-backed chair that had seen better days. The tabletop was clean but had deep scars running through it.

"I'm Jakob Lesser," the priest said, rummaging through the refrigerator and pantry with fluid skill. "Everyone always calls me Jakob." Sandwiches surrounded by pickles and tomatoes, took shape on thick wooden platters.

"I appreciate the hospitality," Light said, "but I'm afraid I don't have the time for this."

The priest waved the comment away. "You have time. Lupu is busy trying to negotiate with Antonescu and the others. It appears they found out about the misfortunes his businesses had in Venice. Besides, Daniel won't be here with your car and other equipment for another twenty minutes." He sat the platters on the table, added a bowl of beef stew from the microwave and a glass of milk.

"How do you know so much about Lupu?" Light asked.

Lesser sat and cut his sandwich in two. "My parishioners, of course. During the week they work for Lupu, Antonescu or one of those men like him. On Sundays they're in the confessional to set things straight with God. Kind of keeping a foot in both camps, you might say."

"Then you know what I'm here for."

"Not exactly. I know Lupu is involved, but the church, sometimes they keep things to themselves. Plus it matters how deeply you're into the rumor mill. I've been out of the main loops for some time since coming to Romania. Would you like to say grace?"

Almost awkwardly Light folded his hands and offered the prayer.

Lesser set to the meal with undisguised gusto when he finished. "When I was told about your impending arrival, I called a few people I still have contact with. Going to play merry hell with the church's monthly phone bill, I promise you. But I don't like surprises. Especially ones tendered by Vatican City."

"I understand."

"You're a Jesuit, I was told."

Light nodded.

"But you haven't been with the church long. You're one of Uccello's boys."

Light looked at the man.

"Oh, there's no need to be surprised," the priest said. "I know Uccello. I know his recruitment policies, his methods and his zealous desires to advance in the church." His eyes narrowed. "And I know his vanity."

A slight burn of anger flooded through Light. Uccello had been one of the major forces in his resurrection. But the anger died away as he remembered the faces of the dead men earlier that morning.

"I see I've hit a nerve," Lesser said. He pursed his lips. "I'm sorry. But I know how charismatic Uccello can be and how strong he is. Whatever mission he's charged you with, whatever you've had to do to come this far, you ask God—and you ask yourself—if this is what He would have you do."

"There is some confusion," Light admitted.

Behind the round lenses of his glasses, Lesser's eyes were blood-shot and penetrating. "I could see it in you. If I hadn't, I would never have spoken to you. Go on and eat up." He leaned back in his chair and rolled a cigarette one-handed, concentrating on the action although Light felt the man could have done it with his eyes closed. "Uccello is a good man,

I think, but his values may be a little skewed. I know he was one of the fathers put in charge of recovering church treasures that were scattered during World War II. In fact, for a time I worked in one of his groups. I found his methods a little too forceful to my taste, but he never quite stepped over that line the Vatican drew for him.''

Light finished the sandwich and soup, then pushed the bowl and platter away.

Taking ceramic mugs from one of the shelves, Lesser poured from a pot of coffee heating on the stove. "Not exactly what you've been getting at the Vatican, I'm afraid."

"I've probably had much worse," Light said.

Lesser sat and regarded the other man frankly. "What is your calling, Father Light?"

"I'm afraid I don't understand."

"Didn't anyone ever ask you why you wanted to join the church?"

"Yes."

"And what did you tell them?"

"That I wanted to serve the church."

"How?"

Light was silent for a moment. "I don't know. I just knew that I couldn't keep living my life the way I had."

"You're a man used to violence." Lesser waved away an answer. "You don't have to tell me. I can see it. My postings have been in Eastern Europe for the past thirty years. Some say those experiences have made me quite cynical even past my age. But the church isn't just a retreat or another way of life, son.

However you were drawn to the church and to God, He has a purpose for you. And I'd wager to say that it's more than merely locating lost art that does nothing for the spiritual needs of His people.''

The older man's words bit deeply into Light, resonating with the conflicting convictions he'd had since the first encounter upon his arrival in Venice.

A low bonging sounded throughout the rectory.

Leaning forward, Lesser put his hand on Light's arm. ''That'll be young Daniel with your car and supplies. Don't blind yourself to the mysteries that may await you, Father. Just trust in Him, for He'll show you what there is to be done. And if ever you need to talk, I'll be here.''

''Thank you.'' Light followed the priest to a back door.

A boy no more than fifteen stood on the back door step. Beyond him a worn Dacia station wagon sat panting in a graveled drive like an asthmatic dog. The boy was slender, dark haired and dark eyed, and had a shy smile. He wore patched jeans, a T-shirt and a flannel coat that hung on his narrow frame. When the older priest gestured, the boy whipped off his watch cap in embarrassment.

''Sorry, Father,'' Daniel said in decent English. ''I meant no disrespect.''

''None taken,'' Light replied. He turned to Lesser, who was pulling a large canvas-colored coat from a rack by the door. ''I'll need directions to Lupu's location.''

''I'll take you, Father,'' Daniel said.

''I don't think—'' Light started.

"Take him," Lesser said. "You'll be safer with him than he'll be with you. Daniel's lived on these streets all his life."

Light nodded, then shook hands with the older man. He followed Daniel to the car.

"Is it okay if I drive?" the boy asked, brushing a lock of hair out of his face.

Nodding, Light went around to the passenger side. "When we get near Lupu's place, I want you to vanish."

Backing out, Daniel said, "No problem." He handled the car with confidence, wheeling it out onto the street and turning on the lights as he shifted into first and rolled forward.

"I'll need a map of the city."

"In the glove box and already marked. The red route will take you back to the airport. The blue one to the rail station. And the green one is the quickest way I know out of the city. In case you forget, there's a key at the bottom of the map."

Light unfolded the map and looked at the streets traced in crayon. Below it, the key was handwritten. "Seems like you've done this before."

"Yes. Before I found Jakob and the church, I worked as a runner for Lupu and some of the others. That's where I learned to handle a car. They didn't ask for driver's licenses or birth certificates."

"And Jakob brought you out of all that."

"Sure. The man is a saint. He took me off the streets, got me off alcohol and gave me a home. But I wasn't the only one. He's helped lots of others." Daniel made a lane change and shrugged. "Not all of them stayed helped, though. Like Jakob says, God can only offer a way out. It's up to the individual to take it. But he keeps trying.''

Light was surprised about the number of children out on the street so early in the morning. They moved and acted like nocturnal creatures, flitting through the shadows at a quick pace. ''Why aren't these children home?''

''They don't have any homes,'' Daniel said, turning again. ''These kids are homeless. When Ceau-şescu was in charge of this country, he made it against the law to have birth control. He ordered every woman to have five children. Well, with the way he was handling things, no family could support five kids. So they abandoned them. Whatever the kids can get on the street, they're convinced that's the best there is.''

Light watched some of them as the car passed by. They looked like scarecrow figures. Some of them caught him watching and made obscene gestures, yelled taunts. He made himself look away. ''Where's the rest of the things I asked for?''

''Back seat.'' Daniel wiped at the fogging windshield with a napkin. The heater labored to keep up but couldn't.

A heavy gym bag was in the back. Light lifted it over the seat and examined the contents. Inside was a Glock Model 21 chambered in .45ACP, and a wicked-looking Skorpion machine pistol. There were extra magazines for both weapons, a paddle holster for the Glock and a sling for the Skorpion.

"That stuff's all first-rate, Father," Daniel said. He eased the station wagon to a stop at a red light, pulling over against the curb. "And that's Lupu's place here in the city." He pointed at the tall building across the street.

"What floor and room?" Light asked, dropping the Glock into his pocket. He stared through the foggy windshield.

"Fifth floor, and he's got it all."

"Okay. Time for you to clear out."

Daniel nodded, then offered a hand covered with a glove that had the fingers cut out. "You take care up there, Father. Mihai Lupu is a mean bastard when he thinks you've done him wrong." The boy stepped out of the car.

Light got out and came around to the driver's side. He drove away, intending to find a place to stash the station wagon, then do a full recon on the building. McKay and Julia DeVincenzo would have to come this way, or he could follow Lupu to them. He glanced in the rearview mirror in time to see Daniel fade into the shadows, looking lost against the night of the city.

Resolutely he made himself focus on the recovery of the art objects. Once he finished this mission and got some kind of closure, he could take a look at what his options were. Until then, it was possible he was going to need all his old skills merely to stay alive.

CHAPTER THIRTEEN

Bucharest

"This is the place," Gabe Valente said to the driver. He pointed to the small building off Virgil Street behind St. Vineri Cemetery.

Staring through his window from the back seat, Alonzo Galvani studied the tall, threatening grave markers that studded the cemetery. The walls and iron bars surrounding the place carried out the Gothic theme he'd seen since his arrival at the city. Fat and pale, the moon looked like some kind of demonic spirit hovering over the place, garbed in wisps of cloth that reminded the old man of shrouds.

Even though he hadn't wanted to admit it to anyone, death had been on his mind since Magaddino's passing. Magaddino had been two years younger than him. All those years ago, when Magaddino had revealed his treachery, Galvani had sworn to outlive his foe and be free of the fear that had festered inside him for fifty years.

Now he had, and yet the fear was more alive in him than ever with the possibility of the DeVincenzo woman turning over his secrets to Mihai Lupu.

The car moved as Valente gave orders, talking rapidly over the walkie-talkie that connected him with the cars following them.

Glancing through the rear window, Galvani watched the other rental cars peel off in different directions, blocking off the streets surrounding their destination. Dark-suited men poured out of the cars even before they stopped rolling.

"Maybe you should stay back here, Mr. Galvani," Valente suggested quietly.

"No." Galvani made his voice harsh enough to draw the driver's attention. He softened it. "No, Gabe. We're putting an end to Lupu tonight, and I'm not going to have it said later that I wasn't there. You understand?"

Chastised, Valente nodded.

The driver pulled the car into the narrow lot beside the rusted-out hulk of a thirty-year-old Volkswagen microbus. The lights went out, barely brushing the building ahead of them. Paint was peeling all over it, and windows had been covered with cardboard and duct tape.

"Now!" Valente breathed into the walkie-talkie. He pushed his door open and got out with a gun in his fist. The other men surrounding the building rushed in at once.

Fisting his .45 Colt Government Model, Galvani got out of the car and walked to the building's front door. His men worked in tandem, obeying Valente's orders like a well-oiled machine. Gunshots sounded inside the building and flashed white-hot lightning against the dirty windows that weren't boarded up.

From inside, a man made a break for it, stepping through the door with an Uzi blazing. The sound rolled like summer thunder, cracking without pause. One of the men in front of Galvani went down. A moment later the man saw Galvani blocking his way and brought up the Uzi.

Bullets whipped through the graveled driveway on their way to Galvani. The fear didn't touch him; he'd lived with much worse. Valente screamed at him to get down, but he ignored that, too. The .45 came up in his hand, solid and secure. Gazing into his enemy's eyes, he squeezed the trigger. Instantly one of those eyes winked out, like a shutter had suddenly been drawn over it. The man pitched back soundlessly, the back of his head blown away.

Galvani kept walking, passing over the corpse of his would-be executioner. That was how a man should face his fears. But Magaddino had never accorded their relationship with honor, instead hiding behind the threat of a death sentence by the other Families or even the damn Jews. When he reached the building, it was over. Valente and his people were in control of the people that remained alive inside.

He ignored the words of praise from the other men, knowing that the story would grow by the time he was back in Venice. Everyone would know to fear him, and he would take what he liked of Magaddino's disintegrating empire. After fifty years he was going to take his due.

The inside of the darkened building looked like a barracks, the wide-open area filled with beds and clusters of furniture that arranged living space and a kitchen. Only one lamp lying on the ground had survived the sudden attack. It threw out an elongated cone of light that lit up a far corner. The men he'd come looking for lived a transient life-style. It had cost him considerably to get their address.

"Where is Palacky?" Galvani asked.

"Here, Mr. Galvani." Valente stood with a group of men to the left. He switched on a flashlight in his hand and revealed a man kneeling at his feet, the guy's face a bloody mask. Another man knelt beside him, his arms held behind his back by some of Galvani's men. He was younger than Palacky, but carried the same dark features and hair.

Galvani approached and stopped in front of them. "You work for Mihai Lupu."

"Fuck you!" Palacky said in broken English.

As quick as an eye blink, Valente backhanded the man, breaking teeth.

"You work for Lupu," Galvani repeated.

Eyes squinted in pain, and from the bright flashlight thrust into his face, Palacky repeated the epithet.

"Who is this man?" Galvani pointed at the younger man with his .45.

"His brother," Valente answered.

Turning back to the younger man, Galvani shot him through the thigh. Both Palackys started screaming. "Shut him up," Galvani ordered, pointing to the one he'd wounded.

A handkerchief was quickly run through the younger Palacky's mouth, then pulled tight, muffling his screams. His brother continued screaming threats until Galvani pressed the .45's muzzle against the wounded man's head.

"Now," Galvani said, "if I ask you questions again and fail to get the answers I want, I'm gonna figure you're just too damn tough for me and kill you both. But you're gonna get to see me do your little brother first. Right?"

"I work for Lupu," Palacky stated. His face was white with rage.

"Good," Galvani said. "This can be easy. Where can I find him?"

"He has some rooms downtown, off Calea Victoriei." He gave the address.

"Is he there now?"

Palacky nodded. "He called. Had me bring some stuff to him a couple hours ago."

Galvani knew the Czech ran guns for Lupu. Over the months of putting his own operations into play in Eastern Europe, there'd been some flare-ups between his people and Palacky's. "You keep munitions here?"

Palacky hesitated.

With a thin, wolfish grin Galvani dropped the muzzle of the pistol to his brother's eye and pressed, drawing more garbled shrieks of pain.

"Yes," Palacky said.

"Where?"

"In the corner." Palacky nodded to the far end of the building. "There's a false floor."

"Gabe," Galvani said.

Valente sent someone to check. An instant after the flooring was lifted and a flashlight flared to life, an affirmative answer came back.

"What do you see?" Galvani knew there would be a police investigation of the shooting but doubted it would arrive before daylight. This was a hard section of Bucharest and not much used to law and order. Police officers were sometimes regarded as good shooting practice.

"Mostly small arms, but there's assault rifles, a couple M-60s, grenades and a few Russian rocket launchers, RPG-7s."

"That'll do fine," Galvani said. Then he dispassionately shot both Palacky brothers through the head. He looked at Valente. "Make sure they're all dead, then get the cars loaded up and let's go find Lupu. One way or another all of this ends tonight."

THE RUMPLED MAN standing in the airport boarding gate wasn't quite five and a half feet tall, had wavy dark hair flecked with gray, and held a placard that read McKay.

"That's a cop," Leo Turrin said as he got his carryon from the automated luggage carousel. "I recognize the hours-without-sleep, my-wife's-been-nagging-me-to-take-some-time-off look, and the effect of too much greasy food and bad coffee."

Bolan silently agreed as he picked up his own bag. He glanced at the man, then back at Julia DeVincenzo, who was showing the strain of not knowing how her son was. "I'll talk to him. Why don't you see to the other arrangements?"

The "other arrangements" included a weapons delivery by a CIA link Barbara Price had set up.

Turrin nodded and set off. "I'll get a car, too."

"A van," Bolan said. "American, if you can get it. The room and the power will be nice to have if we need it."

"Doesn't exactly look like they've got a Hertz office here, but I'll see what I can do."

"Julia," the warrior said.

"Take a powder, right?" Her features showed some of the sting in her words. For a moment he thought she might argue with him. "Don't worry, I learned from my grandfather when I should be seen and not heard." She looked around and spotted a small café. "I'll be in there."

"Fine. I'll be over as soon as I finish up." Bolan watched her walk away, her head up and her shoulders squared. Even worn-out, she still turned heads on her way to the café. He walked toward the cop.

"Mike McKay?" the guy asked.

Bolan said yes.

"Franz Radu." The man flashed his own ID, then offered his hand.

Taking it, Bolan said, "I don't have much time." Kurtzman had briefed him on Radu from Stony Man Farm. The man was one of the highest-ranked and most honest policemen surviving in Bucharest. Before Ceauşescu's fall, he'd been involved in the military, then mustered out to take up the fight for the inner city since that was where most of the carnage came from these days.

"I understand. Follow me. I arranged to have an office."

Bolan followed the man to a small office off the main hallway. The lighting was dim, and graffiti covered the walls under a recent layer of whitewash. A table and two chairs sat in the middle of the room. Radu took one of the chairs, and the warrior took the other.

Putting his briefcase on the table, the Romanian cop worked the combination locks and opened it. "You, of course, know that Mihai Lupu is a very dangerous man."

"Yes."

Radu flipped out pictures, eight-by-tens and 35 mm snapshots, as he talked. "His father was in the military, part of Ceauşescu's organization. After his father's murder by people thought to be loyal to Ceauşescu and the later execution of Ceauşescu himself, Lupu hunted down the people who killed his father. He was seventeen when he started. It took him years, but he got them all."

Bolan nodded, looking through the pictures of a much-younger-looking Lupu accompanied by an older man who had to be his father because the resemblance was so strong.

"Since that time," Radu continued, "he has been working on building a criminal organization of his own." He paused. "He's been very successful, partly due to some involvement with a group of what I think were CIA agents, though I was never able to prove it enough to the satisfaction of our State Department for them to take action."

"They were," Bolan replied honestly. He knew about the CIA connection from the reports Kurtzman had forwarded.

Evidently the answer came as a surprise. The Romanian leaned back in his chair and patted his pockets until he found a package of domestic cigarettes. When he lit one of them, it instantly filled the room with a foul odor and gray smoke. "I hadn't expected you to be so frank."

"I need the information you can give me," Bolan said. "If I start lying to you, then I have to wonder when you're lying to me."

"You're not part of the CIA?"

"No."

Radu nodded thoughtfully. "I was given to understand you were somehow connected to the Justice Department in your country."

"Loosely," Bolan said. "Lupu has become a problem. I'm here to solve it."

"How big of a problem do your people think he's going to be?" Radu asked.

"I know he's at war with Alonzo Galvani of Venice over territory here in Romania. I know he's made some inroads with organized-crime families from Japan, China and some of the Russian Mafia."

"That's more than a lot of my people are willing to admit," the Romanian said. "Why do you think Lupu is so adamant about getting to Galvani?"

"On the surface," Bolan replied, "it looked like a territorial dispute. Then I found out Lupu was more interested in blackmailing Galvani than in destroying him."

"Why?"

"To get Galvani's connections. Open up more business opportunities with the Western world."

Radu nodded in satisfaction. "You're very close to the truth."

"Lupu was trying to expand his operations," Bolan said. "He had an illegal immigration delivery point in Venice, as well as regular smuggling going out of Romania and bootlegged movie videos going back into Romania."

"Had?"

"He doesn't have them anymore," Bolan replied.

"You did this?"

"Yeah."

A fire seemed to kindle in Radu's tired eyes. He leaned forward, more intent now. Dropping his cigarette to the tiled floor, he crushed it underfoot. "Why?"

"To make Galvani more valuable to him."

"To what end?"

"With Galvani suddenly more valuable, Lupu is going to put more pressure on Galvani."

"And this has worked?" Radu asked.

"Galvani's in town, too. From what I gather, he's been in Bucharest about an hour."

Radu nodded. "You think Galvani's ready to deal?"

"Far from it. If he gets the chance, he'll kill Lupu."

"And Lupu knows this, as well as Galvani's arrival in Bucharest?"

"I think so."

"You seek to play them off, one against the other."

"For as long as I can."

A smile showed Radu's teeth to be white and uneven. "You would make a great cop," he said, "but I doubt very much that's what you are."

"A cop can't do what I'm going to," Bolan said.

Reaching back into his briefcase, Radu brought out more papers. "Then let me explain to you why Alonzo Galvani is so important to Lupu." He fanned the pictures out on the table.

Bolan studied them, finding only a few of them that had been in the Stony Man packet.

Radu supplied names, tapping each picture in turn. "Pavel Antonescu, Viktor Petrescu, Michael Borsatti, Stefan Kaulbars, Vassil Sandro, and Boris Svyatoslav. Each of these men are considered Romania's most-violent offenders these days. Between them—and Lupu—they control seventy percent of the crime that goes through this country. Antonescu, Petrescu and Borsatti are all older men and pretty much complacent about the lives they've made for themselves. The others are all hungry. Only one man has suggested to them that they form a union."

"Lupu," Bolan said.

"Yes," Radu replied.

"And he's offered them Galvani."

"Exactly. The three older men, they would probably be content with what they have, except if they don't build new business—"

"Then the younger men will start attacking their holdings to improve their own." Bolan could see the shape of the situation now.

"Lupu has brought this to the attention of the three older men. And he's been able to mollify the demands of the younger men." The Romanian leaned back and lit another cigarette. "Myself, I don't know what to hope for. If the younger men attack the older ones, there's going to be a war in the streets for months. If Lupu is successful in his bid, there won't be any fighting, but there's going to be a hell of a crime machine in place."

"Can I take these pictures?" the warrior asked.

Offering an open hand, Radu said, "Be my guest."

Bolan stacked them neatly, then stored them in his carryon. It would be nice to know all the players. And it was good to know how driven Lupu really was to get the information Julia DeVincenzo was supposed to give him. "What if Lupu were eliminated?"

"At the very least it would slow the battle between the various men involved while they digested his operations. His area is quite large and disparate."

Bolan nodded. "Then we'll start with that. I need to know where Lupu is."

With more energy now, Radu produced maps and reeled off directions. When he was finished, he asked, "What do you want me to do?"

"You're out of it," Bolan said. He could tell the tough little cop wasn't happy with the answer.

"When this goes down, there's no way to keep you clean if you're involved, and I can't guarantee that it'll all be finished. You have to live here."

"Then I'll wish you good hunting," Radu said. He swept his papers into the briefcase and relocked it, then led Bolan out of the room. "If you don't mind, I'll walk with you part of the way."

Bolan nodded, then walked back to the small café Julia had entered. Before he stepped through the door, he noticed that she wasn't alone in her booth.

A swarthy man in a dark suit sat across from her, his face tight with emotion. He talked rapidly, then motioned to two men sitting at another table.

The café was French style, but furnished after a massive budget cut. Imitation lace that looked plastic covered the tables, and the lamps were kept low.

"Those men belong to Lupu," Radu said.

Bolan knew they had to have been waiting. Getting a picture of Julia DeVincenzo was easy. As he watched, the man sitting at the table with Julia grabbed her wrist and twisted.

"Here." Radu thrust a 9 mm Browning Hi-Power into Bolan's hand. A duplicate of it was in his fist. "They won't walk out of there without her, and they'll kill anyone who tries to stop them. When you're ready, I'm right behind you."

Thumbing off the safety and making sure a round was already chambered, Bolan said, "I'm ready."

"LET GO OF MY ARM," Julia DeVincenzo ordered. "You're hurting me."

"You've only just begun to hurt if you don't follow me," the man said in heavily accented Italian.

Noticing the waitresses gathered at the wait station in the back were watching but doing nothing, Julia knew she was on her own. She reached into her purse and found the oversize lipstick inside where she kept it. Pulling it out, she stuck it into the man's face as he began yanking on her arm harder.

"What?" the man demanded with a harsh laugh. "You're going to put graffiti on my face if I don't stop?"

Ignoring the sarcasm, Julia found the safety on the lipstick, then squeezed it the way she'd been shown to activate the internal hammer. One of her grandfather's friends had given her the lipstick as a gift, telling of her of its deadly secret. Housed inside the tube, behind the lipstick, was a .357 Magnum cartridge. She'd never used it and didn't know what to expect.

When the hammer fell, the concussion was deafening. Her hand jumped, instantly numbed yet seared from the burning powder at the same time. The bullet speared into the man's face and drove him backward. There wasn't even a cry of pain as he fell in the booth.

Thinking of Nicky, and how close the man she knew only as McKay had gotten her to rescuing him, Julia shoved herself out of the booth and tried to run for the door.

The other two men who'd closed in on her stood for one frozen moment, allowing her to gain yardage, then they went for their guns. Looking at the doorway, Julia knew she'd never make it.

Then McKay was there, catching her in one arm and dragging her to the side, his black duster whipping around them as he held her in his protective embrace. She felt his stubbled chin against her forehead, rough like his hold on her but gentle underneath. Her head was turned back to the two shooters who were gunning for her.

McKay's pistol came up in his other hand as bullets from the Romanian's weapons sliced through the air where she'd been. Giving herself over to him, she watched as he squeezed the trigger. Harsh percussions ran like a string of exploding firecrackers, and rolling brass spilled out from his pistol.

A haze of gun smoke clouded her vision, but she saw both the men who'd tried to kill her being kicked back by the bullets. It was over before she realized it.

"Are you okay?" Bolan asked.

"Yes. Thank you."

Gently he released her, then turned to the Romanian cop who'd followed him into the café with a drawn pistol. He talked to the cop. "We've got to go. Lupu knows we're here."

"One thing about it," the cop said, "it'll put you in a better negotiating position." He took the gun Bolan offered, then waved them out of the café. "Go on. I'll take care of this."

At his urging, Julia started walking, his hand secure and comforting on her elbow. No one tried to stop them as they walked outside the airport terminal and climbed into the dark maroon Plymouth Voyager Turrin had waiting.

"I thought I heard shots," the little Fed said, helping Julia into one of the back seats. "I was on my way back inside."

"It's over," Bolan said. "Let's move." He walked around, got behind the wheel and fired the ignition.

Turning the passenger seat around, Turrin reached into the canvas bag on the seat next to Julia and removed a couple of handguns. Both were dark and smelled of oil. He passed one to Bolan, who immediately put it away inside his duster. She accidentally caught his eyes in the rearview mirror.

"You did good back there," he said.

"I was scared." Feeling was starting to come back into her hand, making it ache.

"You had good reason to be. I shouldn't have left you alone."

She shook her head. "Lupu didn't have any reason to think we'd be here tonight."

"Maybe."

"He's going to try to double-cross us when we make the exchange for Nicky, isn't he?" She watched the car headlights streaming toward them, seeing how wrecked the city was.

"Yeah," Bolan replied, "he is."

"Then we can't meet him on his terms."

A cool smile lit his lips. "I never planned on it."

HOLDING THE PHONE tightly, Mihai Lupu peered out over the city. Anger burned white-hot inside him as he listened to Pavel Antonescu's words.

"Listen to me for a minute," the club owner told him. "All I'm saying is that if I know, you can bet the others will know by morning. The man they had waiting outside in the car is running his mouth. Doesn't know when to shut up. He let it out to one of my guys that the killing that went down at the airport was over Julia DeVincenzo."

"So what? I told you she was coming to make a deal for her son."

"That deal is turning out to be a two-edged sword for you," Antonescu said. "The others, now they're seeing how you renege on an agreement. They'll remember this even if you get Alonzo Galvani in your pocket."

Lupu turned away from the window. Funar hovered nearby, acting as if he weren't hearing anything. "I'm not going to play games with these people. The bastard who's with her has cost me a lot of money. He's going down, even if I let the woman walk away."

Antonescu sighed heavily over the phone connection. "You've got to remember, not everyone wants this union you're speaking so highly of. If you start dealing in bad faith, you'll never get the others together."

"And what about you, Pavel?" Lupu asked in a hard voice. "How do you feel about this union?"

"I've told you how I feel."

"You don't like it," Lupu said. "Well, that's tough, old man, because it's coming. Whether you or any of the others want it, it's coming. Now, you can make the deal with me and be part of something great, or I'll take you out of the picture myself." Before the other man could respond, he hung up the phone.

Aleksander entered the room, the shotgun canted over one huge shoulder.

"The boy?" Lupu asked.

"Getting dressed," the giant replied.

"Are you having any problems with him?"

Shrugging, Aleksander said, "He's having difficulty adjusting to the medication I gave him to counteract the sedatives. But I told him he's going to see his mother."

"Good." Even though the man in black had thrown the time table off, Lupu knew everything was still well within his control. No matter what, he had the boy, and Julia DeVincenzo and her bodyguard wanted him back in one piece. They wouldn't take chances with his life, and that was Lupu's hole card. "How's the situation with Palacky coming?"

"So far, our people have spread the word that one of the urban gangs hit Palacky and his brother, and that we're going to be seeking retribution," Funar answered. "There's been no mention of Alonzo Galvani or any Italians."

Lupu nodded. That was one of the subjects he'd always heard his father talking so stridently on: suppression of information leaks and never letting an enemy know how closely they'd struck to home.

"Actually, having Galvani in Bucharest may also be a blessing," Lupu said, returning to the window. "This way we get the chance to deal with everyone at once. By morning there's going to be no one to stand in my way. If Galvani can't be bought off after I meet with the DeVincenzo woman, then he's a dead man, too. I can rebuild what I had in Venice, and in the vacuum created by the losses of Magaddino and Galvani, there'll be plenty for us to seize. Antonescu and the others are going to have to deal with me well before they expected to.''

Returning to the window, he looked out over the city that had suckled him like a wolf bitch and made him as strong and as ruthless as he was. All of this would soon be his, and there was no one who could stop him.

The phone rang and he answered it at once. "Lupu."

"You know who this is," the wintry voice said. "We need to meet."

Gesturing at Funar, Lupu had him use the phone-tracing equipment they'd gotten from the CIA people they still did business with on a regular basis. "Yes," he said calmly. "I heard you were in town."

"You lost three more people tonight," the graveyard voice taunted. "Your associates are going to start thinking you're losing your touch."

"Tracking, tracking," Funar said, making adjustments on the machine. He stroked the computer keyboard rapidly, changing screens on the monitor every second. Street maps narrowed to a quarter of the city, then an eighth, sizing down to a specific area.

"I haven't lost anything," Lupu reminded. "I still have the boy."

"And as long as you have him and he's in good health, you've got a chance to make a deal for the blackmail on Galvani."

Screens continued to cycle through on the computer monitor.

Lupu worked hard to keep the man on the phone, wanting to give the tracing program time to work. "How do I know you have the information?"

Without hesitation, the man said, "Galvani worked the wrong side during World War II. Magaddino was the only one who knew that."

"Knowing it isn't enough," Lupu said.

"Magaddino had the proof. Now so do we. If the boy's okay when we get him, so do you."

"You're surely not going to give me the only copy." A blip resolved on the computer monitor. Lupu could tell the area was somewhere in the northwest section of the city.

"Retaining it isn't going to help Mrs. DeVincenzo," the man replied. "She's not interested in his business or her grandfather's. You already know that."

"Got it!" Funar whispered. "He's using a cellular phone. The station access he's using it out of is near Circului Park. We can find him."

Lupu nodded. "Where can we meet?"

"Off Judetului Street. Near the park."

"I know the place. When do you want to be there?"

"Give us an hour," the wintry voice said. The phone connection broke abruptly.

Lupu looked at his watch. It was 4:11 a.m. Evidently the man was hoping to use the park as his getaway, then use the morning traffic to make the run back to the airport.

But the call had been traced. Lupu didn't have to wait at all. Instead of the man getting to set up traps, Lupu would be calling the shots. He looked at Aleksander. "Get the boy. We're leaving."

Aleksander nodded and left the room.

Taking the Skorpion machine pistol from the wet bar, Lupu headed for the door. "Funar, give the men a call and have them meet us out front." There was no more waiting. He was going to take the fight to his enemies and bury them where he found them.

STARING HARD through the night binoculars, Julia DeVinchenzo scanned the entire fifth floor of Lupu's building. She'd understood most of the man's plan, surprised by how simple it sounded yet admiring the twists.

"They're moving, Mike," Leo Turrin said beside her. He was speaking through the ear-throat headset he and Bolan were using, and the woman couldn't hear the big man's side of the conversation.

Bolan was six stories below their building and across from Lupu's, using the second cellular phone they'd brought with them. The first was in a trash can in Circului Park and had been preprogrammed to forward any calls to Lupu's number. He'd told her and Turrin about his suspicions that the man had means of tracing back a call. Now, instead of showing that they might possibly be right outside his building, Lupu thought they were nearly half the city away.

Then her eyes found the bedroom window where Nicky was being kept. Her throat got so thick it hurt, but she made herself speak. "I see him," she whispered hoarsely.

"Where?" Turrin asked. He had a pair of binoculars, too.

"Sixth window from the left," Julia replied. She stared through the distance lenses, seeing Nicky sitting on the bed with his back to her. A huge man was tying his shoes, being gentle with him.

"Okay, Mike," Turrin said calmly. "The boy's in there. They're moving him now." A pause. "Fine, we're on our way down now." He took Julia by the elbow and spoke softly. "Let's go."

"Why aren't they leaving him there?" Julia demanded. She felt the anxiety well up inside her. Reluctantly she trailed after Turrin. Her last sight of Nicky had been of him clinging to the big man, and the thought of him holding on to one of his would-be murderers struck her as obscene.

"Lupu is protecting his interests," Turrin said as they hurried down the fire escape on the other side of the building.

"But you two thought they might leave him there," Julia insisted.

"It was a chance," Turrin agreed. "It didn't pan out. Doesn't mean things won't come together, though. They're still going to split up before they get to the park, do some kind of recon work and set up. Chances are the protection around Nicky will drop to something we can handle for long enough to take him and get the hell lost before Lupu can organize any kind of pursuit."

Julia made the corner at the second-floor landing, coming down fast. "And if they don't?"

"Then we handle that, too." On the ground now, Turrin suddenly caught her and shoved her back up against the wall, staying within the shadows. "Damn." His eyes were locked on a line of cars coming up the street.

"What is it?" Julia asked.

"Galvani," Turrin said in a tight voice. "The son of a bitch just made the party." He pressed his hand against the talk button on the headset. "Mike, we've got problems."

CHAPTER FOURTEEN

"Go, Leo," Mack Bolan answered. Outfitted in the black suit, his face tiger striped by combat cosmetics, the Executioner scanned the terrain, knowing instinctively that it had just become a hellground awaiting battle.

"Galvani made it," Turrin growled. "How do you want to handle this?"

Bolan immediately began planning new logistics. There was no way to call Lupu and warn him without giving away their position, and Nicky De-Vincenzo's life was forfeit if the Romanian crime lord figured out he'd been set up.

"Get the van around to the back of the building," Bolan said. "These streets are going to be too cluttered to move."

"On our way."

The Executioner watched as one of what he suspected was the Galvani cars slowed in front of the building, the ruby taillights flaring for a long beat. Snugged in shoulder leather was a 9 mm Beretta 92-F. Counterpoint to that on his right hip was a Detonics Compmaster .45ACP with nightsights. Webgear kept additional magazines and grenades at the ready.

He moved out, keeping the M-16/M-203 combo he'd chosen as his lead weapon out of sight in the folds of the duster. The numbers clicked into place on the play. Lupu and his group weren't expecting a double cross, not with Nicky's life hanging in the balance, so they were going to walk out to face the brunt of Galvani's attack unsuspecting.

And Galvani didn't give a damn about the boy.

Working the breech of the grenade launcher, the Executioner readied a high-explosive round. The cold air bit into him, bringing an edge to the coming violence and whipping loose debris through the street. He made the curb on the opposite side of the street before Lupu and his men streamed from the building. Other men got into cars along the sidewalk. Plumes of gray exhaust came from the pipes as they started the engines. No one noticed him.

Lupu started for a limousine at the head of the caravan, and some of Galvani's men spotted him. Instantly ruby dots of laser sights flickered across the Romanian. The big man was carrying Nicky only a few feet behind Lupu, directly in the line of fire.

Stepping up to the lamppost near the corner of the building, Bolan took the M-16/M-203 from his side and pulled it to his shoulder, sighting in on the Galvani car he knew from trajectory points had the most shooters that held Lupu in their sights. He tagged the grenade launcher's trigger and rocked with the recoil of the 40 mm warhead jetting from the muzzle.

Lupu's men moved forward to cover their boss from the expected sniper fire, realizing what the ruby dots signified. Then the HE round detonated against the side of the Galvani car and rocked it, turning it into a fiery coffin for the people inside. Orange-and-yellow tongues of flame leaped into the night sky, pummeled by the wind.

Taking advantage of the uncertainty of the moment, Bolan raced through the ranks of Lupu's private army. Brass littered the sidewalk around him as they returned fire against Galvani's forces.

A member of Lupu's group noticed that Bolan wasn't one of them, turned and started to shout a warning. The Executioner burned him where he stood with a 3-round burst.

The big man holding Nicky had retreated to the recessed doorway. He saw Bolan racing at full speed toward him and tried to bring up his gun. Before he could squeeze the trigger, the Executioner cracked him in the face twice with the buttstock, driving him back through the doors to the building's alcove. As the man-mountain went down, his face bleeding, Bolan freed the screaming child from the big man's arms.

"Take it easy," Bolan said. "I've got you, and I'm going to take you to your mother." The boy grabbed his shirt tightly in both fists but didn't stop screaming. Bullets ripped across the door just over the Executioner's head as he ducked and went low into the building.

Two armed men were ahead of him and showed no hesitation about shooting him or the boy. Lifting the M-16/M-203 in one hand, the Executioner punched them to the ground with a vicious figure eight before they could get off a round.

Cutting around the corner, Bolan slung the M-16 over his shoulder and drew the Detonics .45. A man stuck his head inside the mangled door. With two snapped shots, the Executioner sent the decapitated corpse stumbling back out the entryway.

Still holding the boy tight, Bolan took up a position farther back in the lobby, giving himself the option between a corridor running toward the back of the building or the elevator. He tagged the transmit button on the headset. "Leo."

"Go."

"I've got the boy."

"The back way is covered over," Turrin called tightly. "Galvani's people have mounted a rear attack."

Another Romanian gunner tried to come through the door. Bolan led the man, then dropped him with a single shot through the temple. Sheathing the pistol, he yanked a smoke grenade from his combat harness, pulled the pin and lobbed the canister toward the door.

The smoker went off with a loud *bamf* and flooded the entrance with thick black smoke.

Bolan pulled the boy tighter, shifting him so his hands were around the warrior's neck. "Can you hold on?"

The boy nodded, trembling, his cheeks tracked with tears.

"We're going to have to move fast. Your mom's waiting outside."

"Okay." The boy's voice was small, barely audible over the harsh cracking of gunfire.

Shifting the combat webbing and making use of extra straps he could salvage, Bolan looped a couple of ties around the boy, creating a net so he wouldn't lose him easily while he used both hands.

He ejected the depleted magazine from the assault rifle and fed another one in. Fixing the architecture of the building and the streets around it in his mind, he remembered the alley behind the building. No main doors led out that way. "Leo."

"Go."

"What about the alley?"

"Give me a minute."

Bolan moved as fast as he could toward the corridor. Shadows alerted him, driving him to cover around the corner just before bullets ripped into the sides and carpet of the hallway. He kept the M-16 on the sling over his shoulder. With the boy in front of him, shooting the assault rifle would have been difficult. The Detonics Compmaster filled his fist, and he fired a trio of rounds that took out another gunman. The rest of the clip drove the other men into hiding.

He dumped the empty magazine and recharged the .45. Abandoning his position, the warrior raced for the elevator just as a group of Romanian's hardmen broke through the front door. Knowing he was out of running room, he turned in profile to the new arrivals to protect Nicky, then pointed the .45 at them.

"Over here!" one of them shouted. He brought his machine pistol around in a withering arc of 9 mm parabellum rounds.

Grimly aware the numbers were thin, Bolan let his instincts take over, keying into his combat senses. The .45 boomed. Two of his targets went down with head and chest wounds. The third man seemed to sprout an extra pair of eyes just before the top of his head came off.

The fourth man got off a series of rounds, and at least two of them slammed into Bolan's Kevlar vest across his shoulders.

Staggered but still focused, the Executioner squeezed off the final two rounds, putting them both into his target's heart beneath the two-handed grip the guy had on his weapon. After shaking the empty magazine free and fitting another one into place, Bolan sprinted to the elevator. He pressed the button and watched as the cage dropped, then the doors opened.

As the stainless-steel doors slid past him into the recessed areas of the wall, the Executioner caught the grim reflection of Father Gerald "Jericho" Light coming up behind him. He whirled, bringing up the Detonics .45.

CROUCHED BEHIND the windshield already starred by a half-dozen bullet holes, Leo Turrin floored the accelerator and sped through a U-turn. "Stay down!" he told his companion.

Instead, the woman watched, holding a 9 mm Beretta in her fists.

As he came around the corner, turning into the alley, an armed man stepped onto the van's passenger-side running board and took aim at Turrin. The stocky little Fed lifted his pistol, but before he could fire, a pair of shots sounded behind him.

At the same instant the passenger-side window shattered, and the gunner's face became a crimson ruin. He fell away.

"Damn, that was close," Turrin said. The van came around awkwardly, slamming into the security fence and leaving a shower of sparks in its wake. The engine roared as he streaked down the alley.

"Come on, Sarge," Turrin muttered. "I got two doors here. Which one?" He reached for the transmit button on the headset.

STARING DOWN the muzzle of the gun held by the man in combat black, Light kept his hands well to his sides. He hadn't even seen the man until the threatening move was made, hadn't even known the guy was in the vicinity. Coming around the corner of the corridor, he'd never seen him until it was too late.

"I didn't come here to hurt you," the priest said. "Or the boy or his mother. I was looking for Lupu."

"Why?"

"Because if he was out of the way, I thought Mrs. DeVincenzo might be more willing to talk to me about the missing church items." Light paused. The eruption of a fresh wave of gunfire sounded outside. "I can help, if you'll allow me."

For a moment Light didn't think the man would let him. Then the pistol barrel lowered.

"Okay. I don't know if you're exactly on the side of the angels tonight, but you're surely going where they fear to tread.'' His volcanic blue eyes flashed. ''Let's move.''

The man stepped into the elevator cage as someone drove a Land Rover through one of the big windows in the lobby, scattering glass and ripping the security bars from their moorings in the floor and ceiling. The huge 4x4 fishtailed out of control for a moment, then slammed up against the circular seating area near the center of the lobby. A cascade of artificial trees and bushes in stone planters spread before it. Before it had even stopped rocking, miraculously still together, men poured from the four doors.

Light raised the Glock and fired instantly. Trapped inside the elevator cage, the sound was deafening. However, two of their foes wouldn't be getting back up.

''Grenade,'' the man in black said, tossing out a spherical object.

The explosive blew at the same time the doors closed behind them, providing Light only a glimpse of the carnage caused by the fragmentation grenade. He glanced at the control panel and saw the second-floor indicator light up.

''The high ground,'' Bolan said. ''At least a little of it.''

The doors opened with a ping. Taking the lead after pressing more of the elevator buttons, the man in black sprinted for the window at the end of the corridor. Light heard him talking, pressing the button on the headset he wore. No one else was in the corridor.

Lifting the window at the end of the corridor, the man peered out.

Light kept their flank covered but glanced down in time to see the maroon van come to a rubber-shredding stop below the window.

Climbing out the window, Bolan held on to the boy and dropped onto the van, pushing himself off immediately to drop beside the side door as it opened. Julia DeVincenzo reached for her son from inside. The warrior drew a combat knife and slashed the straps holding the boy to his chest.

Without warning, a car rocketed into the alley, the headlights carving long tunnels through the darkness as the woman pulled her son inside the van. Light yelled a warning and started firing at the gunners leaning out of the car's windows, but a wave of autofire rattled across the van, sending Bolan spinning away.

Fisting the Glock, Light fired round after round through the driver's side of the windshield, keeping the bullets to a space that could have been covered by a dinner plate. For the first time since his mission had begun, he'd felt as though he was doing something that was really worth doing. Julia DeVincenzo and her son had been the innocents in the deadly game being played out, and mattered far more than the return of the stolen church artifacts. He'd been following Father Uccello's wishes and not relying on his own view of the situation.

But he knew the answer now and the confusion in his heart was eased. There just didn't seem to be time left to save everyone.

MACK BOLAN FELL BACKWARD, hammered by a tri-burst of large-caliber slugs that robbed his lungs of air. Nearby trash cans broke his fall as brick dust and mortar from the wall behind him rained on his face. Lungs aching, black comets swirling in his vision, he thought for a moment the body armor hadn't held. Then his chest heaved slightly, sucking in the cold air and pushing out a gray plume. There was no warmth of blood.

Diamond chips spit off the approaching vehicle's windshield as the priest's bullets centered over the driver's side.

Willing his body to move despite the agony filling him, Bolan gripped the M-16/M-203 combo and raised it to his shoulder. He slid his finger inside the grenade launcher's trigger, taking up the slack as he sighted on the car. When he touched off the round, the car was less than thirty yards out and closing.

Riding out the M-203's recoil, he watched the HE round pulverize the front tire on the right, dropping the car down and throwing it into an uncontrolled skid. The driver's probable death kept it from being recoverable.

The car swung wild, then nosed around until it was sliding sideways. When the warped axle, remnant from the 40 mm grenade blast, dug into the alley, the car flipped over on its side and kept coming. Sparks flared out behind it, and a man who'd been hanging out of the window was cut in two. Banging up against the stopped van, there was enough force built up to rock the other vehicle.

Looking up into the van, Bolan saw Julia De-Vincenzo sitting on the floorboards hugging her son tightly. Still hurting but breathing better, the warrior forced himself to his feet. Men were starting to crawl from the overturned car. Judging from the assortment of Italian curses, they belonged to Alonzo Galvani.

An instant later the priest dropped lithely to his side. The Glock rolled like a live thing in his fist, killing another man and driving the rest to cover inside the car.

Reaching inside the van, the Executioner took up the squat, sinister-looking Multiround Projectile Launcher from behind the middle seat. The MM-1 held twelve rounds of 38 mm destruction, and Bolan had loaded it so that every two rounds of HE were followed by a fragmentation grenade. The last three were smoke grenades.

"I'll break the way out in just a few minutes," the warrior told Turrin. "You go when I say. Just like we planned it."

Turrin gave him a smile. "Sure. Didn't plan on all the extra frills, though. What about you? We can't leave you here."

"I'll make my own way," Bolan said. "There are a few things here that need to be tied up."

The little Fed didn't look happy with the situation, but he knew better than to argue. "What about you?" he asked the priest.

Light shook his head. "You'll stand a better chance if there are two of us covering your escape."

"Fine. But you're going to need more than a hand blaster." Leaning over the passenger seat, Turrin came back with a Barrett Light Fifty .50-caliber sniper rifle. "Ever used one of these?"

Taking it, Light said, "The bullpup configuration is new to me."

"Makes it easier to use in tight places," Turrin said, adding a couple of extra 11-round magazines. "Good luck with it."

Bolan watched the priest, but there was no indecision in the man. Whatever confusion he'd sensed earlier was gone. Tossing Turrin a salute, the Executioner headed for the front of the building. Light was at his heels.

A metal ladder hugged the corner of the building, evidently for cleaning or maintenance crews who worked on the HVAC units on the rooftop. Hanging the MM-1 from his side, his chest still throbbing from the impact of the bullets, the Executioner grabbed the ladder and scrambled up, feeling the weight of the weapons pull at him.

On the second floor he abandoned the ladder and crept out onto the eaves overhanging the sidewalk in front of the building. The steel support struts kept the unit intact, but it vibrated under his weight. Light's movements created an echo.

Bolan knelt and surveyed the battlezone. Neither side appeared to be gaining an edge. Dead men littered the street, and four cars were burning in addition to the one the Executioner had blown up. Peering over the edge, the warrior found the bulk of Lupu's forces directly under him.

He glanced at the priest. "When we open the ball on this, they're going to figure us out pretty quick."

His face placid, almost serene, Light nodded.

"When we get them out of here," Bolan said, "I figure you and I have a chance at the Land Rover inside the lobby. If that doesn't work, we're on foot."

A ghost of a smile touched the priest's lips. "No medevac on this one."

"Not a chance."

"Let's do it." Light set himself in a sitting position, the Barrett over his shoulder as he looked through the sights.

Bolan ripped five antipersonnel grenades from his combat harness, then tapped the transmit button on the headset. "Leo."

"Go."

"Ready?"

"We've got no choice. Some of Galvani's gunners are coming up the alley." The harsh bark of gunfire crackled over the frequency.

In quick succession Bolan slipped the pins on all the grenades and dropped them among Lupu's ground troops. Then he swept up the MM-1. "Do it," he growled. There was almost no recoil as he fired the rounds, emptying the weapon in under five seconds.

Two of the HE rounds hit cars and started more fires. Counting down, he placed all of the fragmentation grenades among the biggest groups of Mafia hardmen he could find. For a moment the gunfire faded out, swamped by the swell of concussions on the street. The deep basso cracks of the Barrett Light

Fifty were a counterpoint to the destruction sweeping the street.

The frag grenades tossed bodies in all directions from the focal point of the explosions. Some of the survivors were picked off by Light's expertise with the sniper rifle.

Thick clouds of black smoke pooled up from the three 38 mm warheads Bolan fired into the street near the mouth of the alley. Rising quickly, the smoke formed a wall, obscuring the view of the street in that direction.

Bolan tagged the headset. "Go!" Gazing over the side of the eaves after tossing aside the empty MM-1, he saw the van speed out of the alley, taking a wide turn as Turrin fought the wheel for control before straightening. Sparks danced along the top and back of the van as gunners targeted. Then the M-16/ M-203 was in the Executioner's capable hands.

A car peeled off from Galvani's group, swinging after the van. Giving the vehicle a lead, Bolan took up the trigger slack, made certain of his target, then fired. Whooshing out of the grenade launcher, the 40 mm warhead penetrated the driver's window, then blew up inside. The top peeled back like a sardine can, revealing only blackened and flaming corpses.

Below, Lupu's team was in a temporary rout.

"We're clear," Turrin called over the headset.

"Good luck, buddy. If we're not there, get airborne anyway. We may not get a second chance to get the lady and boy clear."

"I read you, but dammit, you'd better be there."

A spray of autofire rattled against the eaves, penetrating the sheet metal easily and leaving puckered shrapnel in its wake.

"Move," Bolan ordered, pushing himself up. Bullets ripped through the area he'd just vacated. Sprinting, he vaulted over the support struts and raced for the ladder. With his hands and feet on the outside of the rails, holding tight, he controlled his slide down the ladder.

A line of bullets cut into the brick and ricocheted with audible whines from the steel rungs over his head. Dropping the last few feet, the gunner already tagged in the periphery of his vision, Bolan collapsed into a crouch and slipped the Beretta 92-F from shoulder leather. Before the gunner could target either himself or the priest, the Executioner fired five times, driving the corpse backward in short, stuttered steps.

Without pause Bolan fired an antipersonnel grenade at the feet of four men rushing his position. Detonating on impact, the grenade shoved four dead men back the way they'd come. Sprinting, Bolan cut around the corner and dived through the broken window the Land Rover had driven through. He raced to the vehicle's side, knowing if it didn't start, he and Light were going to have to fall back into the building and fight their way clear some other way.

Coming around the Land Rover from the other side, using the cover it provided, he yanked open the passenger-side door with difficulty. With a shrill screech, the door fell off at his feet. Ignoring it, he dived inside, seeing that the keys weren't in the ignition. He drew his knife from his combat harness and went to work on the wires under the dash as bullets pecked out what remained of the windows.

"Lupu got away in a car," Light said. Then there was a groan of impact.

Thinking the other man had taken a round, Bolan glanced up in time to see the hulking, bearded giant that had carried Nicky DeVincenzo out of the building trying to slide a knife across the priest's throat from behind. Bolan reached for the Beretta, intending to shoot the bigger man.

Then Light rolled his shoulders, blocked the giant's wrist and drove an elbow into his opponent's eye socket. Bone split loud enough to echo inside the Land Rover. Whirling, controlling the knife wrist, the priest followed up by driving the blade deep into the big man's sternum, then placed a hand on the dying man's forehead and shoved him away. Light had a gun in his hand in time to shoot a rifleman who'd just slid into a prone position in front of the 4x4.

Sparks flew from the wires in Bolan's hands. With a groan the engine turned over and caught. He pulled himself into the seat, staying low, then rammed the transmission into first gear and let out the clutch as Light occupied the passenger seat.

Gaining speed, the Land Rover barreled back through the window it had shattered earlier. The sidewalk was lined with cars.

Bolan kept his foot down as he closed on them, shifting into second. "Hold on," he growled.

There wasn't time for the priest to reply. With a snarl of crunching metal and ruined bodywork, the Land Rover went over the front end and back of the two cars parked in front of it. The transmission momentarily whined as all four wheels left the ground.

Landing with a thump, the 4x4 bucked and protested in a deep ratcheting as the tires found traction. Bolan cut the wheel hard to the left, heeling the big vehicle around. In the seat beside him, Light braced himself with one hand and fired the Glock dry with the other.

Without warning, Alonzo Galvani stepped into the Land Rover's surviving headlight beam. The old Mafia don stood his ground, firing his .45 in defiance. His mouth was open as if he were yelling.

Bolan shifted into third, picking up speed, and felt the seat vibrate as it took a round. He steered for Galvani, running him down in spite of the hail of bullets that invaded the 4x4's interior.

When the reinforced front end hit him, Galvani went up and over, landing with a sickening smack against the almost empty windshield frames.

"Looks like you picked up a genuine imitation General George Patton hood ornament," Light commented. "Or maybe George C. Scott only did that in the movie." Reaching forward, he tugged the corpse across the hood, and it bounced away.

Bolan glanced at the man, smiling slightly.

"I wasn't always a priest," Light explained. "And humor's allowed."

"Sarge," Turrin called over the headset.

"Go," Bolan replied.

"Are you mobile?"

"Yes."

"Good," Turrin said, "because Lupu is coming up fast."

Bolan put his foot down harder on the accelerator. "We'll be there, guy. Just stay on course." He whipped the Land Rover around three cars in a row, barely nipping back in ahead of oncoming traffic. The speedometer needle was quivering around eighty miles per hour. Shivering from the right front wheel let the warrior know the big 4x4 had taken some damage.

His foot on the brake, laying on the horn hard, he downshifted, dropped out into the oncoming lane and made the exchange to Berzei Street around a poultry truck. Just over fifty yards up, the mismatched intersection went in five directions.

Muscling into a milk truck, hoping the four-wheel-drive would help compensate for the other vehicle's greater weight, Bolan held steady and took the left fork along Dinicu Golescu Boulevard. An oncoming car braked to a stop that left it turned sideways in Bolan's wake.

"Gara de Nord?" Light asked, referring to the city's subway system.

For the first time Bolan noticed the man had been wounded. The left shoulder of his jacket was soaked with blood. "Yeah," the Executioner replied. "If the retreat back to the airport proved unfeasible, there was a chance we could regroup in the subway until another route became available."

Opening the first-aid kit attached under the glove compartment, the priest removed a heavy gauze patch, then shoved it under his jacket. "That's the way I'd have worked it, too. Got a plane waiting?"

Bolan cut the Land Rover's wheel and jumped the curb, going down the sidewalk long enough to pass a car that was slowing for a left turn ahead of them. "Red-eye special put up by Seaspray." The outfit was part of the U.S. Army Special Forces, jointly managed by the CIA for clandestine troop-transport around the world. Price had managed the buy-in, pulling in some favors and employing a touch of blackmail.

"They're a good group," Light said, wiping the blood from his gun hand. He glanced over his shoulder. "No one appears to be following us."

"Could change at any moment," Bolan replied. He pulled back onto the street and saw the maroon van only a short distance ahead of them. Directly on the van's tail was a dark blue limousine, closing like a mako shark. The warrior tagged the headset transmit button. "Leo."

"Go."

"I've got you, buddy. On my go, break right and stand on the brakes till we clear you."

"Roger."

Bolan checked his gear, making sure the Detonics .45 and Beretta were secure. He pinned the accelerator to the floor, feeling the Land Rover's power plant surge in response.

"They don't see us," Light said.

"Not yet," Bolan agreed. As he closed, he switched off the headlights. They were less than twenty yards away. He tagged the headset. "Now, Leo!"

The van's remaining brake lights flared on one side, and it shuddered as it slowed. Gray smoke flowed out from the tires.

Lupu's driver tried to stop, as well, but Bolan rammed the heavy luxury car from behind, sending it spinning rear-end forward. He had to fight the Land Rover's wheel to keep it under control, aiming it at the limousine again. This time the contact buckled the big car's rear deck.

Out of control, the limousine spun sideways. Bolan didn't relent, pinning the accelerator again and ramming the luxury car in the side. The vehicles didn't just bump and separate. He stayed buried in the limousine's side, shoving it ahead of him, feeling the 4x4's tires slip as it started to skid, too.

Then the limousine struck the curb on the other side of the street, jumped over it and slammed into the side of the building across from the subway. Torn loose by the big car's sudden stop, the Land Rover lost traction and slid sideways, colliding with a light pole and knocking it over, finally coming around facing the limousine. Electrical sparks jumped from the wrecked light pole, and a number of other lights in the area suddenly went out, turning the area into a sudden nightscape.

With a shudder and a final pop, the Land Rover's engine died.

Bruised and battered from the collision, Bolan forced his door open and got out. Even in the darkness he recognized Lupu as the man shoved his way out of the car and sprinted for the subway station across the street. Drawing a bead on the man, knowing he was still dangerous as long as he lived, the Executioner held his fire because there were too many innocent bystanders in the line of fire. Autofire blasted from the luxury car's windows and drove him to cover.

"Give me the rifle," Light called from the other side of the Land Rover, "and I'll cover you."

Bolan handed over the M-16/M-203. "You've got an HE round in the launcher."

The priest nodded. "Ready?"

"Yeah." Bolan shoved himself into motion as soon as the M-16 opened up. Cars had stopped in their tracks, leaving bare concrete all the way to the subway station. He saw Lupu disappear inside a heartbeat before the 40 mm grenade went off and most of the gunfire died away.

Following, the warrior bolted through the main loading area, knowing the Romanian intended to lose himself in the sewer system that hooked into the subway tunnels if he didn't catch a train. When he saw the people lying on the floor, their hands over their heads defensively, he knew which way the crime lord had gone.

Steps led down into the bowels of the subway tunnel. The power failure from the outside street pole had affected the tunnel area, leaving it drenched in shadows that didn't allow vision much farther than three or four feet. Bolan went through the door in a rush, knowing he'd be skylined against the outside lights.

Muzzle-flashes from less than twenty feet away blew yellow-white, elongated bubbles in the inky darkness, illuminating Lupu's face and hands for a flickering instant.

Bolan held his fire, knowing the man was already in motion, not wanting to give his position away. He listened, but the sound of a distant subway train created an undercurrent of noise that made it impossible to hear his quarry move.

"You're a dead man if you come after me," Lupu said in English. The echoing rumble of the train conflicted with his words as it neared.

Bolan couldn't pinpoint the man's position.

"I know I didn't hit you," Lupu said. "So playing dead isn't going to help you."

Reaching into a pocket on his Webgear, Bolan took out an emergency flare. "I'm not going away without putting you down."

Lupu laughed. "I've taken everything this city can throw at me, and I've conquered it all. You're in my territory."

"Maybe," Bolan responded. "But you're on my street now." He broke the flare against his leg, igniting the chemicals inside, then tossed it to the floor. Instantly the area was limned in the bright emerald dawn.

Standing less than ten feet away in profile, Lupu came around, his pistol lifted and firing.

Taking the Detonics Compmaster in a Weaver's grip, the Executioner pulled the trigger twice, putting both bullets in the center of the Romanian's face.

Driven backward by the heavy .45 rounds, Lupu disappeared over the subway ledge and dropped onto the tracks.

Bolan walked forward, pistol held at the ready to cover the man, wanting to make certain of the kill. Then the subway train arrived, its light flaring brightly. There was no time for it to stop, and Lupu never moved as it rolled over him.

Leaving the subway station, Bolan found Turrin on his way in. "I thought you had somewhere you were supposed to be," the warrior said.

Turrin hooked a thumb over his shoulder. "The lady didn't like the idea of leaving you here. I didn't have much choice, nor much stomach to fight. If you hurry, we can all still make it. I got in touch with our pilot and found out that cop you had the tête-à-tête with is running interference to make sure we're not bothered on our way out of town."

As he walked to the van, taking in the burning wreckage of the limousine and the dead men strewed around it, Bolan noticed the gangs of children and teenagers that had sprung up out of the shadows surrounding the subway station. They watched mutely, a feral look in their eyes.

"I—we couldn't leave you," Julia DeVincenzo said. "Not after you've done so much to help us."

Bolan nodded. "We'd better get a move on. The Bucharest police might be taking their time to react, but Lupu still has got people who might come looking for him.'' He paused at the passenger door and looked at Light. ''There's a ride in this for you, too, if you want it.''

The priest shook his head, a relaxed smile on his face. ''I don't think so. Maybe I followed a fool's errand out here, playing to someone else's vanity, but I think in the end I was meant to be here.'' He pointed up at one of the buildings next to the subway.

There, above the crowd of children thronging the station and the pool of darkness created by the power failure, the building rose up straight and tall. Only some of the lights were on, and the ones that were on went seven stories up and four stories across, with only a few of those dark, inscribing a ragged cross. At the foot of it were the bulk of the children.

''There's another priest I met tonight,'' Light said. ''I think maybe he can use my help. God knows these children can.''

''Then I'll wish you the best,'' Bolan said, offering his hand.

The priest took it.

''For what it's worth,'' Bolan said as he started to get into the van, ''Galvani had the artwork you were looking for.''

''I'll make a phone call,'' Light said. ''Someone else can try to get it.'' With a final wave he stepped off the curb and walked toward the children. At first they receded from him, then a few of the younger ones, led by a teenage boy with dark hair and eyes, started to cluster around him. In seconds they'd disappeared into the shadows.

"Let's go," Bolan told Turrin. He glanced at Julia DeVincenzo sitting in the back seat. The van had been shot to pieces, but the boy was sleeping peacefully in his mother's lap as if nothing had happened.

"I don't understand," Julia said. "Why didn't he come with us? He doesn't know anyone here."

"He will," Bolan said. "What he does know is that he's supposed to be here. That's more than most people ever figure out." The big warrior knew the truth of his words. For men fired in the crucible of war, steeped in the blood of sudden death and hammered into shape by convictions that went soul deep, when that clarion call went out to stand a ground and stand it hard, there was nothing else that could be done.

That was the way it was for the Executioner and the war everlasting. Wherever that last bloody mile took him, Bolan knew he'd meet the challenge head-on. For the warrior there was no other way.

**Gold Eagle Presents
a special three-book in-line continuity**

THE RED DRAGON TRILOGY

Beginning in June 1996, Gold Eagle brings you
another action-packed three-book in-line continuity,
The Red Dragon Trilogy.

In THE EXECUTIONER #210—FIRE LASH, book 1 of The
Red Dragon Trilogy, The Triads and the Red Chinese
have struck a bargain sealed in hell—with a quick payoff
in escalating terrorism, murder and heroin traffic. But
long-range plans include a conspiracy of terrifying
global consequence.

Don't miss the first book of this new trilogy, available in
June at your favorite retail outlet.